Praise for CBA Bestselling Author

Lori Copeland

"[In *A Case of Crooked Letters*] Copeland produces a wacky jumble of humorous characters beset by serious circumstances. Joy wins in the end."
—*Romantic Times*

"[*A Case of Bad Taste* is] a riveting adventure in page-turning mystery and laugh-out-loud humor. Lori Copeland at her best!"
—Karen Kingsbury, bestselling author of the Redemption series

"The characters in *A Case of Bad Taste* are both fun and frustrating, mischievous and maddening. As Maude says, 'Life's a hoot!'"
—Brandilyn Collins, author of *Stain of Guilt*

"Filled with emotion, danger and humor, [*Ruth*] is sure to warm your heart."
—*Romantic Times*

Lori Copeland

Mother of Prevention

Steeple
Hill
Café

Published by Steeple Hill Books™

STEEPLE HILL BOOKS

ISBN 0-373-78536-4

MOTHER OF PREVENTION

www.SteepleHill.com

Printed in U.S.A.

First and foremost, I dedicate this book
to the lonely and grieving. God has not forgotten you.

To Bob and Jo Martin: for your continuing ministry in
Christ and for your watchful eye on this manuscript.

To Barbara Warren, whose love and commitment to God
shows brightly through her work
as my assistant and chief troubleshooter.

To Harlequin Enterprises, Joan Marlow Golan
and Krista Stroever: for allowing me to be part
of the Steeple Hill family.

To the new breed of Christian readers
and buyers who encourage authors
to write books of faith by buying them!

Chapter

1

"Where was the shoe the last time you saw it?"

Kelli, my youngest daughter, is like her father: charming, practical and witty, with enough savoir faire to carry her through two lifetimes. She'd misplaced a sneaker. "Not lost, misplaced," she wheezed. She uncapped her inhaler, took a deep breath, then released it.

"In Sailor's mouth."

Sailor. Our family pooch that carried off anything that wasn't nailed down. I'd warned Neil the animal was going to be nothing but trouble when he brought this...odd-looking creature into our home—rusty black, short legs, very fast, extremely agile. The dog had a domed skull, V-shaped dropped ears, a nose with a straight bridge and large dark brown eyes.

"What is *that*?" I'd asked.

"A puli. Isn't he cute?"

Cute? That long coat looked to me like forty-five minutes a week of professional grooming to prevent matting and felting—and the thing was only a pup!

When I protested, my husband had dropped a noncommittal kiss on my forehead and predicted I'd be in love with Kelli's fifth birthday present before the week was out. I'd proved him wrong. Two hours later I was on the floor, wrestling with the heart stealer, falling head over heels in love with the furry troll. Sailor, unfortunately, captured my daughter's heart, too, but the pet couldn't be around long because Kelli's asthma turned out to be a problem. As long as she submitted to an allergy shot once a week, the doctor agreed Sailor could stay until my daughter decided between breathing and having a dog in the house.

I was still uncertain about the outcome. Sailor had been here two months, and the bond between animal and child had only grown stronger.

"Why did you let Sailor carry off your sneaker?" School started in twenty minutes and I still had to pack two lunches and slap on makeup before we left the house.

She lifted thin shoulders. "It'll be all wet with dog slobbers."

I swiped a lock of long hair out of my face before I turned and dumped coffee into the sink. "Run upstairs and put something on."

My seven-year-old appeared, dragging her backpack across the tile floor. Kris wasn't a morning person. "Have you seen my math book?"

"Not since last night."

"I can't find my math book." She dumped Fruitee Pops into a bowl, grumbling. "Sailor must have carried it off."

The puli skidded around the corner, his nails clicking against the entry's hardwood floor. I gave the canine a warning look, glanced at the clock and thought, Great—now I'm really running behind.

I'd forgotten to put new batteries in the alarm. It had stormed last night, and the power had gone off. Neil and I had dragged the kids out of bed and traipsed over to the neighbors and spent an hour in their basement until the all-clear siren sounded. Never had Oklahoma experienced so many off-season tornadoes, but the weather was freaky everywhere this year. With dead batteries in the alarm, I'd overslept. When I'd awakened and seen the time, I'd thrown the covers back and sprung out of bed. Neil had rolled out on his side, complaining, blaming me for the late start—like he didn't know how to replace batteries?

Ten minutes later the love of my life came through the kitchen door muttering under his breath, "Six minutes to shave, eat and get to the station. Fighting fires is easier than getting out of this house on time."

I handed him a piece of buttered toast and a cup of coffee on his way to the detached garage. He was always cranky during Sooner season. Sooner fever, I called it. The college football team consumed Neil and his friends, and this year the team had an 8–0 record, primed to go for its third league title in four years. Four more wins and the popular Oklahoma Sooners would be one of the teams to play in the Sugar Bowl, the national title game in January.

"Call me!" I shouted to his retreating back. Neil worked a 24-on and 24-off shift. Station 16 was only a couple of miles away, but he would be late.

"And be careful!"

He lifted his right hand, which indicated nothing, and moments later I heard his old pickup leave the drive. We'd been too rushed to kiss goodbye, something that rarely slipped our attention.

Racing up the stairs, I applied foundation, ran an eyeshadow stick over my eyelids, lined the tops and bottoms in slate and brushed a hint of color on my cheeks, all the while yelling instructions to Kelli and Kris. "Ready in five minutes! Be in the car waiting!"

Mom had said there'd be days like this, but like so much of what Mom said, I hadn't listened.

Minutes later I backed the van out of the garage and sped down our residential street.

The usual traffic jam encircled the school yard, so I dropped off the girls half a block from the front entrance. A light rain mixed with sleet coated the windshield and I wondered why I hadn't noticed the weather earlier. The girls should be wearing boots and raincoats. Kelli lost a shoe—which I belatedly noticed didn't match the one on her left foot—when she piled out, and it took a minute for her to scavenge around and locate the foot apparel. By now she'd noticed the difference in colors and she wanted to go home and change. I couldn't go back home—my first appointment was eight forty-five. We had a brief but heated idea exchange before Kris reached down and wedged the shoe onto her sister's foot. The back door slammed, and I peered in my rearview mirror, feeling guilty as sin. I punched the window button and stuck my head out.

"Be careful—don't accept any rides from strangers. Put your hoods up. You'll catch cold!"

I saw Kelli nod, but Kris ignored me.

"And don't get your feet wet! You'll get a...sore throat." By now the girls had disappeared into the building. I rolled the window up and drove on thinking that tonight I'd stop by and pick up Kelli's favorite meal—chicken nuggets and French fries. Nights Neil slept at the station the girls and I bached. We'd eat pizza, tacos—anything junky—but when Daddy was home we ate balanced nutritional meals. Neil had started to tease "his girls"—that's what he called us—that we enjoyed his absence, but nothing could have been further from the truth. Neil Madison had been my life from the first time I laid eyes on him at a junior high dance. I didn't remember how many years I'd loved the husky football quarterback, but it was a long time before he noticed me and even longer before he reciprocated my feelings. But when Neil Madison fell, he fell hard. January 5 we would celebrate nine years of marriage, and I could honestly say that I loved the man more today than I had that stormy winter afternoon I'd walked down the church aisle— in a practically empty church because an ice storm had paralyzed Oklahoma City traffic. Out-of-town guests and relatives were stranded in nearby hotels. Only the pastor, Neil and my parents made the ceremony. We'd spent the first forty-eight hours of our honeymoon in the airport Holiday Inn Express, waiting for flights to Jamaica to resume.

Those had been the most idealistic days of my life. I smiled and signaled, merging onto the expressway. We were young, in love, full of hopes and dreams. Neil had been with the fire department a little over a year and I hated his job—hated the risks his occupation involved. I was a born, certified, card-carrying worrywart. I constantly worried that something would happen to him, but he'd only smile and say when the Lord said his time was up, he could be eating a doughnut at Krispy Kreme. Since we both believed in God and the risen Christ, I consoled myself with the knowledge that He would never hand me more than I could bear, but deep down I knew that if God ever took Neil, I would blame Him till the day I died.

I pulled into the parking lot of La Chic, the trendy salon where I'm employed. The salon was located near various up-scale hotels and shopping malls, and enjoyed a five-star rat-ing. I recognized a couple of vehicles. The red convertible belonged to my client Rody Haver. High Maintenance Rody, her husband called her. Rody permed her long blond hair one week, and the next she'd be back, sick of the curls and want-ing a straight style. I'd cut her hair in a spiky, carefree punk look and when she'd leave she'd give me a huge tip and say she loved it! The next week she'd be back, claiming blond washed her complexion out—could we do something in red? I'd tell Rody I could make her hair any color she wanted, but I'd ad-vise against putting any more product on an already stressed condition. But Rody would want red, so when she left she would be tinted a gorgeous shade of Amber Flame. She would declare this the real Rody. She loved it!

The next week I'd get a call and Rody would say that her husband, an entrepreneur with unlimited resources, didn't care for red; she was thinking maybe something in ash. I'd pencil in a new appointment, but common sense told me Rody would hate ash, which she did.

We'd go back to blond—which she admitted was really her color—but could I do something about extra conditioning? The ends of her hair felt a bit brittle.

Her hair was breaking at the ends, and the last time I'd shampooed, her follicles felt like corn mush.

Rody was already in my chair, thumbing through a hairstyle magazine, when I stashed my purse at my workstation and flipped on the curling irons. Outside rain splattered the front plate glass and I noticed ice was starting to accumulate on sidewalks.

"I need to get home as quickly as possible," Rody said, eyeing the worsening situation.

I glanced at my appointment book and saw that we only had a trim, so that wouldn't take long.

"I love coming to you, Kate. You can fix anything! You're always so cheery and helpful."

I smiled, basking in Rody's compliment. Actually, I was good at my job. Give me a bad color, perm, cut or weave and I could usually send the client out with a smile on her face. I took no credit for my talent, knowing it was a gift, one that I loved and one that gave me more clients and travel than I wanted. A couple of days a week I had to fly to other states to teach classes on perm and color. The remaining three I got to work here in Oklahoma City, and go home to my family at night. I was a born cosmetologist—about the only thing I couldn't fix were my own self-defeating thoughts.

At the shampoo bowl, we chatted. Rody said her husband was taking her to Maui over the holidays. I said that was nice— Neil and I planned to go to Hawaii some day. The trip wouldn't happen until the kids were older; I needed a new stove and refrigerator before I even thought about grass skirts and Hawaiian sunrises.

Back at my station, I fastened a cape around Rody's neck and went to work. There wasn't much to work with, and the improvement would be negligible, but I had a feeling that if Rody wasn't messing with her hair she wasn't happy.

"Neil's talking about retiring at forty-five," I said. Only last night I'd lain in his arms and we had dreamed of the time when I'd quit work, and he'd leave the fire station. He wanted to move to his grandparents' farm in Vermont. He loved the east, loved the smell of sap dripping in his grandfather's woodlot—and even more, loved his grandmother's plates of steaming hotcakes and butter, drenched in maple syrup.

"Just think, Kate. I'll only be forty-five, still considered young, and with my fireman's pension we can make it. I can help Gramps run the farm, and you can stay home and raise the girls—go to PTA meetings, bake cookies, play bridge with your friends."

I'd laughed. I'd worked since I was nineteen and I couldn't imagine staying home, but it was a nice dream. I'd can from the fruit orchard, and make pickles and jam. I'd fallen asleep listening to thunder and rain rattle our old two-story home in a moderate-income subdivision, dreaming of long, color-drenched Vermont autumn days in our new one-story house with dark blue shutters. Neil would build the house next door to his grandparents. His parents lived nearby, so in Vermont the girls would get to see Maws and Paws every day if they wanted.

Mentally sighing, I finished Rody's trim, blew loose hair off her neck with the dryer, then drenched my fingers with repair serum and ran my hands through the blondish, reddish, ash-speckled, shorn locks. In thirteen short years, my worries would be over. No more listening for the phone to ring, no more fear or paralyzing siren wails in the night, no more worrying that my husband, the man who was my life, would not come home.

I would be a woman of leisure—a mother and housewife whose only worry would be what to do with all that maple syrup.

* * *

I left La Chic around three; sleet had turned to a cold rain, but I stopped at the cleaners before I picked up the girls. Frieda Louis was coming out when I was going in. Frieda lived a couple blocks away, and our kids played together occasionally.

"Kate! How nice to see you."

"Frieda." I paused. She always looked as if she'd stepped out of a magazine—every hair in place, flawlessly applied makeup. I felt like an unmade bed next to her.

"Have any storm damage last night?"

I shook my head. "A little wind. We took shelter in the Fowlers' basement and were up most of the night. How about you?"

"The wind took off an awning on the north side, but Jim had it back up by noon. Don't you hate this freaky weather?"

I hated it. Oklahoma had come by the name "tornado alley" legitimately. We exchanged various bits and pieces before I ducked into the cleaners. Tomorrow was travel day: I had to fly to South Carolina and teach a color class to graduating cosmetology students. Except for those awful flights, I enjoyed the brief trips. I handed the clerk my claim ticket and within minutes I was climbing back into the van. One glance at the dash clock, and I realized I still had time for a quick stop by the pharmacy to refill Kelli's inhaler.

I wheeled into Walgreens, braked, exited the car and dashed into the store. When I walked in I noticed a cluster of sales clerks grouped around an overhead television. A news bulletin blared. I caught sight of a billow of smoke, eerily reminiscent of a similar image from years earlier.

I shuddered, recalling that day with a sense of horror. April 19, 1995, at about 9:03 a.m. on a clear spring morning, a bomb inside a moving truck exploded outside the Alfred P. Murrah Federal Building in Oklahoma City. Parents had dropped their children at the building's day-care center and employees had just sat down at their desks to begin the workday when the blast obliterated half of the nine-story building, killing 168 people, many of them children. It was the most deadly terrorist attack to take place on American soil. Until September 11, 2001.

Neil would have been involved in that tragedy, but we were on holiday. I had thanked God my husband had been spared that awful experience. Any time fire broke out, I panicked, even though right now I could see the fire wouldn't involve Neil's station. The pictures were of downtown Oklahoma City, yet a chill slid up my spine. Some other woman's husband—some child's father—was in turnout gear, dragging heavy hoses and racing up crowded stairwells.

I walked to the back of the store and handed the pharmacist Kelli's spare inhaler. "I need a refill, Mac."

"Sure thing, Mrs. Madison. I'll only be a minute."

I turned, perusing the fall decorations. One counter over, Christmas trees blinked, and a revolving Santa was playing a guitar and singing Elvis's "Blue Christmas." I wondered when Fourth of July would collide with the harvest season. I hardly had time to take down decorations for one holiday and put up the next set, which made me think of chocolate chips. Kris needed three dozen chocolate chip cookies for a class party tomorrow, which meant that I had to light the temperamental oven, and the thought sent another chill up my spine.

I left the counter, picked up the chips in the grocery section and returned to see a man kicking up a fuss about his medication.

"I'm telling you," he bellowed. "I'm running out of room to take my medication!"

"Out of room? Mr. Withers, the dosage says to apply a new patch every morning." The white-coated clerk held the carton at arm's length, rereading the instructions out loud. "Says here, one new patch a day."

"I do that!"

"Is the medication too strong?"

"How should I know? I just do what I'm told, but I'm telling you I'm running out of room."

I smiled at the pharmacist, who seemed totally perplexed.

"Look here." The old man suddenly peeled out of his jacket, threw it on the counter, then unbuttoned his shirt and stripped out of it.

A chuckle escaped me, and I covered my hand with my mouth when I saw the problem. The man had at least fifty patches stuck on him in various spots and positions.

Indeed, he was running out of room.

The pharmacist stared at the interstate of patches, and then calmly explained that the man was to *remove* the old patch and apply a new one.

"Well, why didn't they say so?" The man slipped the shirt back on and buttoned it. "Doctors won't tell you a thing."

A few minutes later I'd paid for the medication and was on my way out of the store when I glanced at the overhead TV. A young store clerk was glued to the set.

"That's downtown, isn't it?" I asked.

The young man nodded. "A high-rise office complex is on fire."

I breathed easier. Station 16 was too far away to respond—unless the situation needed more men. I left the store, my mind back on cookies.

I picked Kelli up at Mrs. Murphy's, the woman we called Saint Helen. Retired, husband deceased fifteen years earlier, Helen was a godsend to us. She kept Kelli after kindergarten, and stayed with both girls the days I traveled. I never worried a minute when I was gone; my girls loved Mrs. Murphy as much as Paws and Maws, and Papa and Grandma, and looked forward to the brief visits.

I picked up Kelli, then swung by the school. When Kris got in, her face was somber. "Mommy, my teacher says there's a really bad fire downtown."

"I heard, sweetie. But Daddy's station wouldn't be involved."

"Are you sure?"

I twisted in my seat and gave her leg a reassuring pat. She worried as much as I did about Neil's safety. "Positive. He'll call us at the usual time tonight."

When I pulled into the drive I punched the garage door button. Minutes later I carried the chocolate chips and Kelli's medicine into the kitchen and deposited the bag on the small desk. No light blinked on the message machine.

Stripping out of my coat, I called for the girls to straighten their room before we ate, and then returned to the car for the cleaning. Fish sticks. Fish sticks, macaroni and cheese—that's what I'd fix for dinner. Since I'd forgotten to stop by for the chicken nuggets, I'd fix Kelli's second-favorite meal. I grinned, thinking about Neil and how he was frying hamburger and onions right about now. Tonight was his night to cook, and he'd be making Spaghetti Red, a concoction of onion, hamburger, chili powder and hot pepper.

How the guys' stomachs survived the monthly gastric workout amazed me, but they seemed to thrive on the challenge. Pete Wilson held the station record for most consumed—four bowls and two spoonfuls. Neil had said they'd had a trophy made, which Pete proudly displayed on top of his locker.

I sprayed a cookie sheet with Pam and lined a half dozen fish sticks on the cookware. Then came the challenge. I bent over the old oven and tried to light the gas flame, scared to death. As usual, it wouldn't catch until I'd lit three matches. Then, in a loud *whossssh!* flame exploded. Usually it knocked me backward several feet and tonight was no different. I jumped back and slammed the door, allowing time for the old relic to heat.

Six o'clock. I grinned, taking a box of macaroni and cheese out of the cabinet.

Neil would be calling any minute.

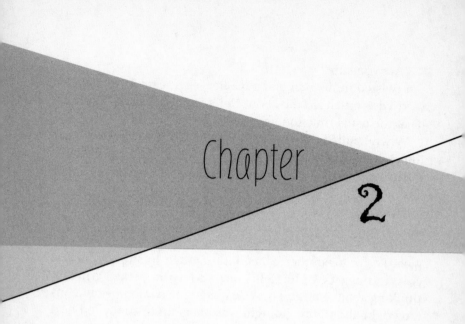

Chapter 2

I glanced at the clock on my way through the kitchen to the utility room. Laundry. Boy, did I have laundry. How could four people get this many clothes dirty?

Seven-thirty. Neil still hadn't called. He seldom went past his self-imposed seven-o'clock deadline, but for once in my life I was too busy to worry. The washer swished away, working on a load of clothes, and I headed for the bedroom to hang up perma press, shake out wrinkles and choose what to take with me. Black pants go with everything. A black, tan and white top and my brand-new cobalt-blue blouse with a vest of flowered tapestry material. Yeah, looking good, Katie, girl.

I dug through my closet hunting for my black flats. They were well broken in and comfortable and I had to stand on my feet all day. A couple of paperbacks to read on the plane. Now, what else?

Kris stuck her head through the doorway. "Mom, are you busy?"

"Oh, well, no. What would give you that idea?"

She glanced at the half-packed bag. "I have to have cookies for the party tomorrow."

"Isn't your class celebrating fall early? October is still a few days away."

"We're having lots of autumn celebrations this year."

"Well, then, lucky I remembered. I bought chocolate chips today. I'll bake them after supper. Maybe you can help."

Sunshine reigned in her smile. "No kidding! Awesome."

She was only seven and would probably make a terrible mess, but it was too late to back out now. I watched her skip from the room and wondered why I worried about her. I liked my job. I enjoyed the out-of-state classes I taught, but I worried. Should I go off and leave my children and husband, to fly to South Carolina for this meeting?

Was I neglecting my duties as a wife and mother, putting my job first? Our lesson in Sunday school this week had dealt with the woman's role in the home. Boy, had I felt singled out.

Was I the only woman in New Freedom Worship Center who had trouble being everything to everybody? A superhero I wasn't. I've always envied that Proverbs 31 woman whose husband and children rose up and called her blessed. When mine rose up and called me, it was usually because I was behind on the laundry.

I left the bedroom and hurried to the utility room to take the clean clothes out of the washer and throw them in the dryer.

I wished I could spend time with the kids tonight, talking and listening, but I was too busy to talk, too busy to listen. It seemed as if I was always rushed, making promises I had difficulty fulfilling. My "want to" kept running ahead of my "can do," and I had enough guilt to fill Kelli's little red wagon.

Neil was good to support me when I had to make these trips. It wasn't the same as me being here, and I knew that. My husband's retirement dream was sounding better all the time.

I went back to the bedroom to throw things into my suitcase. Thank goodness I had made a list. As I crossed off each item and dropped it in my case I felt a sense of relief. I was going to make it after all. I grinned at my lack of faith. I'd never missed a plane yet. But I always worried. Neil claimed if I didn't have anything to worry about I'd invent something. Some days I thought he might have a point.

I closed the suitcase and went back to the laundry room. Kelli was down on her hands and knees trying to pick up a bug off the kitchen floor. One of those water roaches, I think they're called, big, black and very, very ugly. I stared at the roach, and everything I had ever heard or suspected about bugs flashed through my mind. Dirty, creepy, crawly and disease-bearing. And Kelli was going to pick the bug up in her bare hands! The hair on the back of my neck prickled.

I shrieked, "Don't touch that nasty thing!"

Kelli whirled to face me, lost her balance and plopped down on the floor next to the bug. At least the roach had enough sense to run for cover before I could dance the La Cucaracha on its helpless body. Kelli burst into tears.

Why had I screamed like that? I caught myself before I said anything more. We didn't need a crisis tonight, and I recognized the signs of an impending one. Her eyes were as big and as round as gumballs. She was my sensitive child, and when I shrieked, which I did all too often, she panicked. I could see it welling in her eyes. Abject horror.

I reached out and pulled her close, smoothing her hair back from her forehead. "Oh, Kelli, Mommy's sorry. I didn't mean to frighten you."

She sobbed, and the sound tore me apart inside. When would I learn to control my emotions? All my life I'd been frightened by anything that crawled, squirmed or got around without legs, which pretty well included everything in the insect and reptile families. Just the sight of something creepy and crawly was enough to cause me to hit the panic button. I hadn't intended to scare Kelli; I just didn't want her picking up the bug.

"Don't cry, honey," I soothed. "It's all right. Bugs are dirty and they can make you sick."

I marched her over to the sink, ignoring her protests. I wasn't going to have my daughter getting germs or some unknown disease from playing with bugs. She squirmed, but I washed her hands twice with a strong disinfectant. Drat this old house—drat Neil for not calling the exterminator earlier. With any luck we'd have enough money saved next year to purchase a new home.

Kelli sobbed the entire time I scrubbed. "Bugs are nice, Mommy. They're God's helpless creatures."

God's helpless creatures? Where did she come up with this stuff? "They're not as helpless as they look. I'm calling the exterminator the moment I get back."

A look of pure horror filled her eyes. "The Terminator? For a little bug?"

Terminator? Arnold? As in Schwarzenegger? I stifled a laugh, wondering how I could explain the difference between an exterminator and a terminator to a five-year-old. Not that there *was* all that much difference between the two. My daughter was too tenderhearted to approve of either.

The phone rang and I lifted the receiver and snapped, "Hello," thinking I'd hear Neil's voice. Instead I heard the dial tone. I held the receiver out and stared at it. Someone hung up on me? What?

Kris called from the living room. "Doorbell."

The kids weren't allowed to answer the door. You heard such awful things about children disappearing that I was scared to death to let them open the door to a stranger. I hung up the receiver and hurried toward the living room. Telephone. Doorbell. Whatever.

I yelled at Kris to turn the television down from sonic to just plain loud. Why did it always sound like kickoff time at a bowl game around here? A little quiet wouldn't hurt anything. I picked an armload of books and toys on my way to the door, dumping them in a corner of the couch before reaching for the doorknob.

I opened the door to find two men dressed in dark uniforms standing there. One was Neil's fire chief, John Miller, and the other was one of Neil's closest station buddies, Ben Burgess. I smiled and started to speak when I saw the grief in both men's expressions.

My smile faded.

John spoke first. "Kate...I'm sorry."

Sorry? I cocked my head. For what? I gripped the edge of the door. My heart must have stopped beating for a second, because my body suddenly felt wooden, heavy. His mouth moved, but I heard only scattered words.

"Accident...fire...stairway collapsed...lost two men...Neil didn't make it out. So sorry."

Ben had his arm around me helping me to the sofa. My legs felt rubbery, like those foam tubes children use in swimming pools. Kelli and Kris were hanging on to me, begging me not to cry. I tried to reassure them, but my voice failed me. Someone was weeping in great gasping sobs that seemed to come from some deep well of grief. That wasn't me, was it?

"The high rise wasn't in his district," I cried.

"Sorry, Kate, we were called in."

I saw my daughters' fearful faces through a veil of tears. They clung to me and I held them close. Neil... Oh, God...Neil. The words ran through my mind like a prayer, but if God answered I didn't hear Him.

John sat across from me, rolling the brim of his hat in his hands. "Who's your pastor, Kate?"

I stared at him, blank. I couldn't remember the man's name. I had heard him preach every Sunday for four years and I couldn't remember his name.

"Joe Crockett," Kris said.

I shook my head in amazement, thinking how smart she was. I had raised this kid—Neil was so proud of her.... *Neil.*

Then Pastor Crockett and his wife, Eva, arrived. Time had no meaning for me. Pastor Joe took my hand and I saw the compassion in his eyes and I started crying harder. Eva had her arms around Kelli and Kris, leading them from the room. I knew I had to get control of myself. My daughters needed me, but I couldn't think. People talked to me and I answered or nodded, but it was as if I was watching some other woman sitting on the sofa shredding a tissue and trying to cope.

My pastor's words came to me out of a fog. "Neil's in heaven now with his Lord and Savior."

I knew he meant well, but I wanted to lash out that I didn't *want* him to be in heaven. I wanted him here, with me.

Oh, God...why? Had I told him I loved him and kissed him goodbye before he left this morning? I wished I could go back and relive that hurried departure. Hold him a moment longer, say everything I should have said.

Someone had called a doctor, and a man showed up, carrying a black bag. I remember answering his questions to the best of my knowledge, though I was operating in a fog. He shook out a couple of pills, and I swallowed them. He gave the bottle to Eva and reminded me to call him in the morning; I had only enough medication to last through the night. At the moment I couldn't recall if I had a physician. Doctors scared me.

Eventually I stopped crying. The well had run dry. I sat on the sofa in a soggy, wilted lump, blissfully calm. The sedative had started to work.

Sunshine filtered through the bedroom lace curtains. The house had filled up with people, bearing meat loaves and casseroles. A woman I had met—and should have known—went on and on at great lengths in a stage whisper, apologizing for burning a roast.

A bubble of hysteria rose up in my throat, choking me. Burning a roast? When my husband, the love of my life, the father of my two precious children, had burned to death in a high-rise fire?

Neil's parents arrived, and the situation intensified. Madge Madison threw her arms around me and leaned into me for support. Her tears soaked through my sweatshirt. I held her, rocking back and forth the way I did with my daughters when they were hurt.

His father, Harry, short and broad shouldered with a handsome head of white hair, seemed to have shrunk. His hands trembled as he reached out to touch my shoulder. I released my mother-in-law and went into his arms. He awkwardly patted my back, and for the first time I felt a small measure of comfort. Maybe because he reminded me of Neil. With Neil's parents on either side of me, I walked into the kitchen where neighbors were serving coffee.

I stared at my kitchen counters, buried under a deluge of dishes. Salads and desserts and casseroles. How could three people—actually two if you counted Kris and Kelli as one—be expected to eat all of this? My ancient refrigerator was working in overdrive anyway.

Sue Carol, from my Sunday-school class, handed me a cup of coffee I didn't want. What I wanted was to crawl off and lick my wounds and try to deal with the devastating blow, but I guess manners, once learned, go deeper than surface polish. I forced myself to speak to everyone who had taken the time to come and offer comforting words. It occurred to me that friends are one of the greatest unrecognized blessings, and you never fully appreciate them until your world crashes around you.

Eva made up the bed in the guest room for Neil's parents. She was also the one who insisted everyone go home so I could rest. I stared helplessly around the kitchen at the surplus of food, not sure what to do with it all and too tired to care, but to my relief Sue and Eva managed to put away all of the perishables, then filled freezer containers and stashed them in the deep freeze for later.

I locked the door a little after eight o'clock, and turned out the front porch light. Neil's parents had already gone to their room, worn out by the day's emotions. Neil was their only son and the pride of their life. I didn't see how any of us could go on without him.

Losing him had left a crater in my heart.

The girls followed me into my bedroom. *Mine.* Not *ours* any longer. Their eyes were red and swollen from crying. Kelli's lower lip trembled. "Can I sleep with you?"

"Me, too," Kris begged.

I didn't hesitate. "Sure. I'd like that." And I would. The thought of that empty bed had been hanging over my head like that sword of Damocles. Now I would have company.

I helped them into their nightgowns. We could skip baths tonight. I brushed Kris's long, straight blond hair, a feature we shared, along with blue eyes, straight noses and peach complexions.

Kelli, on the other hand, was a miniature replica of Neil with her short cap of dark curls and warm brown eyes. I forced myself to concentrate on drawing the brush through Kris's hair, willing my mind away from the way Neil and I had looked as a couple. My Nordic fairness offset by his dark hair and golden tan. His picture smiled at me from the dresser, held close by the silver frame. But Neil was gone.

I laid down the brush and kissed Kris lightly on the cheek. "Hop into bed, okay."

The girls were docile tonight, none of the usual begging to be allowed to stay up late or demanding a story before they went to sleep. I averted my face so they couldn't see my tears, thinking that their lives had changed irrevocably. Whatever happened now, I was determined that the three of us would stay together, and I'd make the best possible life for my daughters.

Kelli hopped up on the bed and sat cross-legged. "You should have been in the kitchen when Mrs. Hutchinson dropped the bowl of fruit salad."

"She did what?" I turned to stare at her, sure I hadn't heard right. Ida Hutchinson never did anything wrong, to hear her tell it.

Kris's face wrinkled in a smile she tried to suppress. "She almost said a bad word, too. And Reverend Joe was standing right there."

I laughed.

It felt so blessedly good.

The thought of Ida cutting loose in front of our pastor struck me as being extremely funny, although I supposed part of my reaction was due to nerves.

The girls, freed by my laughter, joined me. I sat down beside them on the bed and the three of us had a good laugh. Finally, wiping tears from the corners of my eyes, I said, "Look, girls. We've lost Daddy, but it's still all right to laugh."

Kris nodded. "Daddy liked to laugh."

"Yes, Daddy did." Neil had had a laugh that rang out like church bells. I could be standing on the other side of the yard and hear him and know immediately Neil was enjoying life. That's the way he was—he enjoyed life, and he'd told me a hundred times, *Be happy for the day, Kate. Tomorrow has its own agenda.*

I drew my girls close, breathing in their unique, little-girl scent. "We're going to have sad times," I promised, thinking how ridiculously understated that sounded. "But we will always have laughter. Daddy would want that. That's a promise."

The children hugged me back, then rolled over and crawled beneath the blankets.

I turned out the light and stretched out in the middle of the bed with my clothes still on, holding a precious daughter on each side. "Say the prayer," Kelli said.

I caught my breath. How could I pray tonight? From the depths of my misery, what could I thank God for?

"Go on, Mommy. God's waiting."

All right. I would say the prayer, but other than in front of my children, I would never speak to God again. Never. He had taken the one thing from me He knew I held the dearest. What kind of loving God did that? My praise came haltingly and was brief.

"Thank You for my daughters. Thank You for the years we had their father. Be with us as we go into tomorrow, for we need Your care."

"Amen," the girls said in unison.

I lay in the dark, with the girls sleeping beside me, and let my thoughts drift. I was still too numb and keyed up to sleep. Sudden tears scalded my cheeks. *Dear God. Neil was gone.*

The day of Neil's service dawned clear and sunny. It had rained two days in succession. I had a feeling that the sky had cried itself out.

My mother and dad had arrived from Kansas. I put them in the master bedroom, and fixed a pallet for myself on the floor in Kelli's room. My parents and Neil's had never been what you might call "close." Armed truce was more like it. They were so polite to each other it set my teeth on edge.

Sally Fowler, my next-door neighbor, kept running in and out, keeping peace and striking a note of normalcy. I had a large black-and-blue bruise on my arm, which puzzled me. When I wondered about it out loud, Sally said the day Neil died I had kept pinching my arm, trying to convince myself I was dreaming. I couldn't remember, but I didn't remember much of that awful day. The mental fog had cut deeper than I realized.

My mother was standing at the stove when I entered the kitchen, making her special sour cream flapjacks. Madge Madison was arranging her famous breakfast casserole on the kitchen table.

Mom poured juice. Madge poured hot chocolate.

The tension was so thick you could have cut it with a knife and called it fudge. I sighed. Well, at least nobody was crying.

Kelli padded into the room and cast a jaundiced eye at the set table. "I want Fruitee Pops," she announced.

My mother matched her look for look. "Kelli. I got up early to fix pancakes for you." Her tone said, *Therefore you will eat them.*

Kelli stuck out her lower lip. "I don't want pancakes. I want Fruitee Pops." She sat down at her usual place and propped her elbows on the table. Mom slapped a plate of pancakes down in front of her. Kelli pushed it aside.

Mom burst into tears.

So did Kelli.

Followed by Madge.

I excused myself and went upstairs and locked myself in the bathroom.

Somehow we made it to the funeral home on time. Flowers were banked on both sides of the casket. Neil had a lot of friends, and the auditorium was crowded. I'd let Neil's mother pick out the songs, and now I regretted it.

"'If we never meet again, this side of heaven,'" the soprano trilled, and I sobbed into my handkerchief.

Neil would have liked his service, if that were possible. The church held over six hundred firemen today, all dressed for a solemn occasion. When the funeral cortege left the church for the cemetery, the fire signal system started tapping at regular thirty-second intervals. The procession passed Neil's station, Station 16. His fellow workers and friends—some with tears openly streaming down their cheeks—stood at attention with their caps over their hearts. Behind the hearse was a body of twenty men who were his closest friends. Behind them, one hundred uniformed firemen accompanied my husband on his last run.

The service at the cemetery was mercifully brief. We didn't linger at the grave site. By this time I knew it wasn't Neil in that box—that wasn't my vibrantly alive husband.

As soon as we got back to my house everyone started loading cars, looking for lost items and saying final goodbyes.

Dad hugged me. "Listen, kitten. You need us, you call. Oklahoma isn't that far from Kansas. We'll come in a heartbeat."

I leaned against him, feeling like a little girl again. "I know. Thanks."

Mom wrapped her arms around me. The tip of her nose was red from crying. "Oh, Katie, I'm so sorry. We loved Neil."

I kissed her cheek. "He loved you, too."

"Call me and let me know how you're getting along."

"I will."

"Anything you need, call," Dad reiterated.

I nodded, knowing they couldn't provide what I needed— my life restored, my husband resurrected from the dead.

They both hugged the girls, then they got in their car and drove away, and we went through the whole routine again with Neil's parents.

As suddenly as they had appeared, everyone was gone. Sally and Ron Fowler had offered to take Neil's parents to the airport. I'd agreed, thankful for the reprieve.

That night I sat in the empty living room, holding a cup of tea I didn't want. The kids were in bed, the doors were locked. For the first time in days the house was silent. I had never realized how devastating silence could be.

I was a widow with two small children and I knew I couldn't make it alone. Never mind how I knew, I just knew. Neil's worn Bible lay on the coffee table where he'd left it. We had been strong believers, faithful in our church, but nothing in our Christian walk had prepared me for this. A man didn't die at thirty-two; that wasn't possible. The past week had been a nightmare and I wanted to wake up.

But I wasn't asleep, and I knew it.

Was my faith strong enough to face the future? Neil had left a reasonable insurance policy, so with proper investment I wouldn't have to worry about money. If I kept my job...but I had to do a lot of flying. What if the plane went down? The thought winged through my subconscious and formed a grapefruit-sized knot in my stomach. What would my children do with both parents gone?

Kelli and Kris would be orphans. Neil and I had never gotten around to making a will. Mom and Dad would take the kids...but Neil's parents would want them, too. I gripped my hands in my lap, imagining the war. There'd be a big fight. Split right down the middle along family lines.

My children would live in turmoil; they'd end up in therapy, warped for life because I was a thoughtless parent who was so self-absorbed I'd forgotten to consider my children's future.

I'd never fly again.

What was I saying? If I wanted to keep my job I *had* to fly. It was all too complicated for me in my mixed-up state.

Somehow I'd hold my family together. Life went on, and people went on.

As I recall, that was my last rational thought for a while. I sank into a blue funk. I knew that being a responsible parent meant being there for my children no matter how badly I was hurting, but my mind rebelled. So I slipped away to a private place where I could mourn Neil's passing without the world's interference. If it hadn't been for kind neighbors and my church family, I don't know what would have happened to Kelli and Kris. I loved them—loved them with all my heart—but anguish had rendered me nonfunctional. I faintly recalled someone being in the house at all times, but mentally I was absent. I couldn't explain it; only those who had lived the experience could put the feeling in plain words.

And I stayed that way for maybe two or three weeks. I'm not sure. I'm only sure of how and when my body slowly came back to life. Well, not slowly. Swiftly was more accurate.

It was when Kelli suddenly burst into my bedroom, startling me from my black abyss.

"There's a snake in the attic!"

I blinked, focusing on my daughter. "A *what?* Where?"

"A snake," she repeated. "In our attic. Come and get it Mom."

Chapter 3

A what? My heart jolted, and started beating for the first time in weeks. I was still sleeping on the pallet, unable to return to the bed Neil and I had shared. I jumped up, wide-eyed, hair standing on end. Kris, evidently the calmest Madison, wet a paper towel in the adjoining bath and slapped it across my forehead. I sank back on the pillow, feeling cold water running down my neck.

Snake.

In my attic.

When I found my voice, I asked if Kris was certain.

"Real sure, Mommy."

The snake had slid behind the cubbyhole where we kept Christmas decorations. My natural instinct was to call Neil; my second was to break into frustrated tears.

Kris patted my hand. "Don't cry, Mommy. I'll get the snake."

Although I was tempted, I couldn't let a seven-year-old engage in an attic snake hunt. I had no idea what kind of snake resided in my home other than Kris's description: big.

And black.

Maybe.

"We'll call Ron Fowler," I said. "And what were you doing in the attic so late?"

"Playing." Kris glanced at the clock. "Mr. Fowler will be asleep by now."

Worry kicked into overdrive. If Neil was here he'd dispose of the snake and that would be that, but Neil wasn't here, and this was just the first of a series of problems I would face without him. I couldn't call on my neighbors, the Fowlers, in every crisis. Kris pressed a tissue into my hand, and I tried to get a grip on my fear.

I hated snakes about as much as I hated toads. Both repulsed me, especially toads. One had gotten in my bed when I was a kid. We'd lived in a rural area, and near a pond, so snakes and toads were plentiful, but the critters kept me paranoid. I tried to shake off fear. I had been in a state of shock for, what— weeks? I glanced at the wall calendar—the one Neil had given me last Christmas. Twelve months of sexy, bare-chested firemen. Hot tears filled my eyes.

"What day is this?" I asked.

Kris rolled her eyes pensively. "October, uh, maybe the middle."

Dear Lord. I had sleepwalked through half of October!

I was appalled. I had to pull out of this. I threw back the sheets and told Kelli I was going to shower and wash my hair before we tackled the snake.

I stood under the hot water until the heater ran dry, but I felt more human now. Toweling off, I spotted the bottle of sedatives I had been downing like chocolate-covered almonds. I'd lived on doctor-prescribed medication for the past few weeks. I uncapped the bottle and stared at the blue pills and knew the next few weeks were going to be unbearable, but I had to keep it together for Kelli and Kris. As soon as I was dressed in sweats and clean socks I carried the pills downstairs and crammed them into a jar of sardines, then threw the sardines in the trash. I detested sardines. I knew I wouldn't touch the pills again.

Armed with baseball bats and a butterfly net, my daughters and I climbed the creaking attic stairs. A single overhead bulb lit our way; a bare oak branch scraped the roof. The creepy scenario reminded me of a scene out of a low-budget horror flick. I rarely came up here, but Kris and Kelli played among luggage pieces, old trunks, dress forms and seasonal clothing on occasional rainy afternoons. And of course decorations— Thanksgiving, Christmas, Fourth of July. Madisons were into decorating for every occasion; our house was old and rambling, but always festively lit.

The three of us wore sober expressions; my five-year-old clung tightly to the fabric of my sweats. We made the steep climb, and then stood at the head of the stairs while I flipped on the lone hanging lightbulb that lit the attic itself.

I flashed the light beam across the open rafters. I'd heard snakes like to hang by joists. I swallowed and asked exactly where Kris had spotted the snake. Maybe she'd been mistaken. A seven-year-old's imagination was fertile ground. I felt relieved. That was it—Kris *thought* she'd seen a snake. It could have been anything or nothing. I mean, how would a snake get in the attic this late in the year? Weren't reptiles dormant now? I wasn't sure. Kris pointed toward the stored Christmas decorations. Warning the children to stand back, I crept closer to the danger area. Boxes of bulbs, tinsel and outdoor lights blocked my view. I'd have to move a few to see behind the shelving, but first I took the bat and whacked each box, notifying the snake of my presence. Something darted out. I shrieked and scrabbled for cover, lunging for the nearest refuge. I climbed aboard an army trunk and shouted, "Kelli! Kris—go back downstairs!"

Kelli broke into tears, and Kris, the color of putty, grabbed her sister's hand. I yelled again. "Get away! Run!"

Kris raced toward the stairs, pulling her sobbing sister after her. I could hear their leather soles clattering down the wooden stairway.

I forced myself to think. What had run out at me? The snake? A roach? I hadn't gotten a good enough look to identify the source, but the way I reacted must have made Kris and Kelli think a tyrannosaurus rex was loose in the attic.

Instantly I regretted my emotional outburst. My poor children were going to be paranoid wrecks by the time they were grown. Neil had often accused me of passing my fears onto the kids, but I didn't mean to—after all, how did I know what was slithering around on my attic floor? In my hasty flight, I'd dropped the flashlight. I spotted the beam shining on the floor. I saw nothing but dust bunnies in the intense light.

I eased off the trunk and cautiously approached the enemy zone. When I didn't see anything of the snake, I banged on a box of tinsel and scrambled back onto the trunk. Nothing happened. I could hear Kris and Kelli at the bottom of the stairway, crying.

"It's okay, sweeties!" I called. "Don't let anybody in the house!"

Quivering, high-pitched voices replied in unison, "We won't, Mommy."

I doubted perverts kept these late hours, and I'd drummed into the children repeatedly not to accept rides from strangers, and to never, ever let anyone in the house without permission, including friends and neighbors. Of course, not taking candy from strangers was a given.

Minutes passed, and the snake failed to show its—whatever. I debated my options, worrying my lower lip with my upper teeth. I could lock the attic door, seal it tight with duct tape and call the exterminator in the morning, but I knew neither I nor the girls would sleep a wink knowing what lay in the attic.

Buck up, Kate. You're a big girl now.

I took a swipe at unanticipated tears and could almost hear Neil saying, *You're head honcho now, babe. Take care of the ranch.*

Head honcho. Head coward was more like it. I didn't want to be head anything. I stepped off the trunk and carefully approached the largest box. I tugged and slid the carton away from the wall, then grabbed my bat and waited.

Nothing.

I tackled the next box.

Nothing.

I systematically moved boxes, poised for swift justice. Would I actually beat the thing to death? I'd never gotten close enough to a wild animal to be lethal. My insides churned with hot tar. Soon all the Christmas decorations were sitting in the middle of the attic floor, and still no sign of the snake.

I sank back down on the trunk to think. The kids' crying had fizzled to an occasional hiccup. I pictured my sweet, innocent children huddled below, confused. Worried. *Lord, why am I such a poor role model?*

Why such a wimp and worrywart? Maybe being an only child had created the condition. Mom and Dad had been protective—overly so. Maybe I came by the trait naturally. I thought of all the imagined horrors of my youth, and I cringed. I didn't want Kelli and Kris to grow up afraid of their shadows. Without Neil as a stabilizing force, I would be responsible for how my daughters reacted to fear the rest of their lives. The thought scared me to death.

I had to overcome my uncertainties. I'd prayed about them, but then I would almost immediately revert to my old state. Now that I was alone, I had to change. I had to get a grip. Starting with the snake. Okay. I would shut the attic door, seal the crack and tell the kids not to worry: the snake couldn't harm us. I didn't know beans about snakes, but this one sounded as if it might be a common breed. A cobweb grazed the top of my head, and I reached up to brush it aside, praying a black widow wasn't lurking somewhere in the web. Or brown recluse—that would be more likely.

Stop it, Kate. You didn't ask to be a widow at thirty-two, but you are. It could be Neil left alone, with two children, and I knew, deep in my heart, between Neil and me, God had chosen the right one to take home. Why? Because he couldn't have taken care of kids, the house, baby-sitting and his job. Oh, he could, but it would have been so foreign to him.

I stood up and reached for the butterfly net and flashlight. And then I felt it—something heavy dropped from a rafter, right at my feet.

Peering down, I tried to locate it. Suddenly I couldn't breathe. The snake lay directly in front of me.

Faint now. I was too scared to scream. Hysteria rose, my mouth moved, but nothing came out. Instead, I jumped back, batting at the reptile with the butterfly net.

Stumbling across the attic floor, I engaged in a silent one-on-one war. My heavy shoe trapped the head and I stood frozen. Yewoooooo. I knew I was going to be sick. The snake squirmed and wiggled, thrashing its long body.

"Mommy?" Kris called.

"Yes," I squeaked. The reptile's tail thrashed and whipped back and forth.

"You okay?"

Get a grip, Kate. You don't want them scared of their own shadows.

"Fine," I chirped. My hand tightened on the butterfly net. I couldn't hit the snake—it wasn't in me. Besides, if I missed I would panic and go to pieces.

God, You've got to help me. I cannot do this alone.

I bent over and carefully draped the mesh around the reptile's head and then scooped the writhing snake into the net. Once I had him trapped, I gained power. What now? I could hear Kelli and Kris clumping up the stairs.

The snake was still an alarming sight, even net-trapped.

With a false calm, I snatched the net up and hurried to the east window. Paint had practically sealed the pane, but I discovered strength I didn't think existed. Kris and Kelli reached the top of the stairs about the time I jerked the window open and flung the net, snake and all, outside, praying the mesh wouldn't lodge on the shingles. I slammed the window shut and turned around, smiling as they hit the doorway.

"Hey, guys."

Kelli and Kris hesitantly crept toward me. "Did you find the snake?"

"Taken care of," I said, pretending to wash my hands of the disdainful matter. "Anyone interested in a cup of hot chocolate?"

The kids stared in wonder, relief filling their faces. Kris smiled, and I realized I hadn't seen her smile in weeks. "You got it?"

"I got it."

And I prayed that I had it. A lifetime, my children's lifetime, was an awesome responsibility. I hoped I was up to the challenge.

It was after eleven o'clock before the house settled back to normalcy. I switched out the lamp and climbed into my pallet. Kelli's soft breathing reassured me I was richly blessed, even if I cursed my circumstances.

Streetlight filtered through the eyelet curtains. I rolled to my side and covered my ears with my pillow, hoping the action might blot out my thoughts. No such luck. Worries fought with my need for sleep. Despite my comatose state, I had continued to work. I had a six-o'clock flight; without Neil to help, I'd have to drop the girls and their luggage at Mrs. Murphy's on my way to the airport. My heart ached as though someone had welded the valves shut.

What if I got sick and couldn't work? Neil's insurance should cover the next few years, but the money wouldn't last forever.

I should go back to church; so many of the congregation had supported us, prayed for us, sent encouraging cards and letters. I tried to recall the last Sunday Neil and I were to-gether—couple-together. We'd gone to church, and then taken the girls to Chuck E. Cheese's for a special treat. That night we had taken the family to the local zoo. The kids had de-lighted in the animals and fall decorations. Neil and I had strolled hand in hand beneath a full moon, admiring giraffes and elephants, their habitats decked in colorful lights. I never once thought that would be our last official outing together, but then, who would ever think that? Bad things didn't hap-pen to us.

I tossed my blanket aside and rolled to my back, staring at the ceiling. I knew by heart exactly how many tiles it took to stretch across the room and the number it took to run to the opposite wall. Two hundred and forty.

The house was old, dating back seventy-five years, but it had been the best Neil and I could afford on our budget seven years ago. I was expecting Kris, and Neil was rela-tively new at the fire station. With a baby on the way, we knew we'd need more room than the efficiency apartment we'd moved into after our honeymoon. We'd found the house on a lovely spring afternoon, and even though it was old and run-down, we saw all kinds of possibilities. We'd painted and wallpapered and made a small nursery down-stairs adjoining our bedroom. We'd loved this home, but re-cently we'd talked of buying one of the ranch styles in a new, moderately priced subdivision a few miles away. Kris could stay in her school district, and Mrs. Murphy would still be close.

I rose on an elbow and peered at the clock. Twelve-thirty. I had to get some sleep. Without medication, the hours dragged, but I would not take another pill. I had to resume life. For my children's sake, I had to make an effort to restore normalcy.

One o'clock came.

Then two o'clock. I had to be up and functioning in two hours.

Sleep refused to come. Finally I got up, padded to the kitchen and sat down at the table. A house was so empty this time of night. The furnace was turned low; the floor was cold and unwelcoming to my bare feet.

I stared out the window onto the quiet street. Neighbors were asleep, couples lying next to each other in their beds. I closed my eyes and recalled the years I had taken Neil's presence for granted. Of the hundreds and thousands of times I'd curled next to his warm body, felt his heart beat in sync with mine, and never once thought of the woman or man who lay that same night in an empty bed, alone. Hurting. Pain so intense you wondered if your heart wouldn't succumb to the blackness, and you prayed that it would.

I knew I had to talk to someone. Anyone.

Quietly I walked to the desk phone, not having the slightest idea whom I'd call. Not Mom—I loved her dearly, but she didn't understand, thank God, how deep the pain cut.

If I had a sister...but I didn't. Or a brother. Not even friends close enough to call at this hour of the morning.

My eyes focused on the prayer sheet I'd brought home Neil's and my last Sunday together. The pastor's home phone number stood out. Did I dare? A moment later I picked up the receiver and punched the numerical pad.

Two rings later a man answered. I don't know if Joe Crockett recognized my voice. I don't see how he could have, because I was sobbing by now, incoherent, but he managed to single out who I was.

"Pastor Joe...I...need you," I managed.

"I'll be there in fifteen minutes, Kate."

I got dressed, and when I let him in it was close to two-thirty. Surely the church didn't pay him well enough to climb out of a warm bed on a cold winter's night and come to a distraught female's rescue.

He handed me his topcoat and hat, then quietly followed me into the kitchen. We sat across the table from each other. I didn't know where to begin. So I just admitted the truth.

"I can't do this alone."

"You are not alone," he said. "You feel alone, but God is with you, Kate."

"God." I shook my head, resentment welling up in my throat.

"He's promised never to leave us, Kate, but He hasn't promised that we'll always feel His presence. I know you feel utterly alone and forsaken right now."

"Why did God take Neil?" I looked up, tears running down my cheeks. "I *begged* Him not to take Neil—for years I've begged Him. Why did He do this to me?" My voice broke, tears obstructing my voice.

He shook his head and sighed. "I can't answer that. But I'm here. I care—the church cares. God cares."

I didn't care.

Pastor Joe was kind and the church had been supportive, but Neil was gone, and there was nothing anyone could do or say to bring him back. I knew the next thing he'd be telling me was that God uses our bad experiences to make us stronger, and I didn't want to hear it. I didn't want to be stronger. I wanted my husband back—in this house—laughing, playing with Sailor, teasing Kelli, helping Kris with her homework. Loving me.

We sat in the silent kitchen and he clasped my hand in comfort. The warmth of another living, breathing adult helped, made the dark house feel less threatening and cold.

"Tell me how I go on." I thought of the Colorado flight in a little under three hours. Leaving my girls for the first time since we'd become a family of three. Three was an uneven number....

"It will take time, Kate. Days. Weeks—maybe years. The grieving process is different for all of us. It will be time you won't want to give, but eventually you'll be able to go on. You're a strong young woman. I have utmost confidence in your ability to survive."

I don't know where the conversation would have taken us if the pastor hadn't heard Sailor scratching at the back door. I'd forgotten to let him in before I went to bed.

"That's Sailor. He wants to come in," I said.

"I'll take care of it." He got up and walked to the back door, unlatched and opened it. Sailor entered the house on a rush of cold air.

"Drop it!" Pastor Joe shouted.

Startled, I sat up straighter. "Pardon?"

"Drop it!" He backed up, keeping his distance from the dog. I rose slightly and peered over the edge of the table. My jaw dropped. Sailor had the snake in his mouth. A black tail wildly gyrated back and forth.

"Sailor! Drop it!" Pastor Joe repeated sternly.

"No! Don't drop it!" I sprang up, wondering what I'd done with the bat. This snake was like a plague!

Sailor wagged his tail and dropped it. The snake was badly injured but still alive.

"How in the world?" I breathed.

"Yow." Joe's eyes focused on the disappearing reptile.

"Mommy?" Kris came into the kitchen, rubbing her eyes.

"Kris! Get back!"

My daughter jumped, her eyes darting to the pastor, then back to me. "What...?"

"The snake! Sailor carried it into the house."

What had I done? Committed the unpardonable sin? Was God punishing me? Could I expect a plague of grasshoppers or a swarm of locusts next?

"Where's the ball bat?" I asked.

Wide-eyed, Kris pointed upstairs. "You left it by the attic door."

"Stay where you are," Joe commanded. "I'll take care of it." Joe sidestepped me, grabbed the snake behind the head and took it briskly outside. Kris and I continued to balance on top of a kitchen chair.

Sailor stood in the middle of the floor, obviously proud of his show-and-tell display.

"Sailor. Bad dog," I scolded.

Kris clung to my robe. "Mommy, you said you'd gotten rid of the snake."

"I know, dear. I thought I had." That snake had nine lives—all intended to test me.

When Joe returned, it was close to 4:00 a.m. and time for me to get up.

He had disposed of the snake—where or how I didn't ask. I only hoped this was a permanent riddance. I dragged Kelli out of a warm bed and dressed her. Pastor Joe helped carry two sleepy children outside to the garage.

After stowing our luggage in back, he wished me well, and casually assured a worried Kelli that Mommy would be coming back. He stepped back and watched as I backed the van out of the garage and sped off in the gray dawn.

As I adjusted my rearview mirror I suddenly realized he'd never answered my question. How *did* I go on?

I guess no mere human held the secret. No one could explain how anyone lived through times like this and kept their sanity. Or their faith. I realized that I was mad at God. Livid. He'd taken the best part of my life, other than Kelli and Kris. How could I be anything but bitter?

Chapter 4

Since Neil had died I had been knee-deep in paperwork. I had no idea there was so much involved in dying. Not for the deceased, but for the ones left behind. It was like mopping up after a public disaster; only, this tragedy was private and mine. I had signed papers, taken care of trusts, filed insurance papers and I still wasn't finished. I couldn't believe that Neil died and left me to cope. I gazed out the kitchen window at the two holly trees he had planted six years ago. They'd been just twigs back then. Now they were at least five feet tall and one of them sparkled with bright red berries. He had planted a male and a female tree, explaining that was necessary if we wanted berries.

I blinked back tears. It seemed as if everything came in pairs. Everything except me. *Alone* was a terrible word. The Colorado trip had gone surprisingly well. I had another trip coming up tomorrow—Arizona this time. The girls had made it all right without me, thanks to Mrs. Murphy, but I had still felt guilty about leaving them, and now I was getting ready to leave them again.

The phone rang, jerking me out of my thoughts. I reached for the receiver on the second ring.

"Kate? That you?" It was Nancy Whitaker, one of the stylists I worked with at the salon. Why would she be calling on a Sunday night?

"It's me."

"I stopped by the shop for a minute and found you had forgotten to take your briefcase. Won't you need it on your trip?"

I groaned. My teaching material. Of course I'd need it. How could I have been so careless? "Rats. I'll have to detour by in the morning and pick it up. Or if you're going to be there for a while I can run over now."

"Don't do that." Nancy paused. "Tell you what. I'll drop it by on my way home. Will that work?"

"That would be great. I still have to pack, and the kids haven't eaten yet."

She promised to drop by and we broke the connection. I dug a pizza out of the freezer. Junk food again. I had zero interest in cooking. I fed the girls whatever was handy, and sometimes the meals weren't exactly balanced. Corn chips and baloney sandwiches. Boxed macaroni and cheese. As for me, I'd lost ten pounds I didn't need to lose. My appetite was gone.

I wandered into the bedroom trying to decide what to take with me, although by now I had narrowed my travel outfits down to a few that would pack well with the least amount of wrinkles. I shuffled aimlessly through my side of the closet, not really caring what I wore. I made a few selections, folded them and plopped them in the suitcase.

Kris hovered in the doorway. "You never did bake those chocolate chip cookies."

I stared at her, trying to remember. What cookies?

"For my school party," she prodded.

I shook my head to clear the fog. "Honey, that's long over."

The color in her cheeks heightened. "I know that. I'm not a baby."

"Well, then, your point is?"

"We could still bake cookies." She met my gaze, looking defiant. "I sort of promised."

I sat down on the bed trying to figure out what we were talking about. "Promised what?" I asked gently.

She lifted her eyes to meet mine. "I told Mrs. Harrison that I could bring cookies tomorrow. We don't ever get anything special in class for just because."

I swallowed hard. "Just because" was a catchword in our house. Anytime we did something nice or bought a present for someone for no particular reason, it was a "just because" gift. Just because I love you. My eyes touched a well-known brand of perfume in a cut-glass bottle. Expensive and unexpected. My last just because gift from Neil.

I looked at Kris, noting the flush staining her cheeks, the hesitant expression. Had I actually sent her to school wearing that purple-and-black-plaid skirt with a golden-yellow-and-black-striped shirt? She looked like a walking ad for crepe paper. What had I been thinking? Or more to the point, why wasn't I thinking? I seemed to be lost in a fog most of the time. And had I, in my preoccupation, caused her to look so insecure?

I realized she was still waiting for an answer. "Okay. One batch of cookies coming up. Chocolate chip okay?"

She grinned, relief crossing her youthful features. "That would be great, Mom."

I nodded. "Consider it done. I'll finish up here and then we'll get started."

My daughter took a deep breath, as if steeling herself. "And can we go back to church next week?"

Well, now. I hadn't seen that one coming. We hadn't been back to church since Neil's funeral. I knew the girls missed their friends and church activities, but I wasn't yet ready to face our favorite pew where Neil and I had sat together. Besides, I was uncertain right now that there even was a God. He had ignored my pleas to keep Neil safe. How could I trust Him again?

Kris was still waiting for an answer, and I forced a smile. "We'll see. Run along now and let me finish packing."

She pressed her lips together and nodded. Judging from her expression, I hadn't fooled her. "We'll see" probably meant "no," and she knew it. I sighed. Life had gotten complicated and I wasn't mentally equipped to handle complicated. Maybe I wasn't spiritually equipped, either.

Kris left and I glanced around the room for forgotten items before closing my suitcase. When I got back I'd have to tackle Neil's personal belongings. So far I had kept his side of the closet closed, unable to face the thought of getting rid of anything.

The doorbell rang and I answered, to find Nancy holding my briefcase. Tall, slender, with a head of silver-blond hair she wore in a tousled mop, she looked like the typical feather-brained blonde. Behind that pretty face resided a sharp intellect and a friendly compassionate manner. She was a favorite among La Chic customers.

"You okay, girl?" she asked.

I dredged up a smile. "I'm okay."

"Look, if traveling is too much for you to handle, you need to tell Maria. She can work it out."

The idea sounded tempting, but I knew giving up traveling would amount to a cut in salary, something I wasn't prepared to accept. What if I became incapacitated and couldn't work? We'd need everything I could earn now to get us by without dipping into the insurance money. Maria, the elegant manager of La Chic, would probably be flexible, but for now I'd try to carry on.

Nancy and I attended the same church, and she was aware I had been staying away from services. She didn't mention it, though, probably thinking that I didn't need the pressure right now.

She reached out to grasp both my hands. "I know flying makes you nervous."

"Particularly in winter," I admitted. "Every time I see them deice the wings I start praying."

Nancy nodded encouragement. "We'll both pray that God will see you safely through."

She left, and I shut the door and locked it. I thought about what she had just said. Flying did make me nervous, but I had always trusted in God to bring me safely home. Sometimes I had even enjoyed the takeoffs and landings. But I had lost faith in the power of prayer. My husband had started every day with prayer. Why had God looked the other way when Neil was trapped in that burning building? God owed me some answers.

I wandered into the kitchen and got out the cookbook, looking for my chocolate chip recipe. The weather was unseasonably warm for October. Sailor had been playing out in the backyard all afternoon, but now he scratched at the back door. I let him in and turned my attention to assembling cookie ingredients. It took only a few minutes to mix the dough, and, like the girls, I was looking forward to freshly baked cookies. Maybe I'd put together some ice-cream sandwiches using warm cookies. It sounded good, and for a brief moment I thought perhaps I was regaining my appetite.

Sailor was acting weird tonight, hovering around my feet until I almost tripped over him. "Kelli," I called. "Come get this dog! He's in the way."

My youngest daughter wandered into the kitchen, pouting. "Poor Sailor. Nobody loves him except me."

"Yeah, right," I muttered. "Look, I have to light this oven. I don't need any distractions, okay?" The temperamental thing could blow sky-high. Well, not literally. Last month Neil had called a serviceman to look at the gas monstrosity and he'd pronounced the relic safe. Just old and cranky.

Kelli scooped the dog up in her arms. "All right. Come on, Sailor. We'll watch from here."

"I should sell tickets?" I wiggled my eyebrows at her, in a pitiful imitation of Groucho Marx. My daughter, of course, had never seen the great Groucho, so she simply stared at me as if I had lost my mind.

"All right, I'll provide the evening entertainment, but stand back out of the way."

"Don't worry," Kelli said. "I'll be ready to run if the stove blows up."

"Oh, yeah? You expect that to happen?"

Her expression was way too serious. "You always say it's going to."

That stopped me in my tracks. Had I infected my children with my fear of this stove? I tried to laugh. "Don't worry. There's no danger of the stove blowing up. I was only joking." Wasn't I?

I hunted for the long fireplace matches someone had given us. They had always seemed a strange gift, since we don't have a fireplace. Never had. I found the matches in the top cabinet lurking behind a jar of molasses, bought earlier to make gingerbread houses, which had gone unmade.

Lighting this monstrosity was actually a two-man job, but tonight I'd have to do it on my own. Our house was old and so were our appliances. The stove must have come over on the ark. I paused a foolish moment to wonder if there was a second one out there somewhere making some other woman's life miserable. Or if this was something else that didn't come in pairs?

I knelt in front of the stove and turned on the gas and was rewarded with a furious hiss. Satisfied it was working, I scraped the match across the flint. Nothing. Another match, no spark.

We'd had these matches for ages. They were probably too old to ignite. I fished out another one, forgetting I had left the gas on while I played with matches. This one flamed almost immediately, and I breathed a sigh of relief and extended it toward the oven, neglecting to turn my face to the side the way I usually did.

For a long moment I hung in limbo. Then, *voom!* The mother of all explosions shot a sheet of fire in my direction.

Blue flames rose like a Yellowstone geyser.

I reached out a trembling hand to adjust the controls, and the monster stopped roaring and started purring. Sighing, I shakily got to my feet. My face felt as hot as a roasted marshmallow. I promised myself to replace this stove as soon as possible. Now that I was down to one paycheck per week, and not wanting to tap into our emergency fund, it didn't look as if "possible" would be coming around anytime soon.

"Wow!" Kelli said. "That was awesome."

"Wasn't it?" I agreed. "Better than Fourth of July fireworks."

She frowned. "Are you all right, Mom?"

"Sure. I'm fine. Why wouldn't I be?"

"You look sort of funny."

Well, that was a given. I'd come within an inch of being roasted. Yeah, I probably looked goggle-eyed from the shock. I felt a tremor of pride. I'd lit that stove, and when it spit flames at me, I hadn't even screamed. I was maturing.

"I'm okay. Right now I'm going to bake chocolate chip cookies, and when I'm through we'll make ice-cream sandwiches. How does that sound?"

"Awesome!" She ran from the room, shouting at Kris. "Mom's lit the stove and it didn't blow up!"

I grinned. Kelli was a wordsmith. She collected words and phrases the way other kids collected favorite toys. *Awesome* was her latest.

The day, which had been sunny, was suddenly overcast. I stepped to the back door and cast an anxious glance at the sky. It was too hot for this time of year.

After watching the racing clouds for a few moments I went back inside and turned on the kitchen television. Worry was setting in. Almost immediately a weather crawl appeared across the bottom of the screen. "A tornado warning is in effect for

Oklahoma City from four o'clock central mountain time until 5:30 p.m. Stay tuned to this station for updates."

Tornado. And a warning, not a watch. More serious. Tornado alley again. We'd been hit before and I was familiar with the devastation left behind by the killer funnel clouds. So far we'd been lucky, but if Lady Luck had ever lived in this house, she had moved out.

Kris came into the kitchen. "There's a tornado warning out. I thought we were through with storms."

"I know. I just caught it on the TV." I dropped spoonfuls of cookie dough onto the baking sheet. "You keep a close eye on the set for further warnings."

She paled. "Will it hit us?"

"I hope not." I slid the cookies into the oven.

She stared at me. "What's wrong?"

"Nothing. Why?" I kept an ear tuned to the weather report. Well, maybe both ears, because I didn't hear what she said. She looked worried, but then both girls had worn that strained, anxious expression frequently around me. We were going to have a long talk, as soon as I could get my thoughts straight. It was important to know what you were talking about before you started talking, and right now my thoughts were still tied in a knot and I couldn't find the right string to pull.

"All residents in...are urged to take cover immediately."

I dropped the spoon. It hit against the glass bowl with a clang. "Where? I didn't catch that."

"Us!" Kris cried. "That's us!"

The telephone rang and I snatched up the receiver. My next-door neighbor Ron was on the phone. "Kate? I don't want to alarm you, but I think you and the girls should come over here. Sally and I are going to the basement."

"We'll be right there." I slammed the receiver down and yelled for Kelli. "Come on! We're going next door."

Kelli ran into the kitchen, clutching Sailor. I shoved both girls out the door. "Run." The stove. I whirled and shut off the oven, opened the door and jerked out the pan of half-baked cookies.

The clouds had turned a dirty yellow color. I stood transfixed, watching them boil overhead. A sudden gust of wind whirled debris past me. Trees bent low. I froze, unable to move.

"Kate!" Ron yelled from the door of his house. "Come on. *Hurry.*"

I ran toward him like a scared rabbit scurrying toward the safety of a brush pile. He pushed me toward the basement steps. "Sally and the kids are already down there."

I had started down the steps when he suddenly pulled me back. "What's that you're carrying?"

I looked down and discovered I still held the pan of half-baked cookies. My jaw dropped. I remembered taking them out of the oven, but evidently I had forgotten to put them down.

Ron laughed. "Give them to me and get downstairs."

I shot one more glance toward the sky and saw a dark finger of cloud extending toward the ground. As I watched, it rose again. Tornado. *Dear God, help us.* It really *was* a tornado. I stumbled toward the stairs, aware Ron was right behind me carrying the cookies.

Sally and the kids were huddled in a corner of the basement away from the windows. Vicki, the Fowlers' oldest daughter, had her arms around Kelli and Kris. Mark and Tommy, age thirteen and fifteen, were sitting next to Sally. Mark had brought his ghetto blaster and had it tuned to a rock station. If we didn't already have hearing problems we would be permanently deaf from the volume by the time we got the all clear.

If we got an all clear.

If the tornado hit us we might all wake up in heaven.

Where Neil was waiting for us.

The thought stunned me. As badly as I wanted to see him, I didn't want to die right now. The girls were young. I wanted to see them grow up and get married. I wanted to be a grandmother. The longing caught me by surprise. For weeks I had been mentally moaning that I was ready to die. Apparently that wasn't true.

Kelli clutched Sailor so tightly he whuffled in protest. Tootsie Roll, the Fowlers' yappy little Pekingese, kept running around us in circles, evidently thinking this was some sort of game. Between the dog and the rock music I was about to resort to some very undignified behavior, like yelling "shut up" to the dog and heaving the ghetto blaster to the far side of the basement. Not very wise behavior if I wanted to be invited back.

Since I didn't have anywhere else to go in a tornado warning, I decided to keep my options open.

Ron shouted at Mark to turn off the music so he could catch the weather report. Tommy had picked up a guitar that was lying around, and plucked aimlessly at the strings. If he had a melody hidden in there somewhere I couldn't find it. The kid had been taking lessons for several months. As far as I could tell, he needed a few more.

Ron managed to get a few words of the weather report before Mark turned the radio back to his music. The volume was loud enough to mask the roar of the wind outside, which was one blessing. Ron reached over and turned off the radio and motioned for Tommy to put down the guitar. The boys complied, albeit reluctantly, and their father reached out to grasp their hands. "Let's pray."

I stiffened, eyes wide. Did he think we were in imminent danger? He caught my eye and shook his head. "I don't know if the tornado is coming our way or not, but if it doesn't hit us it will hit others in its path."

I felt tears sting my eyelids. Neil would have said something like that. He had been concerned about others. I realized I'd been concentrating on myself and my children. Me and mine. My husband's death had reduced me to a cold, unfeeling half Christian. I felt chastened as I bowed my head and listened while Ron prayed for our safety and for the safety of those around us. A peace came over me. Not that I knew what was going on outside those basement walls, but because Ron Fowler was a good man; somehow I felt God would hear and answer his prayers. I had even whispered a short prayer of my own. I didn't have confidence in any prayer of mine, but somehow I felt better.

Mark switched on his music again and Ron shook his head and turned the channel to a weather broadcast. The announcer's voice came over the air and I thought I had never heard better news.

"It looks like the tornado system has passed for now, but high winds have caused considerable destruction and a twister did touch down on the north side of the city. No information on damage right now. However, it seems to be all clear for the time being. Stay tuned for further developments."

Ron got to his feet. "Well, looks like the excitement's over for now."

Kelli had climbed into my lap, still clutching Sailor. She lifted a tearstained face to mine. "The tornado went away? We're not going to die?"

I hugged her. "Yes, darling. The tornado went away. We can go home now."

We sorted ourselves out and climbed the stairs. I noticed the boys staring at me with bemused expressions when we trooped through Sally's kitchen. Ron appeared to avoid looking at me at all. I started to feel self-conscious. Was my face dirty, or what? Sally took one good look at me and burst into laughter. "What *happened* to your eyebrows?"

"What do you mean, what happened?" No one had said a word, and I hadn't done anything to my eyebrows. She took my shoulders and turned me to the mirror. I stared back at my reflection in horror. My eyebrows and eyelashes were gone!

Kris was standing at my elbow. "I *tried* to tell you, but you didn't listen."

The stove. That rotten stove. When it exploded into flame it must have singed my eyebrows. No *wonder* I had felt like a marshmallow held too close to the flames. And I had to teach a class in Arizona tomorrow looking like this. I burst into tears.

Sally put her arms around me. "Don't cry, Kate. They'll grow back. Just be glad you weren't hurt."

Of course I was glad I hadn't been burned, but I didn't want to hear my eyebrows would grow back. I wanted them now. The idea startled me. That had been my theme ever since Neil died. Me, I, mine. I wanted my life put back together and I wanted it now. For the first time I realized it wasn't going to be that way. What I wanted had little to do with reality. Life happened. Like it or not.

And I didn't like it one bit.

"You look funny, Mommy." Kelli giggled. I turned and took another look at myself. As a matter of fact, I did look funny. A chuckle started somewhere inside me and I didn't even try to hold back.

When I laughed it was as if the tension in the room shattered into tiny pieces. Part of it was relief because we had escaped the tornado, but it was such a blessing to laugh. To hear my children laugh, to see Ron laugh until the tears ran down his cheeks. I mopped my eyes feeling as if maybe, oh please God, the healing process was starting.

Sally spotted the pan of cookies. "What's this?"

"Well, they started out to be cookies, but they didn't get done," I said.

"Why are they over here?" she asked, peering at the blobs as flat as pancakes.

I snorted again. "I took them out of the oven when Ron yelled for us to come and I forgot to put them down."

Sally shook her head and laughed. "Tell you what, I'll make a pot of coffee and we'll eat the cookies. Deal?"

"Sounds like a first-class deal to me," I agreed.

While they weren't as well-done as I would have liked them, the chewy little blobs tasted a lot better than I had expected.

We sat around the Fowler kitchen table eating and drinking coffee while Vicki styled Kris's hair and Kelli played with Sailor and Tootsie Roll. By the time we were ready to go home I felt as if I had reached my first turning point.

I was slowly working my way out of the fog that had filled my waking moments. We were surviving. That was enough for now.

The girls and I walked home beneath a clearing sky. The first stars were just starting to peek through the clouds, and the air was freshly washed. The yard was full of windblown trash, and broken limbs were tossed everywhere like matchsticks. We'd had some strong winds, but thankfully nothing worse.

The phone rang as I entered the kitchen. I answered to find Pastor Joe Crockett on the line. "Kate, are you and the girls all right?"

"We're fine, Pastor. We were next door with the Fowlers in their basement. What about you?"

"Missed us, but I'm sure you've heard about the damage to the north."

We talked about the storm for a few minutes, and then he said, "Kate, I'm worried about you. I want you to know you can talk to me anytime you feel the need."

"I know that, Joe, and it helps a lot. Really it does."

When I hung up the phone I realized something had happened to me tonight. I had come through a few more minicrises without falling apart. In my own way I was learning to cope. I had read the books on grieving that kind friends and thoughtful neighbors had dropped off; I believed that I had now passed the shock and disbelief stage.

I was lucky to have good friends and a pastor who cared. I was facing a future without Neil whether I liked it or not, and the kind of life I gave my children depended on how well I could handle that future.

I thought I had it all figured out. Little did I know my worst days still lay ahead of me.

Chapter

5

I left La Chic early Wednesday afternoon. On my station calendar, penciled in bold red and circled, was my annual physical appointment. This year I'd have blown it off, only I was in my responsible mode now; I was obligated to take care of myself. Plus, my right ear had been giving me fits on takeoffs and landings. Sometimes the pressure was so bad I was doubled over.

For me, seeing a doctor was like pulling teeth. I had a white-coat phobia—my blood pressure, heart rate and anxiety level all shot through the roof when a doctor or nurse approached. Dad had feared doctors and he'd passed the phobia along to me. Same with storms—every time a dark cloud came on the horizon he'd pace the floor and warn Mother that they'd better get me to shelter. I'd spent half my youth crouching in a dank cellar, praying the storm wouldn't touch us. I knew God promised safe passage to those who loved Him, and in those years I wasn't aware of any gales other than nature's fury. I'd taken God's promise literally. Safe passage to me meant safe passage—it didn't have any hidden meanings like "You might not make it through the storm, but you're promised 'safe passage' into heaven." I was starting to see that life's fury was every bit as lethal as Mother Nature's temperamental displays.

A little before five, a nurse showed me to a small cubicle lab, comically labeled the Vampire's Den. The sign served its purpose and I smiled in spite of my apprehension. Three vials later, I was handed a brown bottle and pointed to the bathroom down the long hallway.

Later I settled on a hard examining table covered in white paper and waited, my eyes roaming the built-in desk with boxes of rubber gloves, lubricant, ear swabs and wooden tongue depressors. Some sort of tool lay in plain sight. Torturous, no doubt.

An hour later, or at least it seemed that long, the doctor breezed in, reading my chart. "Kate. How are you coping?"

"Hi, Dr. Bates." I hadn't been in his office since last year's physical, but he'd been kind enough to make a house call and prescribe medication when Neil died.

He paused, peering at me over the rims of his glasses. "How are you doing, girl?"

Tears smarted in my eyes. When anyone got that tone of voice—the I'm-so-sorry-about-Neil tone—I still lost it. I knew people meant well, but they couldn't help, so the tone was always there, plunging me back to my black pit.

"Not so good, Dr. Bates, but friends say it will take time."

He patted my shoulder and lifted the foot extension, snapping it into place. "I lost my wife a couple years ago."

"I'm sorry," I mumbled, my mind now on what the nurse was doing. This whole process gave me the jitters.

He paused, squeezing my hand with calm reassurance. Dr. Harry Bates had given me my first high school physical, so I should feel comfortable in his presence, but I was jumpy as a pea on a drum.

"People lie," he said. "You never get over losing half of you, Kate. Not entirely, but you manage to go on."

I closed my eyes. "What if I don't want to go on?"

"Well." He went about his business and I tried to think of my "happy place." Sunning on the beach, with plovers and turnstones soaring overhead, rolling surf—ouch!

The mystery tool.

"Trust me," the doctor said. "Given time, the pain will ease and some morning you'll wake up and decide life's a pretty good deal after all."

"If you say so," I said. "I'm pretty sure I'm still in the tearful stage—but making progress."

Later I sat in his plush leather office chair and waited for results. Demons swarmed my mind. Had he found something? Would he walk through that door with a sober expression and regretfully break the news that I had only scant weeks to live? I shuddered, clasping my arms around my middle. There had been an odd pain recently—near the upper rib cage. What organ would that involve? Did they have treatment for my particular case? No. They wouldn't if I had scant weeks to live.

Scant. How many weeks *were* in "scant," anyway?

I had broken out into a cold sweat when Dr. Bates sailed into his office and sat down behind his desk.

"First the good news—you're healthy as a horse."

I felt faint with relief, although the comparison wasn't exactly flattering.

"You're a little anemic, but nothing unusual for a woman your age. And you could use a few extra pounds. So eat up." He scribbled on a pad, then tore off the sheet and handed it to me. "Get this filled and take one a day. With food."

I scanned the prescription. "Okay."

The doctor settled back in his chair, his dark eyes studying me. "Now for the bad news."

I glanced up, heart racing. He'd said I was healthy as a horse. I knew it—healthy as a horse can be in *my* condition.

"Your right eardrum has a small tear, minute but worrisome. You fly almost every week, if I recall."

I nodded. "Twice a week. I teach classes out of state."

He shook his head and steepled his forefingers, resting his mouth against them for a prop. "Sorry, Kate, but I'm going to have to ground you. That tear will heal if we're careful. If not, I'll want to watch it over a period of time before we consider surgery. You'll be running the risk of hearing loss in that particular ear if we don't take care of the problem once and for all. Didn't we talk about this last year?" He glanced at my chart. "You were complaining of pressure, and you had a sinus infection and drainage."

I nodded. He'd touched on the subject, but at the time the eardrum wasn't perforated.

"I have considerable discomfort on takeoffs and landings. Even with the antibiotic and allergy medicine you prescribed last year, the pain is intense."

"Then you've got to stay out of planes for a while."

"But my job..." Did I have to remind him I was sole breadwinner now, and my job necessitated flying?

He shook his head, his expression stern. "That right ear is in jeopardy. You're grounded—at least until the problem is corrected. Talk to your superiors. I'm sure something can be worked out."

I left the sprawling medical complex in a daze. If I couldn't travel, I couldn't teach. If I couldn't teach, La Chic would have to replace me. And who knew for how long or if I'd ever get the position back? Dr. Bates had said the tear might not heal even if I *were* careful. Surgery loomed like an approaching cold front.

I took a chance that Maria, my superior, would still be in her office. When I pulled into the salon, I saw her white Lexus parked in back. I used the employees' entrance.

Maria glanced up when I tapped on her door. The French-born, attractive brunette always seemed rushed, so I stated my case as quickly as possible.

She folded her hands on the desk and stared at me, noncommittal for a moment. I could see my career—and paycheck—flying out the window.

"For how long, *chérie*?"

"The doctor doesn't know—there's no way to know. Maybe as long as a year."

"A year." She gave a French-sounding *tssk*. The row of silver arm bracelets tinkled melodiously when she reached up and touched her cheek. "One year. Disturbing."

"Maybe sooner," I offered. I adored my job, and I didn't want to lose any part of it, though the idea of not flying made me almost giddy. No more angst-filled flights, crowded airports and overbooked airlines. No more cold and impersonal hotel rooms, lugging baggage, cabs in unfamiliar cities. I hadn't realized it before, but now I was stunningly aware I didn't really want to fly anymore. In fact, I didn't care if I never saw another plane.

"Well, you are much too important for us to lose, *ma chérie*." Maria smiled. "I will make a phone call in the morning—perhaps something can be worked out. Your talents are not limited to teaching, Kate. La Chic can work around your condition until you are healed."

For the second time that day I felt faint with relief. I could keep my job. If God and I had been on speaking terms, I would have thanked Him.

"See me tomorrow." Maria dismissed me with a harried glance. "We'll talk then."

When I climbed back into my car I realized I had survived yet another disaster and not come unglued. Life was getting better.

Kate, you're made of Teflon, I told myself.

But in fact I knew I was made of pudding, and one more catastrophe would send me over the edge.

What would La Chic do with me? I could always work in the shop, but I knew that without the teaching challenge I would get bored easily, and I didn't want to dip into the insurance money. I needed something more than cuts and permanents; I needed the adrenaline that came with watching talented students evolve into gifted stylists under my tutelage.

But then beggars can't be choosers, so I would take whatever Maria could find, and baby my right ear until I could resume travel.

No more flights for a while.

Maybe I'd have Kris and Kelli offer a brief thank-you to God tonight in their prayers.

Will Rogers World Airport teemed with travelers when the girls and I climbed out of a shuttle Saturday morning. My head was still spinning from the rapid changes gripping my life.

Maria had called me into her office Thursday morning and broken the news—La Chic's affiliate San Francisco salon needed a manager. The present one had been involved in a car accident two days before and required a lengthy recuperation period. There was only one hitch. The girls and I had to move to California.

At first the idea repulsed me. Leave everything I'd ever known—including irreplaceable memories of Neil? I couldn't do it...yet I couldn't remain immobile forever. Everywhere I looked, every street I drove, every restaurant we'd shared a meal reminded me of Neil. I couldn't face memories of my deceased husband day after day and move on with my life. Maria was offering not only a job, but a new start. So I had agreed to move.

I unloaded backpacks and luggage out of the shuttle and wondered how Dr. Bates would react if he knew I was flying to San Francisco on a house-hunting expedition. I knew what he'd say, and I also knew the risks, but driving to the Bay Area was out of the question, and trains scared me to death. Every time I heard a newscast it seemed some passenger train had been involved in an accident, either here or overseas.

"Is the plane going to crash, Mommy?" Kelli slipped into her backpack, staring up at me with Neil's dark eyes.

"No, honey. The plane isn't going to crash." She'd overheard me talking to Mom on the phone last night, and I'd expressed my usual flying hang-ups.

Kris helped me load bags on a cart and we wheeled our baggage inside the terminal and headed for our airline counter. A long line snaked around the cordoned area. I checked the time and noted that our flight left in a little over an hour; we had plenty of time.

The line moved slowly. Once or twice a new window opened, but only long enough to check in first class or frequent flyers. The girls waited patiently; their behavior made me proud. Neil had always taken care of baggage and checked in when we traveled. Was it only last year that we'd stood in this exact line, happily anticipating one glorious sun-drenched week at Disneyland? The girls had chattered with excitement, and Neil had teased that I was looking forward to the theme park more than Kelli was.

I mentally shook off my thoughts. Stay focused, Kate.

By the time we checked in and the luggage cleared security, we had fifteen minutes. The boarding gate was F12.

The three of us broke into a trot when we cleared security and headed for the assigned gate. I lugged a heavy shoulder bag and my purse, Kelli had her backpack and Kris pulled a small overnighter behind her. Threading our way through the teeming crowd, we sprinted toward the gate with five minutes to spare.

Passengers were on their feet studying their boarding passes when we arrived. It looked to be a full flight this morning.

A woman's voice came over the PA. "Passengers on flight 224 to San Francisco—there has been a gate change. That flight will now be boarding from gate F3."

"F3," I told the girls. I picked up the heavy shoulder bag, and we set off for the eight-gate jaunt.

Breathless, we arrived a few minutes before the other passengers. Kelli peeled out of her backpack and let the canvas sink to the tiled floor. I set the shoulder bag down and rubbed my aching shoulder. An old rotator cuff injury had flared up.

"Mommy, are we going to eat breakfast on the plane?"

"Kelli, there are no meals on shorter flights. Didn't you eat a bowl of cereal this morning?"

My daughter shook her head. "I couldn't see it."

"Couldn't see it? The bowl? You couldn't see the bowl?"

"My eyes wouldn't open."

I grinned. We had left the house around four for the six-o'clock flight. I glanced around trying to spot a snack area, but one wasn't close.

"Maybe I have a meal-replacement bar in my purse."

"Yuck."

The loudspeaker blared. "Passengers on flight 224, there has been another gate change. We are sorry for the inconvenience. The flight will now be boarding out of F12."

"F12!" I muttered. "Make up your mind." I swung the heavy bag over my shoulder and helped Kelli into her gear. "Come on, girls. Back to F12."

"I'm hungry."

"We'll get something before we board."

We passed passengers still streaming from the first gate change, on their way to the second gate.

"Gate change," I called nicely. "Back to F12."

I heard a few grumbles when the word spread through the crowd. The passengers made U-turns and headed back to F12.

I went straight to the desk to confirm that we had the right gate. The woman didn't look up. She kept her eyes on the computer terminal. "The San Francisco flight is loading at F3."

"We were just *at* F3, and they said the gate had been changed back to F12."

The woman shook her head. "I don't know why they would say that. The flight is boarding from F3."

Taking a deep breath, I turned and faced the girls. "F3."

Kelli heaved an exasperated sigh.

"I know—come on." We set off for F3. This time I didn't bother to inform other passengers; I was a coward. Some were getting hostile, and who could blame them? I was feeling a little murderous myself.

We dropped our bags on the floor at gate three and sank into the nearest chairs, trying to catch our breath. Kelli was famished, and grouchy because of it. I rummaged around in my purse and came up with gum, all I had on me. I noticed the flight was loading, so I picked up the shoulder bag and my purse and glanced at our group number. We were Group Six, so we'd have a few minutes. I searched for a kiosk—anything to buy an apple or doughnut.

The overhead speaker said that Group Seven could now load. What happened to Group Six?

I stepped to the desk, rereading seating assignments. The clerk looked up. "Group Six has already loaded?" I asked.

She nodded.

"This is the San Francisco flight." By this time I wasn't taking any chances.

She nodded. Then looked at the monitor. "No, this is the L.A. flight."

"L.A.! What happened to San Francisco?"

She consulted a paper. "I'm sorry—that flight is now boarding out of F12." She smiled. "Better hurry. The flight leaves in three minutes."

Rainy San Francisco. I stared out the windows of the Boeing 727 as the aircraft taxied into the airport. Rain hit the windows in sheets. After we left the plane both girls and I were drenched to the core by the time we hailed a cab and piled into the back seat.

The cab took us to The Crab Corner—four-star accommodations, according to the travel agent. Somehow The Crab had dropped a couple of stars by the time we got there. I opened the door to the dingy-smelling room and dissolved in tears.

Kelli and Kris sat me down on the lumpy bed, and then sat next to me. We all had a good cry. Finally Kris got up and plugged in the small coffeepot and made a cup of hot tea. She carried the offering to me, urging me to drink the warm liquid. By now Kelli had fallen over on the awful-looking crab-patterned spread and fallen asleep. One lone piece of gum rattled around in my daughter's belly.

I took a sip from the cup, and the liquid was so strong my eyes burned, but I drank it anyway.

If I'd been speaking to God, I'd have been asking a lot of questions, demanding to know why He'd do this to me and my girls. He was supposed to be a just and loving God, and there was nothing *just* or *loving* about my situation.

The tea brought me around. Kris had located the thermostat and turned off the air-conditioning and turned on the heat. Warmth filled the smoke-drenched room. I started to come back to life.

"We'd better leave our clothes in the luggage," I told Kris. I didn't trust the old chest of drawers to be bug free.

When Kelli woke, we left the room and the three of us waded deep puddles to a fast-food chain sitting in front of a huge, garish pink crab statue. We ate hamburgers and fries. Later we walked around the hotel pool, the facility looking rather bleak, like an ocean after a hurricane. Leaves floated on brackish water; wind had overturned lounges and chairs. Some kid had left a green beach towel and a pair of white sneakers lying beside the pool.

I turned a chair upright and sat down, staring at the dreary sight, knowing with every ounce of perception that San Francisco wasn't going to be the healing oasis I'd hoped it would be.

* * *

Nine o'clock the following morning, Burt Baker of New Homes Realty picked us up. It would have been nice if we could have started yesterday afternoon, but as long as the real estate agent had houses, I had no complaint. Well, not many. The girls climbed into the back seat of Burt's van, and I took the passenger seat. Burt already knew my budget; it would be hard to find anything in the Bay Area for my price, but he was willing to try, he said, flashing me a three-million-actual-dol-lar-sales-this-year smile.

Kelli leaned forward and told him how much Neil's insur-ance policy was worth, and I reached back and clapped a hand over her mouth. Was nothing sacred to a child?

The first house in my price range scared me. We walked through the "roomy fixer upper," kicking trash out of our path. The occupants had cats. I spotted cat hair hanging off the one overhead fan in the living area. The cat's litter box was in the bathtub adjacent to the guest bedroom. The litter had not been changed in what I guessed to be aeons. My eyes watered from the stench and I quickly left the room. Kris and Kelli were not so discreet; they held their noses, making noises like *gross, eweeee* and my personal favorite, *pea yew,* while we toured the remainder of the house.

"Needs a little work," Burt said, "but fresh paint and new wallpaper will make a huge difference. Lot of possibilities," he added, pausing to admire the pitted oak woodwork.

The only possibilities I could see were a bulldozer and a dump truck to haul off the rubbish.

"Well, I have more!" Burt said when he realized I was un-derwhelmed, to say the least. And indeed Burt did.

For the next six hours the girls and I tramped through equally nauseating possibilities. Then Burt drove us to the "for just a little more" listings. These were minimal improvement; one or two actually demonstrated potential, but the prices were thirty to forty thousand dollars out of my price range. I'd been warned that Bay property was expensive, but I'd never dreamed that an ordinary house—similar to what Neil and I had bought in Oklahoma eight years ago—would cost close to half a million dollars.

I didn't have that kind of money and I couldn't raise it. My job paid well, but not that well. I'd even gotten a raise with the move—now I knew why.

When Burt dropped us back at The Crab, the girls and I headed upstairs and fell across the bed. The three of us lay there in the dingy room, staring sightlessly at the ceiling. Sticker shocked.

"What are we going to do, Mommy? We don't have enough money to buy a house, do we?"

I shook my head. "Not one of those houses, Kris."

I knew the poor thing had more responsibility on her young shoulders than was fair for a seven-year-old. She worried about me, about family finances. It wasn't reasonable what I was putting her or Kelli through, but I was powerless to pull myself together, too discouraged to show any true grit at the moment. I wasn't competent enough to raise these children.

You should have taken me, God.

I realized that I'd spoken to Him for the first time in weeks. Then I couldn't stop. Bitterness tumbled out.

It should have been me. *Neil could have handled this better. He was stronger. Smarter. Wiser. I'll only make a mess out of raising my children. I can't provide a decent home. I fall apart at the first sign of difficulty. How could You have made such a mistake?*

Rain splattered the dingy windows, and I closed my eyes. My head pounded; I hadn't eaten all day. Kris had made coffee this morning, and before Burt picked us up we'd walked to the fast-food restaurant and Kris and Kelli had eaten a breakfast sandwich.

I turned to look at my daughters, now fast asleep on the bed beside me, their young faces so innocent in sleep. What was I going to do?

* * *

"Mommy?"

"Yes, sweetie?" I stirred. The bedside lamp was on, so I must have fallen asleep. I looked up at Kris and smiled. "What is it, honey?"

"Kelli's got a toad cornered in the bathroom."

Her declaration took a second to register. Then I leaped off the mattress and shot into the bathroom in time to see my precious five-year-old reach for the toad.

"S-to-o-o-op!"

She jerked her hand back, eyes wide. "It's a baby, Mommy. Isn't he cute?"

"Don't touch that slimy thing!" I knew I looked and sounded like a wild woman, shrieking, scaring my daughters to death, but amphibians of any kind freaked me out!

Rain, shabby houses, snakes.

What next, God?

I didn't care to know. I had more on my plate than I could handle.

And now toads.

Chapter 6

We arrived home from San Francisco exhausted and a little down from our trip, but safe. The salon phone would be ringing off the hook as usual for appointments between appointments. Now it was Monday morning, and my day had started off on a sour note.

Kelli was up and dressed, ready for school. Kris was still staggering around half-asleep, her hair looking as if she had been caught in an electric fan, and she was still wearing pajamas. How had I managed to give birth to two daughters with such completely different personalities?

The phone rang while I was slapping cereal bowls on the table. I stumbled over Sailor and dropped a jar of grape jelly. The jar hit the floor squarely on its glass bottom. Whoever had used it last hadn't tightened the lid. The lid shot off and a blob of jelly caromed off the ceiling, leaving a lovely purple blotch.

I grabbed the receiver and snapped, "Hello."

"Kate?" Maria? On the phone this early? This would not be good.

"Yes. Sorry." I reached for an attitude adjustment. "Things are a little hectic around here this morning."

Maria accepted the apology at face value and got down to business. "*Chérie*, did you find anything to buy in San Francisco?"

"Nothing I could afford. And the ones I could afford wouldn't make a good doghouse. Why?"

"Well..." She hesitated. "I got word today they need you in your new position by the beginning of December."

I gasped for breath. December! That was barely a month away. Had I heard that right?

Maria's voice came over the line edged with worry. "Kate? Are you there?"

"I'm here," I muttered, staring up at the ceiling as if I expected to see a bevy of angels winging to my rescue. All I saw was grape jelly.

I got my second wind. "December!" I shrieked, probably puncturing Maria's eardrums. I was sure she would never overreact this way. "Are they out of their minds?"

Kelli's head jerked around. Sailor whimpered, and even Kris opened her eyes. I took a deep breath. "Say you're kidding me."

Maria made soothing noises. "I know it's difficult, yes? But it will all work out somehow."

"Can't you do anything?"

"I can't make decisions for San Francisco." I heard the finality in her voice. "I would help if I could, you know that."

Oh yes, I knew. I sighed. "Well...December. How about that?" How would I manage? I hadn't even put the house on the market.

"Kate? Do you need to take a few days off? You're on a salary, you know. It won't make any difference in your paycheck. I *can* take care of that."

I swallowed the lump in my throat. I would miss this woman, miss all my friends and customers. Whatever made me think I'd want to move away? "Thanks, Maria. That would help."

"All right, then it's settled. Take a few days, pack, take care of business. I'll cover for you here."

I thanked her again and we broke the connection.

Sailor scratched at the door and I yelled for Kelli to put him out. I poured orange juice and milk, doled out lunch money, combed Kris's hair and found Kelli's jacket. All the while my mind raced. What was I going to do? I had to sort through seven years' accumulation. Get rid of things we didn't need, sell what I could, choose what I wanted to move. Move where? I didn't have a house in California. I would have to make another trip to San Francisco.

I loaded my daughters into the car and backed out of the drive. I had to break the news to them, and they were not going to be happy.

"Guess what, girls. Maria called this morning and we're going to have to move sooner than I expected."

Kris fixed me with an accusing glare. "When?"

I kept my eyes on the road. "The beginning of December."

Kris gasped. "We won't get to spend Christmas here!"

Christmas? Oh, yeah. That was coming, too. How could I have forgotten our number one major holiday? I sighed. I couldn't do this.

Tears sparkled on Kris's eyelashes. "I don't want to move. Why can't we stay here?"

"I have a chance at a better job, one where I don't have to fly."

"Can we take Mrs. Murphy with us?" Kelli asked.

I could only wish. "No, she has a home and family here."

"Then I'm not going." She stuck out her lower lip in a remarkable imitation of my mother. Why hadn't I noticed the resemblance before? Sensitive to a fault, and determined to have her own way. She was the overly protective type, too. When

Kelli was three years old, on Mother's Day Out at the church, a program for preschool children, there she would be, putting her arm around the smaller children and cooing, "Do you have to potty? Now, if you do, you come tell me. Mr. Potty is our friend!" They thought she was a pain in the neck.

Exactly like my mother.

"Look, girls." I tried to explain. "I don't like the way things are working out either, but we are going to have to make the best of it. Like it or not, we're moving to California by the end of November and I expect you to help me."

"It isn't fair," Kelli burst out. "If Daddy was here..."

I didn't want to go there. I couldn't drive and cry at the same time.

Kris said it for me. "Daddy isn't here."

"No," I agreed. "I'm sorry."

They sat quietly for the rest of the ride. When we reached the school, Kris said, "It's all right, Mom. I'll help. I promise."

Kelli still looked like a thundercloud, but she muttered, "Me, too—but it's not fair."

My heart broke. I swear I heard it crack. I turned to face them, my wonderful, courageous daughters. "Look, girls, California won't be so bad. You'll make new friends and we'll be close to the ocean and Disneyland."

A purely wicked gleam flashed in Kris's eyes. "Can I get my eyebrows pierced?"

"Not on this planet. Don't even think about it."

Kelli's lips curved in a reluctant grin. "I want a nose ring."

Okay, no more television. Or at least not unless I was in the room. "There will be no body piercing. Subject closed."

Kelli hugged me. "Bye, Mom. Have an awesome day."

Kris, who had already got out of the car, popped back in to throw her arms around me. "Don't worry, Mom—it will be all right. We'll like California."

I hugged her tightly. "Oh, Kris, thanks. I'll see you later." She closed the car door and they ran toward the school.

Pulling into traffic, I struggled with fresh tears. How had Neil and I managed to raise two such terrific kids? I didn't deserve them, but somehow I was going to protect them, even if I did have to do it by myself.

I drove to White River Realty and listed my house for sale. Molly Ervin, my new Realtor, filled out the listing. "When can I see the house?"

"Anytime you like. I have to be moved by the first of December, so the sooner the better."

"I see." She pushed her glasses up her nose with one finger and nodded her head, gray curls bouncing. "I'll try to get it in tomorrow's paper and I'll put it on our Internet site. If it's all right with you, I'll stop by in about an hour and take a look. I'll leave a lockbox and put a sign up in the yard."

"That sounds great." I gave her my phone number and she gave me her card. I walked out feeling as if I had just cut an important tie to my past. Events were moving much too fast for me. I started the car and drove home, planning to straighten up the house before Mrs. Ervin arrived.

I didn't go into the house right away. Instead I sat in the driveway looking through the windshield at my home, trying to see it the way a prospective buyer would. The trim needed painting. Neil had put that on his to-do list. The rooms were small, the attic unfinished. You had to jiggle the handle on the toilet tank to make it shut off. Then there was the stove.... Like all old houses it had its shortcomings, but it was home and I loved it.

I got out of the car and went inside, walking through the rooms, picking up the girls' clothing, cleaning the bathroom. So many memories lived here and I was moving away. *God, am I doing the right thing?*

God didn't seem to be speaking to *me,* either.

I stared out the kitchen window, not really seeing anything. I needed help. There was no way I could do all of this myself. I picked up the phone and called my mother.

You'd think at my age I would know better than to give in to impulses.

She answered on the first ring, no doubt anticipating the SOS. Her radar was uncanny.

"Kate! What a pleasant surprise. How are you, dear?"

"I'm fine, Mom, but..."

"How are the girls?"

"They're fine, Mom, but..."

"Are you back to work yet?"

I gritted my teeth. "Mom! Let me finish a sentence, okay?"

"Well, really, dear. By all means, talk." She sounded hurt, and I sighed. I shouldn't have called. I'd forgotten how overwhelming she could be. I loved my mother, but she had a lot in common with a runaway bulldozer.

"I'm selling the house."

"Oh, Kate! You're moving to Kansas!"

I blinked. Where had that come from? "Well, no. Actually I'm moving to San Francisco."

Dead silence.

I had never known my mother to be so quiet for so long. Something was wrong. She'd had a heart attack. I was sure of it.

I yelled, "Mom!"

"What?" She yelled back.

"Are you all right?"

"I was until you yelled at me. What's wrong?"

"Nothing's wrong." I took a deep breath and started over. "You were so quiet I was worried."

"Well. You'd think I was never quiet. I was trying to absorb what you said, and then you yelled at me and I nearly had a heart attack."

Okay, it was all my fault. Somehow I had expected that. And it wouldn't have occurred to me to think that she'd had a heart attack if she wasn't always threatening to have one.

"Why San Francisco?" she asked. "You and the girls belong here, in Kansas. This is your home, dear."

I couldn't go "home." We were two women who couldn't live under the same roof...in the same town...same state.

"Listen, Mom. I have a new job. I'm being transferred to California." I hurried along, afraid she would interrupt again. "I have to be in San Francisco by the beginning of December."

"That's only a month away. Kate, are you sure about this?"

"It's what I have to do, Mom."

She sighed. "Your father and I will come to help."

"Well..." Too late I was having second thoughts.

"No, no. Don't give it another thought. I'll talk to your father and we'll be there as soon as we can get our things together and take the cat by the kennel."

She hung up, cutting me off in midprotest.

What had I done?

She would drive me *insane*. I pictured her in my mind— short, stocky, strawberry-blond hair, although she owed most of that coloring to artificial means these days. She never gave an inch, even when she was wrong. If anyone could motivate this move, she could.

Mrs. Ervin arrived and I showed her through the house while she took notes and asked questions. Trying to see the house through her eyes made my home seem even shabbier. We walked around the backyard trailed by Sailor, who followed me acting nervous, as if he knew something was up. The girls' swing set filled one corner. Just one more thing that would have to be left behind.

"Mrs. Ervin?"

"Call me Molly."

"Molly. Do you think the house will sell quickly?"

She cocked her head to one side and flashed a smile. "I'll certainly do my best. The housing market is strong now and I have a couple of clients who are looking for something in this price range."

We went back into the house and she gathered up her purse and briefcase. "I'll be in touch."

I showed her out and fixed myself a sandwich. While I ate it, I spent a little time digging through the kitchen cabinets trying to decide what to take and what to sell. Definitely take my grandmother's dishes—fine Bavarian china with a rose-and-basket-weave design. I had inherited it when Grandma died, which had really upset Mom because she had expected the dishes to come to her.

The phone rang and I answered it to find my mother's voice spitting out words like a mouthful of pebbles. "We're coming Wednesday. Don't do a thing until I get there. We need to get organized before we start sorting and packing. Your father and I will stay as long as you need us."

"Ah...right."

"Don't worry, dear. I'll take care of everything."

I hung up feeling as if I'd been flattened by a steamroller. She would organize everything. She would sort. She would pack. Mom was coming. Everything would work out. Relax.

So why was I worried?

"You did *what?*" I gaped at my mother, unable to believe my ears. "Tell me you didn't do that."

She raised her eyebrows at me. "I invited our family members in Oklahoma to come here to celebrate Thanksgiving early. Family supports family, and right now you need all the support you can get."

"Where do you think I'm going to put all those people?" I stopped yelling and started mentally calculating the damage. "How many did you actually invite?"

Mom rolled her eyes and looked to be silently counting. I braced for the total.

"Let's see. Clyde and Onie."

Okay, her sister and brother-in-law, I could handle that.

"And their family."

Hoo, boy. Sons, daughters and grandkids. That made fourteen people. Plus Mom and Dad and the girls and me, five more—nineteen. I needed to buy a much bigger turkey than I had planned on. Mom's facial muscles puckered.

"What?" I demanded.

"Well, I just thought. I didn't invite Uncle Frank and Aunt Bossy. I mean Bessie."

"Well, don't. We've got more now than we have room for. Some of them will have to stay at a motel if they're planning to stay overnight."

And no, I didn't need my great-aunt. Put her and my mother in the same room and I'd end up with a catfight supreme. Both women thought they were born to rule, and they didn't brook any interference.

Mom shook her head. "Oh, no. I told them they'd have to leave before night. I made that perfectly clear."

Yeah, that's what concerned me. And with my luck they'd all die on the road—half the guest list couldn't see after dark—and I'd be held responsible.

One more thing to worry about.

"I don't know why you're so upset. This might be the last Thanksgiving we can all be together. California is a long way away, dear."

I grabbed a notepad and started making a grocery list.

Packing started to take shape. Boxes ready to move were taped and labeled and stacked in the garage. The house was a mess, and I was expecting twenty people for our pre-Thanksgiving dinner. Make that twenty-three. Three of the teenagers were insisting on bringing friends.

The girls were going through their things, choosing what they wanted to take. I had placed cardboard boxes outside their rooms for rejects. Last time I'd looked the reject boxes were still empty.

Mom was fixing dinner tonight. Fried chicken, biscuits and gravy, creamed corn, banana pudding and cream cheese brownies. I had spent most of my married life trying to practice good eating habits—except for the nights Neil had worked. And my mother was undoing everything I had accomplished. The girls loved our new diet regime.

Fat, sugar and more fat.

Dad was in the kitchen, too, tossing a ball for Sailor to catch. The dog scampered across the floor and Mom frowned. "Frank, *take* that dog outside to play."

Dad ignored her. As only Dad could do.

"Frank! Did you hear me?"

"Of course I heard you, woman. I'm not deaf."

"Then go out in the yard to play with that dog."

"I like it here. You take care of the cooking—I'll take care of Sailor."

Mom stood arms akimbo. "I will not cook with a dog in my kitchen."

Dad assumed a look of great patience. "Kay, it's not your kitchen. It's Kate's, and she lets the dog stay in the house."

Oh, yeah, right. Drag me into it.

"Maybe you'd have more room to let Sailor run in the living room," I offered.

"He can't run as fast on carpet." Dad tossed the ball again.

Mom folded her arms and primmed her mouth. "All right. If someone falls over that dog and hurts themselves, my conscience is clear."

Dad took the ball from Sailor and tossed it again. "A clear conscience is the result of a poor memory."

Mom stared at him, mouth agape for a couple of seconds. "My memory is just fine, thank you, and I don't remember asking for your opinion."

She took a pan of brownies out of the oven and slapped them down on the countertop.

Dad feigned a sigh. "Of course not. We've been married for forty years and in all that time you've never let me have an *opinion*."

The doorbell rang and I went to answer it, counting to ten.

I loved my parents, but they were really getting on my nerves. I opened the door and stared in dismay. *Mrs. Ervin.* And a young couple who looked to be in their early twenties.

"Uh..." Brilliant, Kate. Get with it. "Mrs. Ervin. Hello."

"Mrs. Madison, this is Mr. and Mrs. Leroy Himes. They'd like to look at the house. I usually call first, but we happened to be in the neighborhood..."

"Oh, yes, of course." I stepped back out of the way. "It's a bit of a mess right now. I'm trying to get packed to move."

The front room looked like the aftermath of an Oklahoma tornado.

Mrs. Ervin appeared apologetic. "I tried to call, but the line was busy."

"It was?" To my knowledge no one had been using the phone. I left the Realtor to give the grand tour and went to the kitchen. "Dad, will you go pick up the girls for me? I can't leave right now."

"Sure." He got up and reached for his coat. I walked over to lift the receiver. It was off the hook. How about that? I turned to face Mom. "Who used the phone last?"

"I did."

"You leave it off the hook?"

She nodded.

"Is there a reason why?"

"You've got so much on your mind, I thought I'd give you a little breathing space. If anyone wants you they'll call back."

"What if the girls had needed to get in touch with me?"

Her cheeks pinked. "Well, I never thought of that."

"So next time think and leave the telephone alone!" I realized I'd been a bit abrupt. "I'm sorry, Mom. It's just that I want the girls to be able to reach me."

"Of course, dear. I'll just tell people you're not talking on the phone at this time."

"No, don't do that, either." I caught myself and turned down the volume, not wanting our visitors to think I'd slipped a cog.

"Look, Mom, don't be so helpful, okay?"

The Himes couple appeared in the doorway and I forced a smile. They looked around the kitchen, opening cabinets, checking out the sink. I bit my tongue. I really wanted someone to buy this house, so I'd have to put up with what seemed like an invasion of privacy. They left and Dad arrived with the kids. We ate our fat-laden dinner in comparative quiet. Mom wasn't speaking to either me or Dad. The silence was heavenly.

The next morning Mom insisted we tackle Neil's clothing. I wasn't ready for that. "No. Not now. We've got enough to handle. I can do it later."

"You'll never heal as long as you are sharing a room with his things. The quicker you get rid of them the better."

I supposed she was right, but I wanted to wait and do it myself.

"Kay, leave Kate alone," Dad ordered. "She'll do it when she's ready."

Up went Mom's eyebrows. "Now, Frank, you can't really expect me to leave Kate to take care of such a painful task by herself."

"No, I don't expect that, but I think it would be best if you did."

"Kate isn't thinking straight at the moment—we have to do her thinking for her. Now, I know what is best in this case."

I stood back and listened to them do battle as if I wasn't standing in the same room. Yada, yada, yada. Finally I couldn't take any more. "*All right.* I give up, Mom. We'll do it today. Happy?"

Mom sniffed. "I think that's a wise decision, darling. I'll get the boxes."

I steeled myself to go through the ordeal. Actually it wasn't as bad as I expected, because Mom did most of the work. When we had the boxes packed, she wanted to call the Salvation Army right then and get the stuff hauled out the same day. I gave in on that, too.

Maybe it was best to get the painful reminders out of the house before the girls came home. I thought I was fine with it until I saw Neil's golf clubs sitting by the front door. The shock was like a giant hand squeezing my heart. Dad saw my face.

"What's wrong, Kate?"

I shook my head and he followed my gaze. "The golf clubs?"

Sighing, I nodded and blinked back hot tears. He patted my shoulder. "I've been thinking of taking up the game. I'd feel right honored to have Neil's clubs, if it's all right with you."

I dissolved in his arms as the Salvation Army truck pulled into the drive. Mom went to the door and Dad carried the golf clubs upstairs. I went to the kitchen, where Sailor licked my hand.

Surprisingly, the slobbered comfort worked.

Our pre-Thanksgiving day dawned clear and cold. Mom insisted on using Grandmother's dishes for the celebration even though they were already packed. I protested, but she unpacked them anyway. All 125 pieces. I clamped my lips together to keep from saying what I thought, and reached for a dish towel. All 125 pieces would have to be washed and dried.

She handed me the gravy boat and I don't know what happened, but it slipped right through my hands to crash in a thousand pieces on the floor.

Mom dissolved in hysterics. "My mother's gravy boat! How *could* you, Kate? Do you have to be so clumsy?"

Dad picked up the pieces. "Calm down, Kay. It was an ugly bowl anyway."

"I can't believe you broke the gravy boat," Mom raged. "You can't *buy* that pattern anymore."

I snapped. "*You're* the one who insisted on using the best dishes. I *wanted* to use paper plates."

That stopped her. She looked horrified. "Paper plates for a *Thanksgiving* dinner? That's sacrilegious."

Dad walked out. I calmed Mom down and went looking for him. He was sitting on a park bench two blocks away. I sat down beside him, stuffing my hands into my coat pockets. What had happened to my sane life? "You all right?"

He nodded. "You know, I love your mother, but there are times I'd like to string her up like a plucked goose."

I grinned. "Me, too. She is a bit overwhelming at times."

"That's an understatement." He turned to look at me. "You've had a rough time, haven't you?"

I nodded. "It's been really bad. Sometimes I've felt like I couldn't handle it, but somehow I seem to muddle through."

"It'll get better. Trust me."

"I don't know. For the first time in my career I gave a bad haircut yesterday."

He laughed. "Now, that is bad."

I grinned. "The woman I gave it to thought so."

We sat in silence for a few minutes, then he got up. "Well, we'd better go back before Kay starts hunting for us."

"Dad, I appreciate all she does. It's just that..."

"I know. She doesn't know when to stop."

"Or when not to start. We still have our Thanksgiving dinner to get through."

People had started arriving by the time we got back to the house. Kelli was fascinated by her teenage cousin Lora, mainly because Lora sported a nose ring. I don't suppose Kelli had ever seen one except on TV, and I hoped seeing the real thing would erase any secret longing she might harbor. I was fairly sure Lora hadn't attended Neil's funeral. Even as distracted as I had been at the time I'd surely have noticed that ring.

Kris was at her seven-year-old best, showing people where to put their coats and the steaming dishes. The relatives had brought food. Dad put up folding tables and carved the turkey. Mom bustled around telling everyone what to do.

Dad asked the blessing, and I thought of all of these good people who had put their own plans on hold to come to "support me."

I thanked God for family and for friends.

Maybe I was slowly working at finding my way back.

After everyone left I went up to my bedroom, which had been cleansed of every visible trace of Neil. I lay down on the bed and closed my eyes, summoning up his memory. His touch. The way his eyes crinkled at the corners when he smiled. The way he smelled after a hot shower.

My mind knew that wherever I lived, Oklahoma or California, Neil would be alive in my memory.

Now, if only I could make my heart believe it.

Chapter

7

So now I was testing emotional waters, slowly but surely starting to function again. For weeks now I'd ignored offers from friends to get out of the house on the weekend, see a movie, have tea. So I chose the safest method—tea. With my friend Livvy Mills. If Livvy couldn't lighten my mood, then no one could. I asked Sally Fowler to keep an eye on the girls, and the following Saturday afternoon, while Neil's parents were at the movies, I dressed in tweed slacks and a cardigan, put my hair in a ponytail and put my best face forward for the outing. The Millses had been "couple friends" at church. Neil and Tom got along well, so we'd attend functions together—concerts, picnics, Christmas cantatas and children's programs. At least once during the week, Liv and I would get together and hash over our children's antics or some menial problem we'd encountered. I hadn't been alone with Liv since the accident.

We met in our favorite haunt—a refurbished brownstone,

now a tearoom and bakery. The establishment's coconut cake was to die for.

We hugged and said all the things we usually said, but I knew Liv was being overly bright, overly bubbly. A regally tall and polished brunette, she never had a hair out of place. She wore large jewelry and more makeup than I ever dared to wear; she was drop-dead gorgeous. I guess she didn't want me falling to pieces on her in a public place, so I promised myself I wouldn't. Today the fog wasn't so dense: I could actually blow my nose without breaking down into fits of weeping.

We ordered tea with 2 percent milk. The waitress recognized us, and gave me a sympathetic smile. "Will you ladies be having your regular?"

I nodded, glancing at Liv. "Chicken salad," we parroted. They made the best in town.

"So many calories," Liv fretted when the waitress walked away.

"Calories are the last thing you need to worry about."

"Look who's talking. Miss Walking Stick herself."

I thought about the way my slacks fit me like a grain sack today. I'd lost weight—the last thing I needed. I was metabolically blessed; I could eat anything, anytime and still lose weight. Friends said they would kill to have the problem, but for me, gaining weight was as grueling as losing it was for them. What a problem, huh?

We chatted, carefully avoiding Neil's name. People did that—as if by avoiding the obvious they could turn back time. All I wanted was to talk—to remember my husband and the good times. It wasn't fair that a young, vibrant man like Neil could be so easily consigned to past tense.

Liv squeezed her tea bag dry with a spoon, and wound the string around the handle before placing it beside her cup. "Why do I feel so awkward? I came today with the intention of cheering you up, but I feel like a clown trying too hard."

I smiled. "You are a clown, Liv."

"I'm serious." She leaned forward, grasping my hand tightly. "I want to help—I *need* to help you. What can I do?"

"Let's see," I deadpanned. "For starters, you can lend me a couple of hundred thou."

Liv stared at me vacantly. "Dollars?"

I nodded. "Dollars."

"What in the world do you need two hundred thousand dollars for? Neil left insurance, didn't he?"

Ordinarily that would be personal information, but not between me and Liv. We'd once even told each other our present weight. Now I had to break it to her about the move; I'd told no one about my plans except Mom and Dad, and cautioned the kids to keep quiet until I could inform friends and Neil's parents. While I talked, tears bubbled to Liv's eyes.

"You're moving to San Francisco?" she whispered.

I nodded, tightening my hold on her hand. "I have to." I explained about the problem with my right eardrum, and how I couldn't fly regularly for maybe a long time. "Maria arranged to transfer me to a La Chic in the Bay Area. The girls and I flew out there to house hunt."

Liv fumbled for a tissue. "Why didn't you *tell* me?"

"I am telling you—now." I sighed and took a sip of tea. "My life has changed so quickly I haven't been able to keep up," I apologized.

"But California. I'll never get to see you!"

"Sure you will—you and Tom and the kids can fly out whenever you want."

"Oh, right." She blew her noise on the tissue. "Six round-trip airfares to California, at today's fares. We'll be there every weekend."

I laughed. "Well, it's going to be hard on me, too." Harder, actually. Who would I pour out all my trivial problems on? I realized now that up until weeks ago my problems had been trifling.

"We have e-mail," I said.

"It isn't the same."

"The phone lines still work. I have unlimited nights and weekends on my cell phone."

She sniffled. "It's not the same."

And it wasn't. But then I'd learned the hard way nothing would ever be the same.

The waitress returned carrying two plates of chicken salad. Conversation momentarily ceased; we busied ourselves dabbing dressing on the accompanying lettuce-and-tomato salad. I knew Liv was hurt and confused that I hadn't told her earlier about the move. Maybe I had thought I'd back out—chicken out—but so far I'd held it all in with the hope of a new beginning.

"So did you find a house?" she asked.

"Nothing that I can afford. Do you have any idea how much the average house costs in the Bay Area?"

"Two hundred thousand?"

"Down payment," I said.

"Mercy. Have you got that kind of money?"

"Do I look like I have that kind of money?" With both salaries, we'd barely been able to make ends meet.

"Then how are you going to buy a house? What about an apartment? Wouldn't that be smarter? An apartment, then if you don't like it there you can move back here where you belong."

"I don't want to raise the girls in an apartment." I couldn't think of anything worse: cramped living space, thin walls, no garage—at least in any unit I could afford.

"Then what will you do? Neil had death benefits, didn't he?"

"Of course he did, but it's not a fortune. I'll have to invest carefully—and you know how squirrelly the stock market is these days. I'll have to put some of it back for Kris and Kelli's college fund, and everything is so expensive."

"Yeah, but I guess you could argue a house would be a sound investment—especially in the Bay Area."

I nodded, agreeing. "Our house should bring over a hundred thousand. We still owe eighty thousand on the mortgage."

"So that means you have to come up with..." Liv paused. "You got a calculator?"

I sighed. "No need. The amount is too much."

"What about your parents—or Neil's parents?"

"I wouldn't think of asking either set for money. They're both living on fixed incomes."

"Yeah, but your dad has to be loaded," she joked. "He's a retired dentist, isn't he?"

"Forget it, Liv. I'm not asking my parents to help." I bit into my roll—or tried. The crust was hard as brick. The last thing I needed was a dentist bill.

"I think the whole idea of moving is nuts. You should stay here. It's not fair to uproot your children and drag them off to another state where they won't know anyone. All of their friends will be back here. With your reputation, you can get a job in any salon in Oklahoma City." She bit into her roll, and frowned.

I glanced up. "What's wrong?"

"Uh-oh," she muttered.

"What?"

Her eyes darted around the crowded room. "Oh no, oh no, augh!"

"What?" I leaned forward, trying to spot the problem. The roll was stuck between her teeth, but she didn't appear to be chewing.

"My upper denture just split in half."

"Your—?" I broke off with a rude snicker. I knew the situation wasn't funny, but I also knew how sensitive Liv was about the artificial appliance. In her teens, she'd been in a bad car accident that had thrown her through the windshield. She was lucky to have survived the incident with nothing more than two broken ribs and dentures. But to Liv dentures meant decrepitude, and the touchy subject had been a long-standing joke between the four of us. And now my beloved, ultrapersnickety friend was sitting in a hotsy-totsy teahouse, toothless as a gold-mining hermit.

"Spit it out in this." I pressed a linen napkin into her hand.

She shook her head passionately. "I have to take it with me." Her voice sounded funny—not like Liv. She lisped. Big time.

"Then I'll get a paper napkin."

"Hurry," she muttered. "And do it discreetly!"

"All right." Did she think I was going to waltz up to the counter and announce that my friend had a mouthful of broken denture?

I got up from the table and casually sauntered to the front. Our waitress was busy with another table, so I asked the first face I encountered. "Could I have some paper napkins?"

The girl smiled. "We don't have paper napkins. Linen napkins are at your table."

Nodding, I smiled faintly. "No paper napkins?"

"None—do you need extra linen napkins?"

"No, thanks."

Now what? I glanced over my shoulder and saw Liv sitting at the table, her right hand clamped over her mouth. I turned and walked back.

Liv looked up mutely.

"No paper napkins," I whispered. "What about a Kleenex?"

She shook her head. "Used all of mine," she lisped.

I searched through my purse and found one, used. I glanced at Liv and she adamantly shook her head.

Okay. Use your head, Kate.

Our waitress spotted the activity and headed for the table, fresh teapot in hand. "More tea?" she asked. She focused on Liv's odd position. Hand over mouth, refusing to look up.

Liv nodded.

"Can I interest you ladies in dessert today? A piece of our special coconut cake or pecan pie?"

Liv shook her head.

"Just fresh tea, thank you." I smiled, trying to get rid of her. Eventually another table needed service and the waitress wandered off.

"Help me," Liv pleaded behind the napkin. "I've *got* to get out of here!"

"Okay. Stay put."

"Like I'm going anywhere in my condition," Liv muttered.

I located the ladies' room. A few minutes later I returned to the table with a pocketful of toilet paper. I inconspicuously put the wad of tissue in Liv's hand. She looked at the offering, horror filling her eyes.

"It's clean," I emphasized. I left her and stepped back to the front to pay the bill.

A short time later I ushered my classy friend through the small shop and its vast array of teapots, charming dishes and other knickknacks, and helped her into her car. Before I even closed the door, Liv was on the cell phone to her dentist, who was at home on a Saturday, advising him she'd be sitting in front of his office in fifteen minutes, and in a lisping threat said he'd better be waiting for her.

I tapped on the driver's window. Liv hit the button, and the glass went down.

"Hey, Liv."

She arched a brow.

"That thing you said about cheering me up?" I broke into laughter—the snorting, not-so-classy kind. Liv shot me a look that would singe tail feathers.

"You did. I feel better. Thanks."

She waved me off in disgust and sped away.

Sticking my hands into my coat pockets, I took a deep breath of cold air and looked up at a faultless blue sky. *Thanks,* I acknowledged.

I wasn't sure if I was talking to Neil or God. If it was God, it'd been a while since we had corresponded.

"Ladies and gentlemen, please remain in your seat with your seat belt securely fastened until the aircraft comes to a complete stop."

I motioned for Kris to put Winter Fantasy Barbie in her backpack, and pick up trash around her seat. All around me I heard the telltale *click* of freed seat belts.

Kelli wiggled into her backpack. "Mommy, are we going to look at dumps again all day?"

"I hope not," I murmured, applying a fresh coat of lipstick. I'd spoken to a new Realtor; the girls and I had this weekend to find a new home. I was still short fifty thousand on a down payment, but I'd asked the church to pray for me. I still couldn't pray. The words stuck in my throat like glue and refused to come out. Mom and Dad had insisted on helping with the down payment, to my dismay, but when they pointed out they didn't want their granddaughters living in squalor, I relented.

Fellow flyers gathered in groups around the luggage carousel. The girls and I watched every single piece go by three times before I faced the obvious. My one large checked bag hadn't made our plane.

The Realtor was probably circling the baggage area, anticipating my immediate appearance.

Carrying a shoulder bag, backpack and pulling Kris's—the only smart one in the bunch—wheeled carry-on, we walked out of the terminal. I'd have to find the Realtor, inform him of the delay and then return and fill out the necessary papers.

A huge Suburban with Moore Realty on the side panels sat idling at the curb. Taxis pulled in and out, cars honked.

I reached for the door handle and stuck my head inside the vehicle. "I'm Kate Madison." The leather interior had a nice, manly aftershave scent.

A good-looking man about my age set a clipboard aside and prepared to exit the truck—to help with our bags, I assumed. I quickly explained what had happened, and since a baggage handler was waving the Realtor on, Gray Mitchell suggested the girls stay with him while I filed the missing-luggage report.

At the suggestion, Kelli turned white as Casper the Ghost. Kris sucked in her breath, staring at me apprehensively.

"Go on, girls. It's okay—" I caught myself. Kate Madison! Are you crazy! You don't know this guy from Adam. He could be some pervert masquerading as a real estate agent, though even the paranoid part of me argued that would be too much of a coincidence. The man was clearly sitting at our agreed-upon meeting place, in a Suburban clearly marked Moore Realty. He had to be on the up-and-up.

Mr. Mitchell promptly withdrew the offer, saying that he'd circle the baggage-claim area until I was finished.

I tucked Kelli's hand firmly in mine, slammed the door and reentered the terminal. The whole process took maybe fifteen minutes, and I was politely assured that when the missing bag was located, it would be delivered to our hotel.

This time I'd booked my own hotel accommodations. "We're staying near the airport—Holiday Inn Express."

The clerk nodded.

Now that I had the girls petrified that we were about to embark on an afternoon with a serial killer, I half dragged them back through the double doors and outside in time to see the Suburban's taillights disappearing around the corner. The girls and I stood in the balmy San Francisco weather and waited for our ride to circle back around.

"Is it safe to go with him, Mommy?"

"It's safe, Kris. Moore Realty is a respected real estate firm. I'm sorry if I frightened you, but I spoke before I thought. I'm sure it would have been fine to let you ride with Mr. Mitchell."

Ha. Those girls wouldn't have come within a country mile of the man without me.

Kelli sidled closer and reached for my hand. "You won't leave us with him, will you, Mommy?"

"Of course not."

Panic disorder—that would be Kelli's first psychiatric session, thanks to you, oh woman of little trust. But a woman—especially a woman alone—couldn't be too careful these days, and I had the girls to protect.

The Suburban rounded the corner and I stepped off the curb and waved. Gray Mitchell swerved out of the line of taxis and braked.

Moments later the girls and I were buckled in the middle seat—a safe distance from Mr. Smells Heavenly real estate agent. I glanced at his left hand, appalled to realize I was looking for a ring. I'd never done anything even remotely like that before, and guilt hit me like a knife in the back. How could I tarnish Neil's memory with such thoughts?

Mitchell chatted away in the front seat and I looked anyway. No ring. He talked about the nice weather, how did we like Oklahoma City, didn't Oklahoma have a lot of tornadoes?

I answered: wonderful weather—hadn't lived anywhere other than Oklahoma, so naturally I loved it—and yes, the state was subject to severe weather.

Then he got into the subject of the *big* Oklahoma City tornado that had hit May 4, some years ago. The National Weather Service had said that a line of severe storms that passed through the Midwest that night produced forty-five tornadoes in Oklahoma, fourteen tornadoes in Kansas and more in Texas the following day. Forty-four people died, hundreds were injured and damage approached a billion dollars. He seemed to know the statistics better than I did. Our house wasn't in the path of the F5, and we were still thanking God for that—at least, most were.

By now we were speeding across an elevated highway. I looked down on both sides of the truck and wondered how I'd ever manage to drive in eight lanes of traffic. There wasn't a car going under seventy on either side, and my mind conjured up the World News scenes of massive pileups, involving hundreds of motorists. I broke into a cold sweat, suddenly wanting to go home.

Eventually he took an exit ramp, and the fast-food stores gradually melted into residential homes. The tree-lined streets resembled scenes out of a magazine—well-maintained houses, older residents. Picturesque. Gray Mitchell brought me back to the present.

"I've given your situation a lot of thought, Mrs. Madison, and your personal preferences as well. After a little research, I've come up with a couple of houses I think might suit you well."

Only two? I thought, thinking about the cost to fly me and my ear and the girls here a second time. La Chic was paying, but still, I spent company money the way I spent my own, and two houses were hardly worth the effort. And I couldn't remember what I had written down in the "preferences" column. An estate for under two hundred thousand?

The Suburban pulled into a curved drive. The girls and I bent forward to get our first glimpse of the house: cottage-style, ivy growing along the front. My gaze focused on the dark green canvas awnings and white porch boxes beneath the windows. The house was adorable.

We got out of the car, and Gray—I wasn't openly calling him by his first name, but he'd assured me that I could—escorted us to the front, double oak door. He turned the key in the lock, and the door swung open.

I stood for a moment with the most bizarre feeling. This was it. This was going to be my new home, my new beginning. I didn't have the faintest idea what the house cost—far more than I had, I knew, but it was as if the house had reached out and purchased me.

We stepped inside the hardwood foyer. From here I could see a small dining room on the right, and an adequate living area with stone fireplace and floor-to-ceiling bookcases on the left. The room had wood shutters on the windows.

"This appeals to a woman's eye," Gray said. We walked toward the kitchen. Small, but arranged nicely. Dark blue cabinets with glass fronts. A center wooden block counter. To the right, a sunny alcove, ideal for a table and four chairs. The floors were wood and carpet. Both needed replacing. Utility room and half bath adjacent to a one-car garage. I lost my heart, room by room.

Gray paused, his eyes roaming the outdated decor. "When I previewed this house, I fell in love with it. It needs work—you can see that—but with a little care you'd have a good home, Mrs. Madison."

"Please call me Kate." Anyone who could come this close to my ideal home had earned the right of familiarity.

"The lady who lived here recently went into a nursing home. She's alone, and she's asked me to find not just an occupant, but a family to live here."

I stared at him trying to discern if this was his usual sales spiel. If it was, he delivered the pitch with grace and sincerity.

Trying not to foam at the mouth, I pretended to casually peruse the rooms, going upstairs several times, talking to the girls to get their feel of the house. I knew it was perfect. Too perfect. I wasn't lucky enough to find the ideal home in one try—I didn't count the previous visit, because those houses were hovels. Affordable hovels. This house was a real home.

Finally we ended up back in the kitchen. I stood at the white porcelain sink, gazing at the garden of Eden: the backyard. Well-maintained, mature plants and bushes, and some sort of stone structure, identical to the house only smaller, far in the rear.

"Storage," Gray said over my shoulder. I shut my eyes, breathing deep of his aftershave, and a blindly intense physical pain assaulted me. Every fiber in me wanted Neil at that moment, wanted the marriage we'd shared.

Swallowing, I stepped back from the window. "I'm afraid the house is out of my price range."

Gray consulted his notes, and then looked up. "The owner is willing to consider offers. I think I mentioned money isn't the primary concern."

I shook my head, wanting to make an offer but embarrassed to do so. This house had to be at least $350,000.

"What is the asking price?"

"Three hundred and twenty-five thousand."

Yep. My hope plummeted.

"We don't have that much money," Kelli said. "We have to be frugal."

Gray grinned, a charming display of white teeth in a California tan. "I understand frugality, Miss Madison."

"You said there was another house?" Why get my hopes up when the effort would only be futile?

"Certainly." Shortly after, we locked the front door to my perfect house and got back in the Suburban.

House number two was nice. It was on a similar residential street, similar floor plan—maybe a little larger and more closet space. Less fixing up to do.

But it didn't buy me. It didn't embrace me. It didn't grab me and say, this is *home*, Kate.

"You like the other one better, don't you?" Gray observed when I stood in the empty living room and covered my eyes with my hands in frustration. Our words echoed throughout the empty dwelling.

"Love it," I admitted. "But I don't love the asking price." Sighing, I knew I'd come to the inevitable. "I think I'm going to have to rent."

"I understand." He didn't push; he didn't insist that we go back and take a second look. He seemed to understand my dilemma and I was grateful.

We climbed back into the Suburban, and Gray backed out of the drive.

"I liked the other one better," Kris murmured. My seven-year-old snuggled closer to me and laid her head on my lap. Kelli wiggled and made a place for her head.

"I did, too," I confessed. "Sorry, girls."

"Maybe we could sell some of my toys." Kelli yawned, rubbing her eyes. "The big bear, the wagon. My dolls. That might help, huh, Mommy?"

I patted my daughter's head, thinking how proud Neil had been of this baby.

Later, the Suburban swung into the Holiday Inn Express and stopped at the entrance. The girls were sleeping soundly.

Gray whispered, "You go check in, and then I'll help you carry them to the room."

"Oh, no—" I protested.

"Please, Kate. I don't mind. The children have had a big day."

I slid out of the truck and within minutes I was back with a key.

Gray carried Kris, and I took Kelli. We rode up the elevator in silence. I suddenly felt awkward and tongue-tied around him.

He unlocked the door, and we carried the sleeping children to one of the double beds and gently deposited the girls on the mattress. Kelli stirred briefly, opened her eyes and then dropped instantly back to sleep. Kris never moved.

"Thank you so much," I whispered.

"No problem." We tiptoed quietly to the door.

Gray stopped, turning to face me. "You know, I'm an Exclusive Buyer's Agent."

I didn't know what that meant.

"It means that I work for you, not the seller. I can advise you whether the seller will accept a lower price, the seller's reason for selling, how long the home has been on the market, true house value, previous offers, if any, strengths and weaknesses of the home and comparable market data."

I nodded as though I understood every detail of real estate buying. Neil and I had gone through a dual agent when we bought our house, and whether the agent listed or sold the home, he was legally bound to represent the seller.

"You want that house, don't you?"

I nodded again. "It's perfect."

"Then make an offer."

"I couldn't—the price would be insulting. I can't afford anywhere near the asking price, honest. My husband was killed in an on-the-job accident a month and a half ago, and while he left insurance, I have to be careful. I adore the house—so do Kelli and Kris—but it's out of our price range."

"Make an offer. And I'll do everything within my power to get that house for you."

I stared at him. "Why would you do that?"

"Because I lost my wife to breast cancer last year, and I know what it's like to be alone and up against the world."

Tears smarted in my eyes. "The owner wouldn't be insulted?"

"She doesn't insult easily, and she wants to sell the house." He bent closer and informed me in a stage whisper, "She's leaving her millions to her three cats."

My mind raced. Exactly how much *could* I pay and not cheat the woman? Not nearly enough; but an offer. That's all it would be. The owner could take it or leave it. We'd never personally meet.

After a moment I said, "Two hundred and seventy-five thousand. That's it—that's all I can pay, and even that will be stretching me." Not only would I have to sell our house in Oklahoma City, but I'd have to borrow more from Mom and Dad than I'd intended, and take a second mortgage on this house to come up with that kind of money.

Gray pulled out his pen. "Take a chair, Kate. I'll write up a contract."

By the time he'd left, I had made an offer on a home. I knew in my heart I wouldn't get the house; my offer was fifty thousand short of the asking price. But Gray assured me that all the owner could say was no. She couldn't shoot me.

When I locked the hotel door behind him, I kicked off my shoes and sat down on the edge of my bed. Six o'clock. The children would be hungry when they woke. I hoped there was a fast-food restaurant nearby.

Lying across the spread, I closed my eyes and pictured the house. A rosy fire in the fireplace, new carpet—someday—refinished floors.

I wouldn't get the house.

If Neil's death had taught me anything, it had taught me cynicism. Bad things do happen to people like me. Even if the woman was out of her mind and accepted the contract, the house would have termites—or dry rot. Or both.

Sewer problems.

Boundary line disputes.

Tax liens...

Chapter 8

Kelli stirred and sat up in the bed, rubbing sleep from her eyes. I was aware of the movement, but too exhausted to respond. Outside the hotel window lights flashed.

"Mommy."

I breathed deeply, pretending to be asleep. I didn't want to cope. Not now. The day had been emotional and physically draining. Five more minutes...

"Mama!"

Kris awoke from a deep sleep to a sitting position. "What?"

I patted my eldest daughter's back. "Nothing, sweetie. Kelli's calling me." Yawning, I rolled on my side and peered at the bedside clock. Eight-thirty. My stars. We'd slept two and a half hours!

"Mommy, I'm hungry." Kelli leaned over and patted both of my cheeks, peering sleepily into my eyes.

"What would you like to eat?"

"Chicken."

"You're going to grow tail feathers," I teased. "How about some nice steamed broccoli, carrots—"

"Yuck!"

We had a good laugh at the thought of Kelli eating vegetables of any sort. I had to work on the child's finicky eating habits.

I rolled off the bed and we straightened our appearances before we rode the elevator downstairs. The evening clerk informed us there was a fast-food chicken place across the highway. I froze at the thought of getting two children across the busy interstate. We walked the mile to the intersection, and crossed at the light.

We returned to the room carrying shopping bags of chicken wings—they had no nuggets—French fries and coleslaw; as I said, I needed to work on my children's dietary habits. Mine, too. I'd bypassed the salad bar, with scattered bag lettuce and salad dressing, smeared the length of the bar. It looked as if chickens had been roosting in the croutons, and the fresh fruit was canned, swimming in sugar, a last-ditch attempt for dedicated low-fat dieters.

Inside our room I spread fresh towels over the bed and set out the bounty. The three of us kicked off our shoes, climbed on the buffet table and started foraging. By now we were hungry as wolves.

Kelli paused, looking sternly at me. "I will say the blessing."

I guiltily spat out a piece of fry into a napkin. "Sure, honey." Kris and I bowed our heads.

"Thank You, Jesus, for the hot wings and French fries. Could You please help the nice lady to get some chicken nuggets, 'cause kids like chicken nuggets better'n hot wings, but Mom says chicken's chicken and I can tear the skin off and the meat won't be so hot.

"Thank You for letting us house hunt and not get hurt by some bad person or bad thing. Please let us find a good home, God. Amen... Oh. Wait!"

I quickly bowed my head again.

"Please tell Daddy hi, and we love and miss him, but if he's having a good time, like playing golf all he wants, and he don't have to fight dangerous fires, and his back don't hurt so much when he plays football, 'cause he loves to play football but he can't because it hurts his back, then let him stay with You. Mommy says we'll just come there and join him one of these days. Really amen this time."

I quickly dashed a hot tear from the corner of my eye and echoed, "Amen."

Kelli dived into the French fries. "Do you think God will let us have that good house, Mommy? I really like it."

"I don't think so, honey, but we'll find another—maybe one even better." My mind pictured the cramped, two-bedroom apartment we'd most likely be occupying, and my heart ached. I wanted so much more for the girls. If I stayed in Oklahoma we could live in the house, old and decrepit as it was, but also roomy and comfortable. Though one could happen anytime, tornado season was usually confined to early spring and summer.

Should I go home and tell Maria I wasn't going to take the new job, that I was going to quit La Chic and maybe open a small shop of my own? Start with a couple of experienced cosmetologists and build. I rubbed my temple, massaging the tight ache. I'd thought I would be so comfortable with the "new beginning," but suddenly I wasn't. I had all kinds of doubts.

I'd lost all trace of hunger, too.

I fixed Kelli's plate—Kris was steadily stuffing fries into her mouth—and slid off the bed.

"Aren't you going to eat, Mommy?"

"I'm not hungry. I'm going to call Liv."

The children seemed content with my choice, so while they ate I took the prepaid phone card out of my wallet, praying that Liv would be home tonight. I pecked out the series of numbers and waited until the phone rang once before I pulled up a chair and settled in for a long, badly needed talk.

Tom answered.

"Hi! It's me!"

"Kate? Well, son of a gun. How are you—thought you were in San Francisco this weekend."

"I am—we are. I'm in a room at the Holiday Inn Express, eating chicken wings and French fries." I frowned, consulting my watch. There was a two-hour time difference between Oklahoma and California. So it was eleven-thirty there... "I'm sorry about the time."

"No, we were up. We had dinner with the Brysons tonight and got back late."

"Jill and Tony?" One of my favorite church couples. Neil and I had gone to a movie and pizza with them a week before he died. A wave of homesickness engulfed me, and I gripped the receiver tighter. "Can I speak to Liv a minute?"

"Sure thing—hold on." Tom put his hand over the phone and I heard his muted voice call, "Hey, gorgeous, somebody wants to talk to you."

A few seconds later Liv picked up.

"Hey," I said, suddenly losing interest in the phone call. I missed Neil so badly it hurt.

"Hey, yourself! What's going on? Did you find a house?"

"Yep, found the house of my dreams."

"No kidding! Well, praise the Lord!"

"But I can't afford it," I added, bursting Liv's bubble.

"Oh, shoot."

"Oh, Liv, I wish you were here to see it. It's perfect—three bedrooms, ivy growing on the front of the house. Porch boxes and green canvas awnings."

"So how much are you short?"

"Fifty thousand. Plus repairs. It needs some updating, but it's still a great price."

"Oh, man." Like most of us, Tom and Liv made a comfortable living, but they clipped coupons and ate chicken more often than steak. I told her about how Gray had encouraged me to make an offer, and how he said the owner wasn't as interested in money as she was in finding a home for the house.

"It's okay," I told her. "I love the house and there isn't even a remote chance that I'll get it, but it's probably a blessing. It needs new floors and carpeting, and then there'd be all that upkeep—taxes, insurance, lawn to mow." I made enough excuses to make me feel better, at least.

"Well, you know what Pastor Joe says—God doesn't work on our time frame. If He wants to bless you by giving you that particular house, a mere fifty thousand isn't going to deter Him."

"I wouldn't hold my breath. If I get that house, it will be tantamount to God parting the Red Sea."

Liv laughed. "You think God couldn't get you that house?"

"He could. I just don't think that Kate Madison is uppermost in His mind right now." After all, the world was in turmoil. Maybe once every terrorist on earth was disarmed, then peace came to the Holy Land, and poverty, child abuse and racial hatred were wiped out, then God might give my piddly situation some thought. Still—and here it was again—I could hope. Hope that the phone might ring and Gray Mitchell would be calling to say the owner accepted the offer and the girls and I were free to move immediately.

"I'll let you get to bed," I apologized. "I'll call you when I get home."

"Okay—are you all right, Kate?"

"As good as I'm going to get," I predicted.

"I wish I was there with you. You're coming home tomorrow, right?"

"We have a late-afternoon flight."

Liv's tone sobered. "Tom says to remind you that we're all praying for you, praying that through this darkness you'll find an even greater purpose for your life."

When I got through this I was going to remind Liv to be careful when she tried to console. How easy it was to say things like *There's always a reason for your pain.* Or *You're young, you'll remarry someday.* Then there were the practical soothers. *Get a grip. Life goes on.* Losing Neil had taught me one thing—until I'd walked in that person's shoes I couldn't console, I could only be there. Be a friend.

"I'll talk to you tomorrow evening."

"Safe flight, Kate."

Thanks for reminding me. I hung up, smiling. Liv was God's gift to me tonight.

"Mom, we're eating all the chicken," Kris reminded me.

"Okay." Resigned to apartment living, I got up and headed to the "buffet."

The phone jangled.

I turned and picked up the receiver wondering what Livvy had forgotten to tell me.

But Gray Mitchell's voice was on the line. "Kate, hope I'm not disturbing you."

"No." I gripped the receiver. Had he presented the offer so quickly?

"I'm just walking out of the nursing home."

"And?"

"The owner needs time to think about the offer."

My heart dropped. I knew it. I knew the offer was preposterous, so why did I feel so deflated—like a pricked balloon?

"She's promised to read the four-page summary I wrote about you and your particular situation, and she promises she'll get back to me soon."

"Did she say when?" The stubborn part of me still clung to the notion that I could be lucky enough to buy something in the Bay Area for fifty thousand under asking price.

"Not an exact time, but I expect to hear something within the next couple of weeks."

"Two weeks." I shook my head. "I don't have two weeks. The girls and I have to be moved by the end of November."

"She could get back to me sooner, and if she accepts I can have a closing date and date of possession faster than most contracts."

"Can you suggest the name of a rental agency?" I gave up. I didn't want to move to an apartment, but time and circumstances left me no choice. With any luck, maybe someday the owner's cats would put the house on the market and I could have enough saved by then to purchase the home. But then, with my luck the cats would be greedy and double the price.

I could hear doubt and a hint of impatience creep into Gray's voice, but he rattled off a couple of rental agencies and phone numbers.

"I'll call first thing in the morning and make arrangements to see an apartment before our flight leaves."

"I wish you'd reconsider. I believe eventually the owner will come around."

"Honestly, I see no reason why she should. The home is lovely. She should have no problem selling the property at the asking price."

I hung up, my appetite gone again.

"We didn't get the house," Kris surmised.

"We didn't. Sorry."

"Bugs," Kelli said. That was her choice expletive.

I helped clean up the dinner remains, and later carried the trash to a hallway receptacle; I didn't want the room to smell like coleslaw.

I took a hot shower and put on clean pajamas. I waited in the bathroom until I heard Kelli and Kris say their prayers. Then I turned out the light and crawled into bed with my two daughters.

We lay in the darkness listening to sirens shrill up and down the expressway. Overhead an occasional outgoing flight roared over the hotel roof. San Francisco was noisy.

I dropped off to sleep the way I did every night: worrying. How would Kelli and Kris take to living in an apartment? Leaving their friends, their school and the church family they'd been born into. Kris's Brownie group.

Kelli's gymnastics.

God, if You'll just somehow let me get a house, any house instead of an apartment, I'll make it. You can't take Neil away and leave me to face this alone without help from You.

I paused. Oh, great. Now I was in the bargaining stage, and I resented every moment of it.

The male flight attendant proceeded down the aisle closing overhead bins. I helped Kelli with her seat belt, then sat back and fastened mine. No house. No future. The dreaded return home flight looked like a piece of cake.

I popped an antihistamine into my mouth, thinking I'd sleep through most of the three-hour flight; I knew the children would. Kelli's head was already bobbing.

The standard pilot's patter came over the intercom. Clear weather—should have a nice flight. He gave the flight path. Sit back, relax and enjoy the view.

I closed my eyes and thought about the morning's events. I'd phoned the rental agency around eight, and by ten o'clock someone from the office had come to pick us up. We looked at three possibilities. The apartment complexes were nicer than expected—and why shouldn't they be for the price? All had pools, palms, shuffleboard and centrally located laundry rooms. In addition, the apartments each had their own hookups for folks with washers and dryers.

Disheartened, I'd let the girls pick the complex and apartment they both favored, which was the exact opposite of the one I'd picked, but at this juncture I really didn't care if I lived under a rock. I couldn't rid myself of the desire to own that house—the cute porch flower boxes. Green awnings. Picture-book perfect.

Neil would have loved it.

By now the jet had taxied to takeoff position. The aircraft sat waiting for tower clearance. I was already starting to feel the antihistamine; I lay back against the thin pillow, snuggling deeper into the blue, lint-covered airline blanket. Vaguely I heard the pilot tell the flight attendants that the plane had been cleared for takeoff.

Gradually, then picking up speed, the plane streaked down the runway. I automatically gripped the armrests, waiting for the sensation of wheels leaving the ground, then the gentle bump as they retracted into the belly of the 727.

I dozed in the hushed pressurized cabin, aware of voices around me. Businessmen discussing their day, a woman trying to comfort a crying infant.

The plane climbed and then banked east, encountering small air pockets as it gained altitude. I'd once heard the crucial times in a flight were takeoff and landing. I opened my eyes and gazed out the window. Fluffy cumulus clouds ballooned below; above me, an aquamarine sky spread a dazzling awning over the craft. The plane leveled, and I relaxed, closing my eyes, breathing a sigh of relief after the uneventful takeoff.

I didn't hear the flight attendant offering drinks and pretzels from the service cart—I slept right through that. What I did feel two hours into the flight was a large jolt, so violent the force shook me awake. I blinked and looked at the flashing seat-belt sign. Suddenly the plane dipped, soared, then leveled again.

And then plunged. I grabbed at my throbbing eardrum.

Kelli stirred, opening her eyes a crack. "Are we crashing, Mommy?"

I tried to assess fellow passengers' reactions. Some were reading; others were working on laptops. None appeared unduly concerned.

The plane jolted hard. The pilot's voice came over the intercom. "Flight attendants discontinue food service and please take your seats."

I glanced at the young woman attendant who brushed past me on the way to her jump seat.

"Is something wrong?"

She smiled. "Turbulence. Nothing to worry about." She sat down and strapped herself in. Tightly.

The front of the plane dipped. Shook. Once the craft dropped so quickly and so steeply that three overhead bins popped open and oxygen masks fell down.

I swallowed, gripping the arm of my seat so hard that I could see the veins in my arms. Kelli and Kris, white-faced and shaking, sat paralyzed beside me.

Dear Lord...please. I know You've tried Your best to keep me off planes and I won't listen. Perforated eardrum should be enough, but if You'll just keep this thing in the air—

A couple of women's voices rose in panic when the plane hit a series of pockets.

The pilot's voice came over the intercom. "Ladies and gentlemen, I'm sorry about the rough ride. I've tried several altitudes, but so far I haven't found any smooth air. There's no need for alarm. Please remain in your seat with your seat belt tightly fastened. As soon as the tower gives me clearance, I'm going to take the craft up to 33,000 feet and see if I can't find you a better ride."

The plane bucked and vibrated. I broke into a cold sweat. I'd worried that I'd go down and leave the kids orphans, but maybe God's plan was to take us all at the same time.

Poor Mom and Dad—and Neil's parents. They'd been through enough lately. It would kill Dad. He had loved Neil so much—now to lose me and the children.

I reached over and took my girls' hands, aware I should be putting on a brave front. Ha, ha—look death straight in the face, but right now death didn't seem very funny, though the thought of seeing Neil made it easier.

Passengers in the back panicked. A couple of young mothers screamed, clutching infants tightly to their breasts.

I clamped my eyes shut and prayed, holding my throbbing right ear with my right hand, and bending over to keep hold of the girls' hands with the other. The cabin pressure was suddenly excruciating in my eardrum. Funny how I went straight to God in times like this but could barely speak to Him about Neil.

I didn't want to discuss Neil with Him. He shouldn't have taken my husband. There wasn't one single reason Neil should have been on that stairway the exact moment the structure collapsed. Two minutes more and he would have cleared the corridor, been safely on the twelfth floor. The fire had raged on the sixteenth floor.

Friends and well-meaning co-workers had been quick to mention that God is seldom early, but He's never late, and we don't always know why life happens the way it does.

Well, that day His timing was perfect. It could have been any other husband or father on that stairwell that day, but it was my husband.

Kelli and Kris's father.

And why? What had Neil ever done to God other than serve Him and rear his family in a Christian path?

More oxygen masks popped open as the plane seesawed through unstable air. I was so tense that my insides set up like concrete. The elderly gentleman on my left ate from a bag of airline pretzels, his expression calm under bushy white brows. How could he *eat* through this?

Faith, I heard an inner voice whisper. *You should try a dose, Kate.*

For over twenty minutes—which seemed more like twenty hours—we rode out the severe instability. Then gradually, mercifully, I felt the plane start to climb. The rocking lessened and then eventually leveled off. Now it felt as if we were traveling down an incredibly rocky road—like being in a boat and hitting rough water—but the nose of the plane held steady.

My grip on the seat arm started to relax; my muscles throbbed from the exertion. *Faith.* I heard Neil's voice in my mind. *What good is faith if you don't practice it?*

What good, indeed? I glanced at my panic-stricken daughters and thought, Kate Madison, what are you doing? By instilling constant fear in their young minds, they'll never fly or take any risks when they grow up. And if they never take risks they'll miss out on the best parts of their lives. Paris. Hawaii. Scotland. You couldn't drive to those adventures.

I had to stop this. I had to portray a more positive attitude. I made myself smile, and told the girls that turbulence was just a part of flying, nothing to worry about in the least.

I wasn't sure they believed me; I don't know if I believed myself. But I was tired of constant worry.

An hour later the aircraft touched safely down in Oklahoma City and screamed down the runway.

We were home. And we were safe. I pointed this out to the girls.

I think they still didn't believe me.

We arrived back at the house weary and disappointed. The girls headed straight for their bedrooms. Mom and Dad got in only a few brief questions before I headed up the stairs.

"How was the flight?"

"Awful. I thought we were going down twice."

Mom tssked. "Kate, you're always so dramatic."

I didn't want to argue. I believed God was trying to tell me to swear off flying. This time I was going to listen.

I dragged my bag up the stairway.

"Oh, Kate?"

"Yeah, Mom."

"There's a message on the machine for you. It's from some Realtor."

"The rental agency?" I paused. Now what? Had the apartment been leased after all? There had been some confusion, but the lady had clearly said the apartment that Kelli and Kris wanted would be vacated by the twenty-ninth.

"From whom?"

"Some man by the name of Gray. Mitchell, I believe he said."

I turned and peered over the railing. "Gray Mitchell? What's the message?"

Mom pursed her lips thoughtfully. "Let's see—oh, yes. He said to tell you congratulations. You got the house, and not to worry. He'd called on a friend for a personal favor and you have a closing date and date of possession. One week from yesterday, if that's what you want."

I sank down on the steps, my legs too weak to hold me. The words beat a tattoo in my heart. *You got the house.*

It was as if God had spoken.

Chapter 9

It was the day before we had to load up everything we owned and move all the way across country to California. I picked up the kids at school and drove home. What was I, a transplanted Okie, going to do in California? Well, for starters I was going to have to make our first Christmas without Neil a good one, for Kris's and Kelli's sakes. I had to admit God had thrown me a curve on the house, but I still wasn't prepared to admit that I'd been the one to step away, not Him.

I would begin a new life, and I would have to do it in a new house where everything was still packed in boxes. Right now I couldn't even remember which box held the Christmas tree.

"Mom? Are we going to open presents tonight?" Kelli asked, her face screwed up in anticipation.

"Only the ones from Grandma and Papa. They want to see you open your gifts. The rest we'll open on Christmas morning in our new home."

Kelli already knew the answer, mainly because she asked the same question on an average of five times every day. It seemed as if her grief for Neil had solidified around an anxiety that they might not have a good Christmas. It wasn't that Kelli was greedy. Usually she wasn't all that concerned about gifts. I thought it must be a security thing. Christmas was supposed to come, therefore in a world where nothing else was working out the way it should, Kelli wanted Christmas to be the same as it always had been. I could identify with that.

Kris sighed. "Are Grandma and Papa going to move with us?"

"No." I felt an involuntary shiver. I love my parents to pieces—I just like a little distance between us. "Did you think they would?"

Kris shook her head. "I just wondered."

I didn't want to pursue that line of thought any further. I loved my mother, of course I did. It was just that Mom could be so overwhelming sometimes. Maybe Kris was feeling over-whelmed. I knew I was.

I sat in my driveway missing the decorations we usually put up. Even if I had been in the mood this year, which I wasn't, it was too early. And since we were moving tomorrow, it would have been foolish to put up decorations and take them down a few days later, but still I missed the lights, the electric candles, the crèche we always displayed in the picture window in the living room.

Neil always made a ceremony out of putting up the crèche. He would read the story from the Bible, and at the proper times the girls would arrange the figurines. Like everything else, the crèche was packed away. Maybe next year we could get back to the well-loved tradition. I doubted if I could have gotten through it this year without dissolving in a puddle of tears. Oh, Neil! I missed him more with every passing day.

The girls had already run into the house, and I followed slowly, realizing this was the last night I would spend here.

The Himeses were anxious to move in. Loretta Himes had already been over twice to measure for drapes, and the second time she was accompanied by carpet and appliance salesmen. She was going to get the new stove. I felt as if I had sold a piece of my heart.

The house smelled of turkey and sage and cherry pies. A nice homey smell. Mom was in the kitchen, dressed in black pants and a black chiffon top with flowing sleeves and a glittery pattern of iridescent swirls lighting the somber fabric. Not exactly the perfect garb for cooking, but at least it was festive. I felt like a drab little wren in my tan pants, cream sweater and tweed jacket, but then I had never been as flamboyant as Mom.

"What can I do?"

Mom waved her hand. "Nothing. I've got it all ready. You go wash up. Frank can help me get the food on the table."

Dad stuck his head around the door. "See, you can't get by without me."

Mom cocked an eyebrow and smirked. "It might be fun to try. You sure weren't much help with the Thanksgiving crowd."

"Fun! Everything has to be fun." Dad picked up the turkey. "How much fun do you think it is for the turkey? Ever think about that? And if you hadn't invited half the state for our pre-Thanksgiving dinner I wouldn't have been so nuts!" With the last words he raised his voice and mocked Mom so perfectly, even she had to laugh.

Mom shook her head. "Just carve the thing. We're ready to eat."

We gathered around the table, and I tried not to think of the one family member who should have been here doing the carving and leading the family in the Christmas dinner blessing. I would have preferred to skip this celebration, but my parents had insisted we observe tradition, albeit early.

Mom nodded. "Frank, say the blessing."

"I carved the turkey."

"Don't be cute. Say the blessing."

He stretched his lips in a phony smile and wiggled his eyebrows. "You think I'm cute?"

Kelli giggled and Mom batted her eyelashes. "Not as cute as Tom Cruise. Say the blessing."

I shook my head, looking at them, Mom with her strawberry-blond hair fluffed out around her face in a halo, Dad tall and lanky, bald and acting goofy. They were trying to give the girls a Christmas send-off. I loved them. They were a special gift from God...as long as I didn't have to live in the same state with them.

We had a hurried breakfast the next morning before the moving van arrived. Kelli had lost her shoes. Sailor was having a nervous breakdown, running from room to room barking, and Kris was on the phone calling everyone she knew to say goodbye.

Mom was busy telling the moving men how to do their job; they didn't seem to be paying too much attention to her. Dad helped me load the car. I stood for a minute looking up at our house, remembering the good times and blinking back tears.

He reached over and put his arms around me. "Don't cry, kid. It's just a house. What goes on in the house is what makes it a home. You'll build a home in California."

"It won't be the same."

"Nothing is ever the same."

I smiled up at him. "Why, Dad. That's profound. Are you turning into a sage?"

"Either that or I'm quoting your mother. Is that all you want to take in the car?"

"I guess so. I have to leave room for the girls and the dog."

"In that case, I'd better go find your mother before they seal her in a box and load her in the van to get rid of her."

I laughed and followed him back to the house. An hour later we said goodbye in the driveway, and my parents got in their car and left for Kansas. The girls and I drove away, following the moving van.

"California, here we come," I sang, trying to sound cheerful for the girls' sake.

"I'm not going to like California," Kelli said.

"How do you know you won't?"

"I've made up my mind not to like it," she said, a trifle smugly. "I don't have to like it if I don't want to."

Kris rolled her eyes. "You sound just like Grandma."

Amen, I thought, but I said, "Give it a chance, girls. There are a lot of fun things to do in California. You'll see. We can go to the beach. And, oh...lots of things."

Deep down, I felt like Kelli. I wasn't going to like California. I had already made up my mind. I kept my eyes on the moving van, afraid if I lost sight of it I might lose sight of my new life. Not in my wildest dreams had I ever imagined I would be driving to San Francisco with everything I owned, two disgruntled girls and a dog that wanted to go to the bathroom at every rest stop.

Three days later we arrived in San Francisco in the middle of a citywide garbage strike. Plastic bags overflowed garbage bins and the odor reminded me of the time Neil had unplugged the freezer during a lightning storm and forgotten to plug it back in. We had hauled out tons of rotten food. Multiply that by an entire city and it didn't smell like Chanel No 5.

Kelli wrinkled her nose. "California stinks."

I ignored her. The van stopped in front of our house, and three hours later drove away. I looked around at the furniture and the boxes to be unpacked. I felt like sitting down and crying. A knock on the door interrupted my brewing pity party.

I answered to find a short, chubby woman dressed in blue-and-black-checked cropped pants, a blue sweater and blue leather mules. The stylist in me didn't miss her cute brown bob.

Her brown eyes twinkled with fun and her smile had enough wattage to light up all of San Francisco.

"I'm your neighbor Mazi Hollingsworth. I just wanted to stop in and say welcome to the neighborhood!"

She extended a plate of Christmas cookies, the cutout kind shaped like trees and angels and wreaths. There was even a Santa Claus decorated with red sugar. The kind of cookies I always planned to make and could never find the time.

I took the plate of goodies and ushered our visitor inside. "Sorry the place is such a mess. I'd offer you a cup of coffee, but I haven't found the pot yet."

Mazi laughed. "Don't worry about it. I'll come back some other time for coffee. So, how do you like San Francisco?"

"I haven't had time to see much of it." I set the tray on the table and pulled out a chair. "You're my neighbor on which side?"

"Left side," Mazi said. "Handy enough to be a pest."

I couldn't see this warm, friendly person being a pest. Somehow the day seemed brighter since she had arrived. "You're the first neighbor I've met." I looked around at the cluttered room with boxes of things to be put away. "This is only the second time I've ever moved. And I sure don't plan on doing it again anytime soon."

Mazi grinned. "I'm a navy brat. I've moved more times than I can count."

"Are you married?" Kris asked.

I frowned at her. Hadn't I taught her not to ask personal questions?

Mazi laughed. "Yes, I have a husband. He's not home much. He's a pharmaceutical salesman, so he travels. In fact, he's gone more than he's here."

"Do you have kids?" Kelli sneaked a cookie shaped like a star and bit off one of the points.

"No. I do have three cats, though. Persians."

Kelli bit off another point. "I like dogs."

Yep, my mother incarnate. I gave Kelli a look intended to convey my disapproval, which she completely ignored. "Don't you girls have something to do?"

"No." Kris took an angel and bit off its head.

Mazi laughed. "I don't mind. We're going to be close neighbors and before long we'll know quite a bit about each other. I love kids."

I smiled. "I'm glad you came over, Mazi. I was feeling sorry for myself before you came."

Having a friendly neighbor would go a long way toward my new adjustment. By the time Mazi went home we were on the way toward a solid friendship.

I woke from a sound sleep with the impression someone was shaking my bed. I jerked to a sitting position, staring around the room. The pictures on the wall swung back and forth. The house vibrated. The girls ran down the hall toward my bedroom, their bare feet slapping against the floorboards.

Earthquake! I leaped from the bed and met them in the doorway. We clung together as Sailor galloped down the hall to join us. I could feel him quivering against my legs. The tremor lasted only a minute or two, but it felt like an eternity. I had fled Oklahoma for this? What were a few dust storms and a couple of tornadoes compared to an earthquake?

I wanted to go home.

When the motion stopped, I led the girls to the kitchen and turned on the light. One look at their white faces and I knew I had to put my own fear aside and comfort them.

"Well, that was fun, wasn't it?" I couldn't *believe* I had said something so silly. Evidently they couldn't, either

Kelli stared at me in disbelief. "Fun?"

Kris shook her head. "*Mom!* That was an earthquake."

"Well, yes, it was, wasn't it? Our first."

Like our first case of the plague? Had I lost my mind? I searched for something half-intelligent to say. "At least we didn't have to go next door to the basement like we did in tornado season in Oklahoma."

Had I made a mistake bringing my children out here to California where the ground could open up and swallow them?

My cell phone rang and I punched the on button. "Hello?"

"Kate? This is Mazi. Are you and the girls all right?"

"We're fine." I heard the unease in my voice.

"Sure you are." Mazi's cheerful voice came over the line. "It was a baby tremor. Nothing to worry about. You'll get used to them."

"If you say so." If she was trying to comfort me, she was definitely choosing the wrong words. My house shaking like a bowl of jelly wasn't anything I wanted to get used to. "I was just getting ready to fix the girls some hot chocolate."

"That's the ticket. Hot chocolate will cure a lot of ills. No matter what the problem, chocolate helps." Mazi laughed, a rich, warm chuckle. "What do you think contributed to my excess baggage?"

"Silly—you're the perfect size." I laughed. "I'm buying a box of the best chocolates tomorrow. The next time I have a quake I'll sit on my bed and eat them."

"That's the spirit. I'll talk to you later."

I hung up the phone and looked at the girls, who had calmed down. "What say we skip the hot chocolate and get back to bed? Tomorrow we'll put up the tree and place the presents around it. Make it look more like Christmas. Okay?"

They agreed, and surprisingly I didn't have any trouble going back to sleep.

Sunday dawned warm and clear. After a thorough search we managed to find the tree and the decorations. I strung the lights on the tree and the girls hung the ornaments. When they were finished I found the star and placed it on top. That had been Neil's job immediately after Thanksgiving. Now it was mine.

"Are we going to open our gifts Christmas Eve?" Kelli asked.

"Do you want to, or would you rather wait until morning?" I stood back to admire our handiwork. The tree looked lovely.

My daughter thought about it. "Morning, I guess."

"Okay, then let's set out the candles." I unpacked the electric candles and the girls placed them in the windows, where they glowed like a bit of the home we had left behind.

Kris stepped back to look at the result. "Where is the crèche?"

"It's here somewhere. I know we packed it." I had a sudden inspiration. "I know what. How about inviting Mazi to come over tonight and we can have a party? I'll fix dips and snacks. Does that sound like fun?"

It had been so long since we'd had fun.

Kelli's expression brightened. "Can we go over and ask her? I mean me and Kris?"

I nodded. "Do you want to make an invitation?"

Kris smiled. "Sure. I know which box has the crayons and paper in it."

I left them designing the invitation and set about trying to put my kitchen in order. Soon I had the dishes unpacked and arranged in the freshly washed cabinets. I made out the grocery list while the girls walked next door with Mazi's invitation. They returned with the news that she would be delighted to attend our party.

At seven o'clock that night, Mazi showed up dressed in black stretch pants, which were definitely stretched to full capacity, and a black sweater decorated with a sequined picture of Santa Claus surrounded by tiny Christmas lights that flashed on and off. I looked down at my jeans and navy blue sweatshirt. I might have to update my wardrobe. Surely they wore jeans out here.

Mazi exclaimed in delight over the Christmas tree. "I never put one up. Warren is usually gone over the holidays and it seems a waste of time to decorate just for me."

"You can share ours," I assured her.

After stuffing ourselves on chips, dip and more junk food, we settled down in the living room, where the girls insisted on singing Christmas carols. Mazi didn't know some of the words, but she joined in the best she could. She had a lovely soprano.

We were just sitting and talking when Kelli and Kris brought in the crèche. I caught my breath. Not tonight. I couldn't. But one look at their faces and I knew I had to. They placed the figurines on the floor by a table already arranged next to the front window. Kris brought me her father's Bible.

"Read the story."

I swallowed and turned to the second chapter of Luke.

"'And it came to pass in those days that there went out from Caesar Augustus a decree that all the world should be taxed.'"

The familiar words stuck in my throat, but I ploughed on. The girls placed the figures in the proper place at the proper time until I finished reading and let my hands rest on the open Bible. Neil's baritone echoed in my mind. *Good girl, Kate. I knew you could do it.*

Subtle warmth filled my heart. It was almost as if he was there with me. Almost.

Mazi smiled. "That was beautiful, Kate. I've never heard the Christmas story read like that."

Kris knelt beside my chair. "Dad would be pleased, wouldn't he?"

Kelli dropped down on my other side. I rested my hands on their heads. "He would have been very pleased."

The girls' new school was half a mile away, nestled in a wooded lot. We drove there one afternoon and I let them spend a few moments out of the car getting acquainted with their new surroundings. The low brick building looked like a nice place to spend a school term.

Then I tackled the interviews—women to take care of Kelli and Kris after school. My new job would require me to work some late nights and Saturdays.

Four people had made appointments for the job, and I was nervous. We had never left the girls with anyone except Helen Murphy and I was worried about leaving them with a stranger. The first applicant arrived in a bright yellow Volkswagen with all four wheels painted to look like daisies.

A young woman looking to be in her late twenties got out and strode toward the door. I lifted the window shutter and peeked out, standing back where she couldn't see me, and I almost decided not to open the door. She was tall, dressed in orange-and-green-striped stockings, clunky shoes and a black skirt cut thigh-high. Her skimpy attire barely covered the essentials.

My gaze focused on the yellow sweater and long lavender scarf wrapped around her throat and draped over her shoulders like Tiny Tim's muffler in Dickens's *A Christmas Carol*. It seemed hardly appropriate "work dress"—at least in Oklahoma. But then, I was in California now.

The doorbell rang and I answered, tempted to tell her I gave at the office. Up close I had a very good look at her short spiked blond hair, the blue eye shadow, the magenta lips. Leave my girls with this...this...whatever she was? I didn't think so.

She chomped gum. "Hi. I'm Tina. I'm here about the, you know, the job."

"Ah, yes. Come right in." I indicated the chair I had placed where the light would shine the brightest. A trick I had learned from reading mystery novels. "Now, Tina, what do you have in the way of references?"

She blinked. "You mean like...credentials?"

"Not exactly. I mean like previous work history. You know—people you've worked for before? Have you ever taken care of children before?"

Kelli already wanted a nose ring. What would she want after being around Tina a week?

She shook her head, her eyes glazed. "No. I've never done that. But I know I'd be good at it."

"Are you employed now?"

"No. I'm an actress."

"Oh." I paused. "Aren't you a long way from Hollywood?"

She leaned forward. "See, that's part of my strategy. Everyone goes to Hollywood. I'm going to be discovered here in San Francisco."

"Discovered doing what?" I asked, totally confused.

She looked at me as if I was abysmally stupid. "You always read about the big stars being discovered waiting tables or something. Well, that's what I'm going to do. I'm going to be discovered."

"Ah."

I wasn't sure what to say next. I was all for free spirits, just not taking care of my daughters. I stood up. "Well, Tina, I have a few more applicants to interview. We'll be in touch."

"Sure. Could you let me know by, say, around four o'clock? I have a shot at a waitress job at Fisherman's Wharf. I only came because I'd already asked you for an interview."

"I think your chances of being discovered would be better there."

She nodded. "Just what I was thinking. Well, I'll be going. Thanks for your time."

I watched her clunk back to her car. She had come to be interviewed for a job she didn't really want because I had agreed to see her.

Maybe there was more to her than wild makeup and weird clothing.

The second applicant arrived thirty minutes later. Eloise Ferguson. This one looked much more normal—short, dumpy, graying hair curling around her face, and a sweet, benign expression.

Lavender and lace and tea cozies.

I expelled a breath I hadn't realized I was holding. After Tina, this one was a touch of sanity.

I opened the door and ushered her in. "Mrs. Ferguson?"

"Yes. Mrs. Madison? I have an appointment." Her voice was soft and high, reminiscent of a chirping canary.

I indicated a chair. "Would you like a cup of coffee?" I was so eager for her to like me I'd have baked cookies if she had requested them.

"Oh, no, dear. We'll only be here a moment."

I felt my brows rise. "We?"

"Oh, yes." She glanced to her left and smiled, her eyes aimed slightly above her eye level. Just at the height where someone would be...if someone were there.... The hair on the back of my neck prickled. She nodded. "Homer doesn't care for coffee."

"Homer?" My gaze slowly—and I hope discreetly—searched the room. There was no Homer.

She glanced to her left again, smiling, and I found myself staring at that spot beside her. I jerked my eyes back to hers. She simpered. "He has a very delicate stomach, and coffee is too strong for his taste. Not that he's finicky, though."

My mouth snapped shut.

Her eyes roamed the room with a pleased expression, lingering in approval on the crèche. She looked at her invisible companion, eyebrows raised. "You think it will be all right, dear?"

She nodded, glancing in my direction. "Homer likes your house," she informed me. "We'll be very happy here."

I offered a faint smile as my mind slid over the possibilities of sharing my home with an invisible man. I could think of plenty of scenarios where that might be a trifle embarrassing.

"Who's Homer?" I asked in only a barely perceptible, quivering voice.

She smiled and fluttered her eyelashes...at Homer, I guess. She sure wasn't looking at me. "Why, my husband, of course."

"Oh, of course." I swallowed. "Uh...does he go everywhere with you?"

"Oh, my, yes." Her china-blue eyes grew wide and childlike. "I wouldn't think of leaving him at home." She lightly touched her temple. "He...he tends to be forgetful." She smiled.

"Really...I had an uncle once who forgot to turn off the stove. That can be dangerous."

I was babbling, but I couldn't stop. "I am so sorry, Mrs. Ferguson. I fear I have brought you all the way over here, and the position has been filled."

The sweetness slipped from her expression. A hint of disapproval tinged her voice. "Oh, that's too bad."

"Well, yes, that's the way the cookie crumbles." I decided that didn't sound very sympathetic or respectful. "I mean, I'm awfully sorry."

I got to my feet, wondering what I would do if she refused to leave. To my relief she stood up, too.

Her expression was stony. "Come along, Homer. The position has been filled." She crooked her elbow and I glanced involuntarily to her left, half expecting to see Homer materialize.

Eloise swept out, head high, looking more royal than the queen. I shut the door behind her and leaned against it, surprised to find I wasn't even trembling. Evidently my troubles were coming so thick and fast I no longer had time to be afraid.

The third applicant was a large woman with iron-gray hair twisted in a bun. She approached my front door with all the dignity and bearing of a battleship. I opened the door, wondering what to expect this time.

She looked me up and down as if she wasn't sure what species I belonged to. "Mrs. Madison? Letha Harrod. I have an appointment with you and I believe I am one minute early."

"Oh, no p-problem," I stammered. "Please. Come in."

She raised her eyebrows. "You're sure? I am one minute early, and I can assure you I am always accurate."

And never wrong. The words flitted through my mind, and for one horrible instant I thought I had spoken them out loud, judging from her expression. Then I realized she was looking past me.

"What is that?"

"A s-sailor," I stammered. "I mean...no! A dog. A puli. His *name* is Sailor."

"He'll have to go."

"Go?" I stared at her wondering where I had missed a turn in this conversation. "Go where?"

She drew herself into a formidable fort. "I will not work in a house where there is a dog. Miserable, dirty creatures."

Sailor took one look at her and backed away, whimpering.

I dredged up the last remnants of my courage. "I'm sorry. My daughters adore Sailor. He stays."

But yes, he could be a dirty little foul-smelling creature— at times.

"Then obviously I would not find you a suitable employer. The interview is over."

She stepped off the porch and surged down the street like the Queen Mary in full steam. I watched her go and then headed back inside, totally overwhelmed.

Lord, all I want is someone reliable and normal...to stay with my children. Is that too much to ask? Please help me out here.

I barely had time to consider that I still wasn't asking anything of Him.

Thirty minutes later, a young woman, looking to be in her early twenties, dressed in jeans and a blue sweatshirt, came up the walk. She wore her long brown hair straight, shiny and clean. I quickly tallied her attributes in my mind. Her expression was open and friendly.

I almost hugged her.

"Mrs. Madison? I'm Alissa Devon." The young woman paused on the steps. "I called about the baby-sitting job?"

"Please, come in." I glanced past her to see a late-model Chevy parked at my curb and drew a sigh of relief.

Well, God, maybe our relationship is beginning to thaw.

Inside, Alissa smiled. "You will want references."

"References?" I held my breath. "You do have them?"

She reached into her purse. "I'm a college student, working on my thesis in child care. I don't have any previous employers, but I have references from my school professors. Names and phone numbers are listed. My pastor also is willing to offer his recommendation."

I leafed through the pages she handed me, skimming the type. Friendly, trustworthy, honest, loves children.

Thank You, Lord.

Alissa was so fresh and so open she reminded me of Oklahoma. For a moment I was homesick.

"The job is very basic. I need someone to be here when my daughters get home from school. Usually you will leave around six o'clock—but there will be times I'm required to work late. Of course I would compensate you for your extra time."

She nodded. "That would work fine for me. I have classes until one every afternoon, and I don't mind staying late when you need me." She flashed an affable grin. "I can use the extra money."

So. As simple as that, God had sent me a lovely young woman I felt reasonably sure I could entrust with my daughters' security. And once more, I hadn't asked Him to.

Chapter 10

Saturday morning I stepped back and admired the new kitchen border I'd just hung. I still had umpteen boxes to unpack, but I'd spotted the border at a chic shop not far from the salon on my lunch hour yesterday and I had to have it. My choice wasn't all that bad—blue background with tiny buttercup colored irises that looked as if the wall covering came right out of the pages of *House Beautiful*. Sighing, I poured a second cup of coffee and anticipated my day. Through careful scheduling, I'd penciled out the last three hours on my appointment book. I'd promised Kelli and Kris a Christmas shopping expedition, though none of us was exactly in a festive mood. Everywhere I turned sparked old memories. I'd thought if I moved and started over, thoughts of Neil would be less frequent. How wrong could anyone be? I thought of him day and night, in places we'd never even visited together. When I saw egg rolls I cried; Neil had a passion for egg rolls. Our ninth anniversary would be coming up in January and I worried how I would get through the poignant day.

On the plus side, the girls adored Alissa. The three had formed an instant friendship.

And Mazi. Well, Mazi was another one of those gifts from God that I hadn't asked for but He'd given me. She had a dichotomous personality: happy, depressed, full of energy, fatigued—you never knew which Mazi would breeze through the doorway. But I adored them all.

The phone rang and I jerked up the handset, glancing at the clock. The salon: my eight-thirty had canceled.

But instead of Wendy Curry, I recognized Gray Mitchell's baritone.

"Hope I'm not calling too early."

"No, not at all." I perched on the step stool and wondered what time the man got up. Certainly earlier than I, because if it wasn't the holiday season, and I wasn't scheduled to work today I would still be snoozing away.

"How's the new house?"

"I love it. I still can't thank you enough for all your help."

He'd earlier mentioned that he'd returned to the nursing home after our talk that night, and had a long visit with the owner. He'd wanted to make sure she understood the terms, and who the new owners would be. After she'd read the informational sheet Gray had prepared she had asked for a pen and immediately signed the offer.

"She and her deceased husband built the house," Gray said. "They lived there their entire married life, so the residence is more than a house to her—it's a symbol of happiness. When she learned of your circumstances, and that you have two small children to raise, she smiled and said she would pray that the home would bring you as much happiness as it has her."

"She sounds like a wonderful person."

I made a mental note to take Kelli and Kris by the nursing home before Christmas and introduce ourselves. I thought of

La Chic's outrageous poinsettia display filling the leather-and-cherry-wood sitting area, and decided that I'd stop by the florist before we went and purchase a plant for this lovely and compassionate woman.

"Kate, I was wondering if you had plans for this evening."

The question took me by surprise, and I answered honestly. "Tonight? No."

Were there more papers to sign? Something I had failed to do?

"There's this Realtors' dinner tonight. Would you like to go with me?"

Oh, boy. I felt faint. I was being asked for a date? The very word felt heavy on my tongue. I wouldn't know how to act on a date—I hadn't been on a "date" in close to nine years. Alarm bells sounded in my head. Too soon! Too soon! The mere thought of going anywhere with a man other than Neil left me faint with guilt and disloyalty. I would have murdered Neil had I died and he dated this soon. Or ever, actually.

"Oh—thank you, Gray. I'm flattered. But I..."

"I know this is early for you, Kate. And we wouldn't consider it a date, per se, just a relaxing evening—if you think of office parties as relaxing."

No, I didn't. The mere thought left me lukewarm. I'd have to have a new dress, arrange for one of the stylists to do my hair and makeup.

"Thanks, but it is early—too early for me to—"

He interrupted. "Tell you what. Would you feel differently if I skipped the office party and invited the girls to go? We could make it a foursome—hamburgers and fries at a local restaurant. What do you think?"

Hamburgers and fries. The plan sounded innocent enough, and the girls would enjoy a little socializing. When Neil was alive, we ate out often, shopped together, visited theme parks, and zoos.... I shook the memories aside.

"Kate?"

"Yes?"

"How about I meet you, say..." I pictured him consulting his watch. "Around five. There's a great restaurant about two blocks from your salon. Parlyvista's?"

I knew the place; I'd seen the trendy restaurant on my drive to work. A far cry from a hamburgers-and-fries joint.

"I know the restaurant."

"Okay. Five o'clock. If you get there first put our name in for a table."

"All right." I still had plenty of reservations about the whole idea, but apparently I'd accepted the invitation—though I didn't remember accepting. I shook off the mental fog.

"Got to run—got a call on the other line. See you at five."

I nodded, and punched the off button. Now what had I done?

You have just cut out an hour and a half Christmas shopping from your planned expedition, my petulant conscience informed me.

One hour in holiday crowds and you're pulling your hair out by the roots anyway, I smarted back, but I didn't know why. I didn't want to go to dinner with Gray Mitchell. Oh, he was nice enough—very nice, in fact. Helpful. Great personality and sense of humor—all traits I admired in a man. Without him I wouldn't have gotten the house.

Is that right?

I didn't know where *that* voice came from—I had my suspicions, but they were suspicions only.

Sighing, I got up and dumped the remains of my cold coffee in the sink. Alissa would bring the girls to La Chic at two o'clock for our shopping expedition. I had exactly an hour and a half to dress and get to work. Weekend holiday traffic would be murder; I would be lucky to make my eight-thirty on time.

I shook my head as I sailed through the kitchen's double louvered doors.

I had a date.

Neil, if you're watching, I don't have an actual *date*. Hamburgers and fries—that's all, honey. The real estate agent's way of saying, "Thank you for your business."

If the explanation failed to comfort Neil, then at least it made me feel more at peace.

Four o'clock. I dropped into a mall patio chair and kicked off my shoes. The sprawling shopping complex teemed with holiday shoppers. Kris and Kelli set their bags next to mine, and then plopped down on a wooden bench. Coward that I was, I had yet to mention our "dinner engagement."

"Mom, can I have a corn dog?" Kris loved the wiener on a stick. The seven-year-old could polish off two without exhaling.

"Me, too. And some chicken nuggets," Kelli seconded.

The loudspeaker blared "Grandma Got Run Over by a Reindeer." I rubbed my aching feet. Five and a half hours at the salon, four updos and a cut, then another two hours here in the crowded mall. I thought maybe I'd have to crawl to the car.

"Girls, I have a big surprise!" They were going to freak out on this one. We'd just had a tearful scene in a men's clothing store. The girls wanted to buy Neil's present; we did. A light blue shirt, tie and two pairs of dark blue socks. I had to promise to wrap the gift and put it under the tree.

Kelli's eyes lit with expectancy. "Surprise! What, Mommy?"

"Yeah, Mom. What!" Kris echoed.

"We're going to have dinner with Gray Mitchell!" Upbeat, Kate, upbeat!

Pleased expectancy slid off their expressions like hot butter, replaced by mild confusion.

"The house guy?" Kris asked

"Him?" Kelli frowned. "Why?"

"Why? Because he was nice enough to ask us to have dinner with him. He wants to thank us for buying the house from him."

Kris, wiser than her years, eyed me dubiously. "He already sent us flowers."

"Yes. That was nice, too. Now he wants to take us out to eat."

"Can we have chicken nuggets?" Kelli asked.

"You can have anything you like."

"But, Mom." Kris heaved a deep sigh. "I want a corn dog. Can Mr. Mitchell meet us here, and we have corn dogs?"

"No, we're supposed to meet him at Parlyvista."

The girls stared at me blankly. Even I knew "Parlyvista" didn't have the ring of a corn dog joint.

"Look," I said, consulting my watch, "how about you each have a corn dog—and chicken nuggets for you, Kelli. We aren't scheduled to meet Mr. Mitchell for another hour."

There would be over an hour's wait for a table at Parlyvista. I could count on it. "If you promise to eat your dinner later," I continued.

"Okay." They both agreed.

We purchased the food, and I drank a diet soda while the girls polished off the fast food. I put my foot down when Kris wanted a second corn dog; I knew there'd be no way she'd eat dinner with two of those grease-coated battered fried dogs churning around in her stomach.

After trash cleanup, we rode the escalator to the third level.

"Be careful where you step. You could hurt yourself."

The girls reached for my hand.

"And be leery of anyone trying to talk you into going to look for me if we get separated. I don't want you kidnapped—"

I stopped short when I saw Kelli's expression turn to one of wretched alarm.

"What I mean to say is, don't wander off alone."

Now they stuck to me like leeches.

As I exited the moving steps, someone in back of me stepped on the heel of my shoe and I pitched forward. Stumbling, I hit an elderly man's back, shoving him into a flashing, colorful Christmas bulb display.

The display upended, sending delicate red and green glass balls shattering to the floor. The pop! pop! pop! drew the attention of every shopper and nearby clerk. The poor man looked dazed.

"I am so sorry," I murmured. Kris and Kelli scampered around trying to locate my missing shoe.

I slipped the loafer back on my foot and limped on with as much dignity as possible after the humiliating incident. The last I saw of the disaster scene—and clerks' distorted faces—the gentleman was pointing to me, saying I had pushed him.

I hurriedly ducked into Sharper Image, with my girls hot on my trail.

"Don't touch anything in here," I warned. "I wouldn't want to have to pay for anything you break."

Kris gave me one of her patented "I wouldn't talk if I were you" looks.

We browsed the store, admiring the really cool, really "sweet" merchandise. Kris and Kelli stalled at the "Saxy" display—a tuba-clarinet-saxophone-synthesizer-kazoo instrument—while I wandered deeper into the store looking for gifts for Mom and Dad and Neil's parents.

We left the store and went into Brookstone, where I purchased four fat, puffy travel pillows. All four parents had complained about stiff necks, so this year's gift might actually be used. Why my optimism ran high I couldn't say. The last time I'd looked in Mom's closet I'd found unused Christmas gifts from me ranging back to premarriage days.

Around a quarter to five we left the mall, toting heavy sacks. I'd thought about taking the merchandise to the car, but the restaurant was two blocks away and the parking garage was half a mile; my sore feet won out. We carried the bags to the restaurant. Now all I had to do was get through the meal, excuse myself early, saying the girls were exhausted, and I could go home, kick off my shoes and take a long soak in a hot tub.

* * *

"The wait is an hour and forty minutes right now."

Parlyvista's smiling hostess wrote my name and number in party down on her clipboard, then handed me a buzzer. My eyes scanned the crowded waiting area. Potential diners were lined out the door, spilling onto the sidewalk.

"Mommy, I'm tired." Kelli slumped against me, holding the sack of pillows. Though bulky, the package was the lightest to carry.

I gently soothed her hair. "I know, sweetie. We're all tired."

My feet were coming through the soles of my shoes. My gaze searched for an empty spot—anywhere we could get out of the traffic flow. Waiters and waitresses ducked around us carrying steaming platters to anxious customers. I checked the time: 5:03. Gray was threading his way through the blocked doorway.

I stood on tiptoe and waved. After several attempts at trying to snag his attention, he finally saw me and worked his way over.

"Hello—sorry I'm a few minutes late."

"We just got here."

His eyes skimmed the crowd. "What's the wait?"

"An hour and forty minutes."

"Not bad." He smiled at Kelli and Kris. "Good afternoon, ladies."

Kelli buried her face in my skirt; Kris mumbled something. He turned back to me. "Care for a drink from the bar?"

I shook my head. "I'll wait and have tea with dinner...but if you—"

"No, I don't drink," he said. "The stuff gives me a headache." We backed up to allow another set of waitresses to pass by.

"Did you ladies have a successful shopping expedition?"

I briefly told him about the crowds, and how I knew better than to shop on weekends. Kelli was pressing into my side, deadweight. I tried to straighten her. She jerked away and buried her face in my skirt.

The thing about dating—it's so awkward. I remember the first time Neil and I went out, he took me to a movie and then later for a soda. I bet we hadn't said fifteen words to each other that night, but he called again the following weekend. The second date we played miniature golf; I beat him double the score. I thought he wouldn't call again. But the third weekend he called, and by then it seemed as if we couldn't talk enough.

I glanced at Gray, melancholy washing over me. I couldn't start crying now—not in front of him.

I straightened Kelli, and she whined. "Stand up, honey. Mommy's tired, too."

My daughter—my precious angel who rarely gave me an ounce of trouble—suddenly sat down in the middle of the floor, screwed up her face and let out a bawl that would make a guernsey proud.

Horrified, I watched fat tears run down her cheeks; her nose ran, and between squalls she blubbered something about chicken nuggets.

Gray stooped and tried to console her but she kicked out at him, catching him on the shin.

Pain shot across his face, and he quickly backed off.

"Kelli Madison!" I bent and tried to pull the child to her feet, but she threw her head back and howled more loudly. By now every eye in the place was on the ruckus.

I lowered my tone. "Kelli. Get up this instant."

"I want chicken nuggets!" She pounded her heels on the floor and I wondered if she had suddenly become possessed while shopping.

Kris came over and made the situation worse. "Stop acting like a baby."

"I'm *not* a baby!" The screeching jacked up another level.

I pulled Kris back and asked her to stand beside Gray, who by this time was standing way clear of the embarrassing fracas.

After several aborted attempts to calm my daughter, I decided to practice tough medicine. I knew the child was exhausted. She'd never acted this way in her life, but she wasn't going to get away with public tantrums.

"Kelli, you are pushing my patience to the limit. Get up off that floor right now!"

She ignored me, continuing to wail like a fire siren. If we'd been at home I could have cut this tantrum short in a hurry, but standing in the crowded lobby of Parlyvista made the situation more difficult. I gave her shoulder a shake and frowned down at her, trying to get my point across. If this evening ever ended, I'd give her a lecture she wouldn't forget in a hurry. Kelli scrunched up her face and glared at me, and I knew at this point, anything I said would only make matters worse.

I stood up, pretending to ignore her. The provocation only made her cry harder.

"So," I said to Gray, "did you have a good day?"

His eyes were on the squirming kid creating a public spectacle in the middle of Parlyvista's polished floor.

A departing couple paused, greeting Gray. He shook hands with the man, and above Kelli's screams I overheard the guy thanking Gray for handling their house closing so efficiently. I heard the conversation only because the participants were talking above my daughter's bellowing fit.

A waitress stopped and handed Kelli a small package of saltines. She took the crackers, sobbing.

When she'd sufficiently calmed, I picked her up. Five-year-olds were too heavy for me to carry, but I felt that she needed assurance that I wasn't going to let her starve. I also had a strong urge to march her out to the car for some "back-seat parenting."

"Will she let me hold her?" Gray inquired. Poor man. By now he was probably longing to bolt for cover.

Kelli jerked sideways, clamping her arms around my neck. That's how I stood for the next hour and a half, holding Kelli, shuffling her from one hip to the other. My feet were meshed with my soles now.

Eventually someone called our name; maybe it was God being benevolent. I would have fainted dead away if I'd had to stand one minute longer.

We followed the waitress to a booth, and Kris sat beside Gray. I took charge of Kelli.

Round two began when the waitress informed us they had served the last chicken strip fifteen minutes ago.

My heart pounded. Kelli was on a chicken binge and refused to consider anything else.

"I want chicken nuggets," she said.

"Darling." I glanced up and smiled reassuringly at Gray. "They're out of chicken nuggets. How about grilled cheese—"

"No!"

Where had this *brat* materialized from? Not once since Neil's death had Kelli been anything but cooperative and pleasant. She appeared to be testing her limits in front of Gray.

"Hamburger?" I tried.

She shook her head.

"Make her eat grilled cheese," Kris said. "Kelli, they don't *have* chicken nuggets."

Kelli sulked and buried her face in my lap. I smiled at Gray. "Kids," I offered lamely.

The meals were ordered. Gray even ordered appetizers, hoping to coax Kelli into a better mood. The ploy failed. If anything, the five-year-old turned more surly.

Over dinner—which Kelli refused to touch—I tried to carry on an intelligent, stimulating conversation. I knew a little about football because of Neil's Sooner obsession; Gray was a Redskins fanatic. We managed to keep the conversation flowing while we ate. Kris had ordered fries and a hamburger that she now picked at. The earlier corn dog had spoiled her appetite.

Kelli's grilled cheese congealed on the plate.

I leaned over and—knowing better—tried to force her to take a bite. She gagged and hawked up a chunk, which I managed to catch in a napkin.

Gray looked in the other direction.

Diners were starting to vacate tables by the time we ordered coffee. The girls sat quietly. Kris nodded off once. I finally relaxed enough to thank Gray again for helping us purchase the house, although I was fairly certain that by now the man considered the Madison family a notch below the Munsters.

"My pleasure. My wife and I never had children, but if we had, I would have liked to have raised them in that particular home."

"Well, it is lovely. It needs a few repairs..." Roof, heating and air-conditioning—but I did get a bargain.

"All houses that age need repairs," he assured me.

He took a sip of coffee, and a French fry missile hit him squarely between the eyes. He blinked, choked and set the cup back on the table.

I wasn't sure I'd seen what I thought I'd seen. I glanced at Kelli. She was sitting up, pretty as a picture, refreshed now.

"Did I tell you that I hung a new kitchen border this morning? It's blue with—"

A second missile hit his left cheek and stuck.

Aghast, I caught Kelli's movement from the corner of my eye. She was *throwing* food. I jerked around to face her, wishing we weren't in a crowded restaurant. I seldom disciplined my children in public, but Kelli was pushing it. She knew better than to behave like this.

"Kelli!" I snapped.

She turned innocent eyes on me. "Yes, Mommy?"

"Did you *throw* that French fry?"

Her guiltless look said I must be hallucinating.

I wanted to jerk her out of that booth and give her a time-out she'd never forget—or give her a strong talking-to, whatever it was the baby books suggested these days. I shot her a stern look, trying to convey the "just wait until we get home" message. She glowered at me, her mouth twisted into a pout. I reached over and touched my napkin to Gray's cheek, muttering an apology. "I am so sorry. I have never seen her act this way."

He took the napkin and finished mopping grease off his face.

Kelli suddenly bolted upright, knocking over her glass of soda. The dark fizzy liquid shot across the table and ran a foamy stream into Gray's lap. He sprang to his feet. The table china rattled and I reached out to steady Kris's water glass, in the process upsetting my coffee cup. Now two stains zigzagged across the white linen cloth. I could hear a steady stream splattering the floor. The couple in the opposite booth signaled for their check.

Seizing the opportunity, Kris picked up a fry and zinged it at her sister. I reached across the table and grabbed her hand. "Stop that right now."

She ignored me.

French fries flew.

Groaning, I buried my face in my hands and prayed for a hole to climb into and shut behind me.

After baths that night, I sat my girls on their beds and prepared to deliver the riot act. Matters like this were usually left to Neil, but now I had to fight the battle. When Gray had left the restaurant he had an ugly stain on the front of his trousers. Of course I'd profusely apologized. Needless to say, I didn't think I'd have to worry about his calling again.

Not in my lifetime.

My eyes focused on my daughters. Fresh from their baths, hair curling around their cheeks, they looked like perfect angels. I hardened my heart. They had to understand just how rude they had been tonight.

"I cannot *tell* you how disappointed I am in your behavior." Disappointed was too mild a word. I was furious. And it felt good. I'd cried so much it was a relief to experience an emotion that had nothing to do with grief.

Kelli, repentant now, gazed at the floor with lowered lashes. "I'm sorry, Mommy."

"Sorry doesn't cut it, Kelli. You have never acted this way before. Mr. Mitchell will think you're a hooligan."

She stared at me vacantly, swinging her feet. "Uh-uh."

"What do you mean, uh-uh? What else could he think of such rude behavior?"

She looked up. "*You* told him we were Irish."

Kris rolled her eyes. "That's not the same as hooligans, goofus."

Kelli took a swat at her. "Don't call me goofus!"

"Stop it!" I trapped Kelli's hand in midair. "Young lady, you are out of control!"

Kelli shrugged, dropping her head to the pillow. "I want my daddy."

"Well, you can't have your daddy!" My breath caught, and I suddenly couldn't speak for the tight knot in my throat. Kris sat looking at me like a thundercloud about ready to explode.

I fought my anger. "You can't...have your daddy." And neither could I. I gathered my girls into my arms, and we had a solid cry. Certainly not our first, nor the last, but the bouts were getting more evenly spaced. If I concentrated hard enough I'd count that as today's blessing.

Trouble was I still wasn't trying hard enough. It bothered me that the only way I could break my pattern of bawling about everything was to get upset at my daughters. Was that normal? I didn't want to admit how angry I had been. The girls had been through a great emotional upheaval, losing their father and moving away from everything familiar. I didn't like the way I had behaved tonight, either.

But since God supposedly knew all and saw all, how was I going to hide something like that from Him?

Chapter

11

I dropped the girls off early Monday morning and drove to La Chic, dreading whatever this day would bring. I was used to the Oklahoma City salon, where under Maria's experienced management all the employees worked together in relative harmony, and the customers were an extended part of the family.

Things were different in San Francisco. Tremors were as common as mounting garbage sitting at the curb.

Every customer at La Chic was convinced she was descended from royalty. I wondered if I could ever get used to the demands. I missed Rody and my other clients. Missed the gabfests we'd had while I was cutting their hair. I actually missed the hot, sultry Oklahoma weather. Given another week, I could probably work up nostalgia for an Oklahoma tornado.

I braked for a red light, tapping my fingers on the steering wheel. My first appointment would arrive in thirty minutes. I'd barely have time to turn on the curling irons and do the shop paperwork before Mrs. Josephine Hinkle, self-appointed overseer of San Francisco society, would sweep in on a fragrant cloud of perfume. Mrs. Hinkle would personally supervise every brush stroke, every scissor snip and every strand of her shampoo, trim and set. This would be my second time to do Mrs. Hinkle's hair and she was royal, all right—a royal pain. She was almost as fussy as Angel, the sparkly-collared pug she carried everywhere.

Lisa, one of the stylists, claimed Mrs. Hinkle had even carried Angel into church once. Evidently her fellow members had taken a dim view of sharing their worship service with a dog and Mrs. Hinkle had taken Angel and left, never to come back. A clear case of *love me, love my dog,* which would have been a lot easier if they hadn't been so much alike.

The narrow parking lot next to the salon was nearly full, mostly with cars belonging to people who worked at the strip mall across from the salon. I'd have to do something about them taking our space. Parking was at a premium, I knew, but I needed this lot for my customers. I locked my car and walked to the front entrance wondering what major crises I would encounter today. Every day brought a skirmish of some kind.

The stylists were as independent and temperamental as Hollywood divas. So far I was getting along with them, which was a good thing, since it was the holiday season. San Francisco must hold the record for parties. Our appointment books were filled with people begging to be fitted in.

I pushed the door open and walked in to find Mary, Kitty and Brittany screaming at each other. Lisa cowered in the background looking as if she was close to tears. I considered joining her until I remembered I was in charge. I hadn't a clue what this catastrophe was about, but I *was* reminded of a picture I had seen once of a herd of ducklings followed by a frantic mama duck. The inscription read, "There they go, I must catch them. I'm their leader." Well, as the leader of this menagerie I was clueless regarding the current donnybrook.

I glanced at Lisa, eyebrows raised in a questioning manner, trying to convey the notion that someone needed to fill me in on what was happening. She sort of whimpered, which didn't do much to boost my morale. We didn't have time for this. Our first appointments would be arriving soon. I would prefer the client didn't walk into a contest between three of my top stylists over who could scream the loudest.

"You couldn't do a decent *trim* if your life depended on it," Mary screeched. Her green eyes sparkled with fury. "A preschooler with a pair of dull scissors could beat you any day of the week."

"Oh, yeah?" Kitty snarled. "Well, you've missed your calling. You'd make an excellent dog groomer."

Short, wide and pugnacious, Kitty had a knack for going straight for the jugular.

Brittany, tall, thin and artificial in almost every conceivable way, apparently determined not to be outdone, planted her hands on her hips and narrowed her eyes. "Will you two shut up? I not only am the top stylist in this salon, I have seniority."

"Well, you know what you can do with your seniority." Mary grabbed up her bag and headed for the door. "I don't have to take this kind of treatment. I quit."

"Quit?" I moaned. "Mary, wait a minute."

"That works for me." Kitty headed for the door, leaving Brittany standing alone.

Brittany transferred her gaze to me. "This is a crummy place to work," she announced. "I can do better."

The door slammed behind her and I turned to Lisa, feeling as if I had taken a sharp blow to the stomach. "What was that all about?"

She shrugged. "Artistic differences, they said."

I rubbed my temples where a definite headache had started to bloom. "Artistic differences? What does that mean?"

"I guess it means they each thought they would get the manager's job and then you came along."

"Oh." I chewed on that for a minute. "What did that have to do with today?"

"They were arguing over who would get the job when you quit."

"I'm supposed to quit?"

Lisa smiled. "I never said that."

"But they did?"

Lisa shrugged. "You're from out of town. Oklahoma, of all places. No one really *comes* from Oklahoma, according to them. You haven't seemed happy. They felt it was a foregone conclusion you'd give up and go back home."

"What do you think?"

She grinned. "I think you'd better get busy and find three stylists to hire or we're going to be burning the midnight oil, and I happen to have a date with a real hunk. You wouldn't want to make me cancel, would you?"

I caught a mischievous glint in her eyes. "Definitely not. Any suggestions?"

"You might try the beauty school on Elm Boulevard. They turn out pretty good graduates."

"Thanks. Can you do Mrs. Hinkle for me this morning?"

"Not a problem—as long as I get off by six."

"Not a problem."

I headed for the office and the telephone as the door opened behind me. I didn't look back. Lisa could take on Mrs. Hinkle with my blessings.

Life rolled along. My new life. The one I'd started over and that was supposed to be good. I was putting in eighty hours a week. Kris and Kelli hardly saw me, and when I was home I was so exhausted I could barely function. I had hired three new stylists and they tried, but we were still having trouble keeping up with appointments. It seemed every client was fussy, dissatisfied and in need of extra service. We fell further and further behind.

I couldn't have survived without Mazi. If she hadn't been there to take up the slack, my daughters would have felt like orphans. She fed them, saw that their clothes were clean and helped with homework while I walked like a zombie through their lives, too tired to comprehend what was going on around me.

Mazi was at the house this evening when I got home. "Hey, girls, look who's here. It's Mommy!"

At this point I wasn't sure of my identity.

"Hey," I muttered, trying to be upbeat and not whine.

My cheery next-door neighbor had chicken nuggets and macaroni and cheese on the table. Kelli must have planned the menu. I had to start taking a bigger interest in my children's lives. I ran my hand through my hair. "Oh, Mazi, what am I going to do? My daughters are growing up without me."

She leaned over in the process of dishing up macaroni and gave me a much-needed hug. "It will get better, Kate. Really it will. Give it time."

Time? There wasn't enough time left in this world to put my life back together.

We ate supper, and Mazi walked the girls through their homework while I took a bath and pulled on a pair of jeans and faded sweatshirt. Later I strolled through the living room and saw that the three were watching a Three Stooges tape, drinking hot chocolate and eating popcorn. I stood just inside the door watching them, feeling like an outsider. I missed my time with the girls.

I missed Neil.

I missed my old relic of a stove.

Sailor sniffed at my ankles. Even the dog seemed to be suspicious of me.

The next day I called Mazi in a panic.

"Hold on—slow down. What's the problem?"

I glanced at the clock. "I'm in a bind. Could you help me out?"

"Of course, hon. Just tell me what you need."

I breathed a silent prayer of thanks for this woman who had rapidly become my best friend.

"I have to drop Kelli by school, and two of the stylists called in sick, which I doubt since I overheard them talking about taking a day trip shopping for antiques. Kris really is sick, though. Could you take her to the doctor?"

This was breaking my heart. I had never allowed anyone, not even Neil, to take my children to a doctor without me. I had always been there to comfort and take care of them. I realized Mazi was talking.

Her voice sharpened. "Kate? You there?"

"I'm here. My mind was wandering."

"Well, call it back home." Her rich, deep contralto warmed. "I'd love to take Kris. Just tell me where and when."

"Dr. Harvey Wilkins. He's a pediatrician."

"No problem. His office is in the same building as my doctor. Don't worry, Kate. I'll take care of her."

"I know you will. I owe you one."

"No, darlin', you don't owe me anything. Friends are there for friends."

"And you're a real friend." I hung up the receiver and thought, *Well, God, there's another one in Your column.*

He had been good to me, giving me a friend like Mazi. So far, she was my only friend in California. Alissa kept the girls while I was gone. She was sweet and friendly, but she was so much younger that we had little in common except the girls, and besides, there was a difference between friend and friendly. Mazi was a *friend.*

Work started to run more smoothly. The new stylists began to settle in, but I was learning running the salon was different than just working *in* the salon; being in charge set me apart. Exactly what I didn't need. I understood now why Maria always seemed different, more aloof, not a part of the group. It wasn't smart to be overly friendly with someone you might have to discipline or even let go.

The days passed somehow. Christmas was next week. When I did have a little free time I had too much to do at home to indulge in much self-pity.

Kris had turned out to have strep throat. Mazi filled her prescription and nursed her back to health. My kindhearted neighbor filled in for me at Kelli's preschool aquarium visit when I got tied up at the salon. She picked up the girls at school, dropped off dry cleaning, made sure we had milk and bread, and stayed late many evenings until I got home. The girls adored her. So did Sailor. Alissa missed the extra money.

I was jealous.

While doing some emergency shopping, I passed the boutique where Mazi liked to shop. There in the window was a handbag she had raved about. Mazi dressed in the latest fashions whether it suited her or not, and most of the time her choices were rather far out. The bag was tall with patches of faux-fur animal print: tiger, leopard and something else with spots I didn't recognize, interspersed with patches of some velvety-looking ethnic print in shades of brown. An irregular brown leather fringe hung along the bottom of the bag and a fluff of black feathers circled the opening.

Actually it was pretty awful, but characteristically Mazi. I eyed a second bag that I considered even more far out. Smaller, black with hot-pink lip prints scattered over it. I shuddered and went inside. There was only one faux-fur bag left, not counting the one in the window. I squinted at the price tag and gulped. Mazi didn't shop at inexpensive stores. I'd never in my life paid that much for a bag, but I owed the woman big-time.

I took the bag home and tried to plan how to give it to her, finally deciding to take her out to dinner. She accepted the invitation with exclamations of pleasure, as usual. We chose a small Italian restaurant about ten minutes from where we lived. The place was crowded and there was an enticing scent of tomato and basil and Parmesan. I sniffed appreciatively. One of the things I did like about San Francisco was its selection of really good eating establishments.

The girls ordered pizza, and I chose pasta primavera. Mazi settled on fettuccine Alfredo. The waitress brought my iced tea and the girls' sodas. Mazi, who hadn't ordered anything to drink, smiled brightly.

"This is such a special treat and I'm feeling festive. I think I'll eat a whole dessert tonight."

"My treat." I grinned. "Knock yourself out."

"Oh..." She suddenly backed off the impulse. "I shouldn't. Warren thinks I'm too fat now."

"He said that?" I couldn't imagine Neil saying such a thing— even if I had to stop by the stockyard to weigh myself.

Kris's eyes were round as saucers and Kelli wore my mother's expression of deep disapproval. She looked like a little carbon copy of Neil, which at times comforted me and at others broke my heart. She had a lot of her father's mannerisms and behavior, but somewhere inside her was a hard core of the woman who had raised me.

Now she frowned at Mazi. "You're not fat. You're just fluffy."

"Kelli!" I reprimanded.

"Well, you know. She's not *fat*."

Mazi bent forward and grinned. "That's okay, sweetie. I know what you mean. I'm a little pudgy, but I'm healthy."

I watched as she slathered bread thickly with butter. "I'm going to hate myself when I get on the scales in the morning."

The waitress refilled my iced-tea glass and brought more butter. The girls were nodding off, and I decided we'd better eat while they still had their eyes open. I handed Mazi the brightly colored gift sack and her eyes widened.

"What's this?"

"Just a little something from the three of us."

She opened the sack and peered inside. "Oh, Kate." She shut the bag, and then opened it again to look inside. "It's the exact bag that I wanted." She raised her eyes to mine. "Why?"

I shrugged. "Because you're you."

"But I don't understand why you would do this for me."

"Because we love you," Kris said.

"We love you lots," Kelli echoed. "You've made our life bearable."

I smiled, wondering where she'd heard that.

Mazi wiped tears off her cheeks. "You don't know how much this means to me. I'll treasure this bag forever."

"Yeah, or until next week," I joked. I'd seen her purse collection.

We drove home with Mazi still exclaiming over her bag. When we got out of the car she hugged each of us again before stepping over the box elder hedge to her drive.

The girls and I went inside, and as I listened to the girls getting ready for bed I realized how lucky I was to have them. Mazi was sitting alone in her house. Her husband came home occasionally, but I had never met him.

I vowed to be as good a friend to her as she had been to me.

The following Sunday, the kids wore me down. We finally attended church. The congregation was mostly younger people with children. I enjoyed the welcoming smiles. The music was livelier than we were used to, dominated by praise choruses. The kind Brother Joe Crockett used to call seven-eleven songs. Seven words sung eleven times. To my surprise, I enjoyed them. I enjoyed the sermon, too, finding it inspiring, and I could see Kelli and Kris taking notice of the number of kids. Since Neil had never attended this church, I didn't have the incomplete feeling I'd had back at our home church.

When the service ended, several people stopped to shake hands and invited us to come back. On the way out, a young woman dressed in a brown suede skirt and matching vest with fringe and a white silk blouse stopped us. She wore brown suede boots, and her bronze, closely cropped hair framed her face, pixie fashion. Her smile was dazzling.

"Hi. I'm Beni. We're so happy to have you with us this morning."

I took her outstretched hand. "Thank you. I'm Kate Madison. We've enjoyed it."

"Are you looking for a home church?"

I felt this was going a bit too fast. I'd have preferred to have time to look around, but her smile was so infectious that I had to smile back. "I guess we are. We've recently moved here from Oklahoma."

Her smile had a sincere effect. "How nice. Is Mr. Madison with you?" She glanced at my left hand.

"I'm a widow." The words didn't stick in my throat the way they usually did. Maybe I was making progress.

Her smile faded. "I'm so sorry. Tell you what, we have a great singles group here at the church. Why don't you come by and get acquainted? I think you would enjoy it, and you'll find others who know what you're going through."

I doubted that, but I took the church calendar she pressed on me and promised to think about it. Beni followed us out to the car. "I really mean it, Kate. I'm divorced myself, and I know what it is to need people who understand. I've got a couple of girls, too. Mine are older than yours."

I wouldn't have taken her to be that old. "I'm not looking for a man yet." I couldn't believe I'd said something so gauche. Beni didn't seem to mind, though.

"Most singles aren't looking for anything other than friendship and fellowship. We can offer lots of both. Give it a try, Kate. I think you'll like it."

Suddenly the idea didn't sound all that bad. "Okay, Beni. I'll drop in. Maybe not this week, but sometime. I promise."

"That's all I ask." She smiled and hurried across the parking lot to join a couple of girls who looked like preteens, pretty girls with her bronze hair and her sense of style. I got in my car with the girls and drove home, thinking that I knew I shouldn't have come this morning.

Christmas morning I fixed waffles with maple syrup, a Christmas-morning tradition, but no one was hungry. We pushed the sticky treat around on our plates. We tried. That about covered it.

After breakfast we gathered around the tree to open gifts. I handed out the gaily wrapped packages, a full dozen for each girl. Neil's parents had mailed their presents—Barbies wearing shimmering dresses, and new nightgowns for each girl, with matching robes and fluffy house slippers.

Kris held up her new lavender-flowered robe. "Look, Mom, isn't this pretty?"

"Lovely," I agreed "and it's a good color for you."

"Is mine a good color for me?" Kelli held up one exactly like Kris's but in soft peach.

"Perfect with your coloring," I said, which it was with her dark hair and eyes so like her father's.

They each received a large box wrapped in silver-and-blue paper from Mazi. Art supplies. Lots of art supplies. Mazi dealt with a generous hand.

Kris examined a box of pastels. "Mazi has good taste, doesn't she?"

I thought of some of the outlandish costumes I'd seen her wear. All high fashion, of course, but definitely not "her."

Kris waited, her blue eyes locked with mine. "Very good," I agreed. I was all for truth, but not when it might hurt a friend, and Mazi was top of the line in the friendship department.

I had gone overboard, buying clothes, games, bath products and hair stuff. At the last minute I had picked up bead kits so they could make their own jewelry.

Kelli poked at a package of hot-pink plastic beads. "I'll make you a necklace. Mazi, too."

"I think that would be nice," I said. "I know she would appreciate it."

Finally there was only one gift left under the tree. Neil's present. Kelli ceased playing with her bead supplies, her lower lip quivering. Kris's expression turned solemn. I could have kicked myself for not removing it from under the tree and hiding it away somewhere. I wished I'd never given in and let them buy it.

The front doorbell rang. Thankful for the momentary reprieve, I went to answer. It was Mazi, dressed in black pants and red sweater with a Christmas pin that outshone the northern lights. "Ho ho ho, Merry Christmas."

"Merry Christmas to you, too. What are you doing out so early?" She usually wasn't out of bed until much later.

"I'm bored. Warren got stranded in Cincinnati and didn't make it home. How about the four of us going out to eat?"

Well, it prevented tears. The girls' faces lit up with anticipation. I didn't really want to go anywhere, but I didn't want to stay home and try to pretend everything was jolly, either.

"Sure. Let us change and we'll be right with you."

The girls scampered to their rooms, carrying the new outfits they'd gotten for Christmas. I remembered Mazi's nice pants and sweater and turned my back on my favorite jeans for dress pants and a coral-pink top.

When I got back to the living room Mazi had picked up the discarded paper and ribbons, stuffing them into a plastic trash bag.

I ran a brush through Kelli's hair. "So where are we eating?"

"I thought Chinatown."

For Christmas? Well, why not. At least it would be different. "You driving or am I?"

She laughed. "You don't drive to Chinatown. Parking places are practically nonexistent. We'll drive partway and take a cab."

So I had a lot to learn. The taxi let us off at the green-tiled Dragon Crested Gate, at Grant Avenue and Bush Streets, the traditional entrance to Chinatown and a favorite place for tourist photo taking.

Kelli stared wide-eyed at the ornate gate and the exotic street signs. They didn't have anything like this back in Oklahoma. We strolled along, looking in shop windows.

Kris grabbed my hand. "Look at the streetlights."

The famed dragon lights, looking like little pagodas, sat atop the tall poles. The glass lenses shone as if they had been newly cleaned; red-tiled roofs gleamed in the sun.

"Can we come back some night and see them lit?" Kelli asked.

"Sure." Mazi nodded. "In fact, if we can make it, let's come back for the Chinese New Year Parade. I'll buy bleacher seats along the parade route."

"A parade!" Kris adored parades.

"Like you've never seen!" Mazi stopped in her tracks, her eyes gleaming. Evidently she and Kris had something in common. "The most gorgeous floats and costumes. There'll be acrobatics, Miss Chinatown U.S.A. and, of course, the Golden Dragon."

Kelli grabbed my hand. "A real dragon?"

Mazi laughed. "No, honey. It was made in Foshan, a little town in China. It has a six-foot-long head with rainbow-colored pom-poms and colored lights from nose to tail, with silver rivets on its scaly sides. And it's trimmed in white rabbit fur. It takes one hundred men and women to carry the thing and it's considered an honor to be chosen to take part."

Kris sighed. "Oh, we *have* to see that."

Mazi paused in front of the Grand Palace Restaurant. We went inside to find snowy-white tablecloths with hot-pink napkins on each table. The girls needed help with the menu, but Kelli finally decided on cashew nut chicken. Kris wanted spicy chicken, but settled for sweet and sour when I pointed out she didn't really like spicy foods.

I settled for chicken with double mushrooms and Mazi chose Mongolian beef. She also ordered creamed chicken corn soup for the girls and sliced chicken breast shark fin soup for the two of us. In addition she chose steamed chicken bun, deep-fried spring roll and pot stickers from the dim sum menu.

"We'll never eat all of this."

"So we'll get a doggy bag. I want the girls to taste as many things as possible."

To my surprise, the girls relished Chinese food. Even Kelli, my picky child, sampled everything, and while she wasn't crazy about the Mongolian beef, she said it wasn't too bad. High praise coming from her. I was surprised to see Mazi merely picking at her food. A feast like this and she didn't eat a third of the goodies on her plate. I, however, had cleaned mine and pigged out on pot stickers. It wasn't that I had overeaten, not at all. Just a healthy appetite. I took a deep breath. Why had I worn this belt?

We spent the afternoon window-shopping. Kelli stood transfixed in front of a window filled with dolls dressed in bright colors with their straight black hair cut in bangs. Her favorite, though, was in the shop that sold pearls. It was a baby doll dressed in pink with a bonnet made of fluffy pink feathers and loops of pearls hanging around the face. Totally adorable.

I was amazed at the twisted ropes of pearls, in every conceivable color, and Kris stood transfixed in front of the kite shop. I got her to move on only by promising we'd come back in the spring and buy kites to fly.

The girls were quiet on the way home, but it was a contented silence. I silently blessed Mazi for helping us through this day. Instead of a day of sorrow and memories she had introduced Kris and Kelli to a whole new world, one they'd never seen before, and she had given them a happy memory to temper the sad ones.

When we pulled into the drive, she declined to come in, saying she needed to call Warren. I put my arms around her. "Thanks so much, Mazi. You've made this a wonderful holiday for us."

A note of sadness tinged her voice. "You've made it special for me, too, Kate."

I watched her walk away down the drive and step over the hedge. She seemed so alone. Suddenly I realized that Mazi needed us as much as we needed her.

I couldn't take Warren's place, but the girls and I could be the family she was missing.

Chapter

12

On Friday I drove home from work with a light heart and a sense of anticipation. I actually had a full Saturday off. The salon was closed on Sunday. The new stylists were working out well and business had slacked off, so I could actually spend a day at home. I had a to-do list a mile long, and I planned to spend the day playing catch-up.

I walked into the house to find it empty and the telephone ringing. My heart skipped a beat. Where were my daughters? Where was Mazi? I grasped the receiver, my hand slick with nervous perspiration.

"Hello?" My voice cracked.

"Mom? Hi."

"Kris?" I sank to the kitchen stool. "Where are you?"

Her voice dropped until I could barely hear it. "We're at Mazi's."

"Oh." Complete silence while I tried to pull myself together.

They hadn't been snatched off a street corner, or run over by a bus. "That's nice. I wondered."

"It's all right, isn't it?"

"Sure—of course." I had to get a grip before I turned my daughters into neurotic robots.

Kris sounded more assured. "Mazi wants us to eat with her tonight. That's okay, isn't it?"

"I suppose so. Let me change into something comfortable and I'll come over."

"Okay, Mom. I'll tell her."

I hurried to change into jeans and a sweatshirt and crossed the hedge to Mazi's low-slung brick house. The shutters were painted a dark green and the door chime played the opening notes of the *William Tell* Overture.

Classy.

If I ever installed door chimes, mine would probably be more in the line of "Old MacDonald Had a Farm."

Mazi met me at the door wearing a leopard-print caftan. "Kate, come in! We're about ready to eat."

A smoke-gray Persian cat with three black stripes running from his ears to his topaz eyes curled around her feet. Mazi picked him up and stroked his soft fur. "Minto's my best bud."

I scratched under his chin and was rewarded with a rumbling purr.

In the kitchen Kris cuddled a silver-gray Persian named Mystic and Kelli held a shaded silver female. The three stripes on her forehead gave her a perpetual frowning expression. Her green eyes cast a cool glance my way.

The queen surveying her subjects.

Kelli held her up for my inspection. "Say hi to Mimi."

I admired the feline beauties, while Mazi bustled around the kitchen. She refused my offer to help, so I settled in one of the oak captain chairs and watched as she set out a large bowl of salad, followed by grilled chicken breasts and roasted potatoes with garlic. A basket lined with a red-and-white-checked napkin held thick slices of freshly baked French bread. Not one thing my finicky Kelli would eat. She liked chicken, but hers usually came fried.

When Mazi sent the girls to the bathroom to wash their hands I braced myself for the explosion.

We took our places at the table and I saw Kelli cast a questioning glance at the salad. Her face settled into her "I won't eat vegetables" expression.

Mazi placed glasses of fresh lemonade at each place and sat down. "I know you pray before eating, Kate. Would you like to do that now?"

I bowed my head and thanked God for His blessings and for my friends and family and for the food we were about to eat. Mazi looked thoughtful when I finished. She didn't say anything, just looked rather curious.

"Kelli, would you start the salad around, please?" Kelli started to protest and then caught my eye and clamped her mouth shut. The look she sent my way spoke volumes.

I reached for the salad bowl and peered at the contents in surprise. An assortment of greens blended with red and green grapes, red and green chopped apples, kiwi and strawberries in a sweet poppy-seed dressing. I took a tentative bite. It was delicious.

Kris forked out a strawberry. "I love this salad, Mazi."

"It's so different." I added my praise and was rewarded by Kelli trying a bite.

She looked up, surprise registering on her features. "It *is* good."

So maybe she would eat her vegetables if I smothered them in something sweet? Wouldn't that nullify the benefits?

Mazi cut into a bite of grilled chicken. "Kate, do you have to work tomorrow?"

"No." I almost laughed with joy. "I actually have two days off together and I'm going to catch up on all the work I've had to let go."

Mazi sipped her lemonade, looking as if she wanted to say something.

I frowned. "What?"

"I was just thinking. This is the first weekend you've had off. Maybe we could take the girls out to Cliff House."

I stared at her. "Are you kidding? I have so much to do...."

"Which will wait." She nodded at Kris and Kelli. "They won't."

I closed my mouth, my mind racing. How many times had I complained that I didn't have time for the girls, and here I had time, but I hadn't given a thought to my daughters. They gazed at me, their eyes watchful, their expressions still, as if they already knew what the answer would be.

I forced myself to relax and dredge up a smile. The last way I wanted to spend my one day off was playing tourist, but Mazi was right. The work would wait. My daughters came first. "Okay," I said. "We'll go to Cliff House."

Their delighted expressions were reward enough for me.

Before we left that evening, it had been decided we would leave at nine and Mazi would drive. I was secretly relieved. I was getting used to San Francisco traffic, but I didn't want to spend my only day off manipulating a car through a weekend demolition derby to one of the state's major tourist attractions.

This was Mazi's idea—let Mazi do it. I noticed she left most of her dinner on her plate tonight.

The following day the girls and I were up early and happily anticipating our day. Mazi showed up in a short black skirt, calf-length high-heeled boots, a V-neck tan knit top and a black jacket with a faux-fur collar and cuffs. The outfit would have been fabulous on a tall, skinny model. Mazi was neither tall nor skinny. Kelli, for once, was too excited about the coming trip to make one of her outspoken observances.

We piled into the car and started off. The girls and Mazi were in a holiday mood, excited, laughing and talking. I forced myself to look on the bright side and not think about all the chores awaiting me when we got home. I'd always wanted to see Cliff House, and now I was going to.

The attraction was all I had expected. I stood at the window in the dining room, looking at miles of sandy beach with surf breaking along the shoreline. I could see the Golden Gate Bridge and even old Dutch windmills, although what they were doing here I hadn't a clue.

"Look!" Kris pointed. "A ship."

"Ships come from all over the world to the San Francisco harbor," Mazi explained. We watched as the vessel moved with majestic aplomb past the bridge.

Mazi showed us around. She stopped before a framed photograph. "This is the way Cliff House used to look before it burned to the ground."

I looked at the seven-story hotel built like a French château and wished I could have seen it before tourism took over. Mazi pointed to a framed menu. "Just think, girls. At the original Cliff House an abalone dinner only cost three dollars and fifty cents."

"Baloney?" Kris asked.

"Abalone—fish, dear."

I figured a glass of tea would cost that much. Times changed. We ended our tour back at the window, fascinated by the view. Trees on the hilltops were permanently bent shoreward by the strong oceanic winds. The blue of the sky and the darker blue of the ocean blended in graduated shades. Waves rippled the surface of the water and churned into a lacy froth on the sandy beach.

Kris was enraptured. "Can we go to the beach?"

"Not today," I said. I'd wanted to take the girls to the seashore, but now that I had seen it, I was afraid. That was an enormous body of water and they were so small.

Mazi sensed what I was thinking. "Let them go, Kate. They have to live."

I nodded, but inside I was upset that she could read me so easily. She pointed out Seal Rocks, looking like miniature pyramids.

"I see a seal!" Kelli exclaimed. "Look, Mom!"

"The seals are only here from September to June," Mazi explained. "They go south for July and August. They're fun to watch."

At the Musée Mécanique, Kelli fell in love with the coin-operated figures. Her favorite was a grandmotherly looking figure in purple vest and frilly white blouse who would tell your fortune.

"It's not a real fortune," Kris said.

"I know that," Kelli retorted. "But it's fun."

Fun? I wasn't having any fun. Neil should have been here. Neil should have been pointing out the sights and buying the girls popcorn.

I turned away so the others couldn't see my expression. I didn't want to ruin this trip for the girls.

"Okay, next the Camera Obscura," Mazi said, tottering away in her high-heeled boots.

I felt like a schoolkid on a field trip. I followed, because there wasn't anything else to do. The building, shaped like a camera, didn't seem appealing to me, but to my surprise, Kris was fascinated. We walked past the huge brass arrows pointing to the entrance. Once inside we watched as the camera obscura chugged around on its motorized axis, panning the surf, the rocks and the sinking sun, while we listened to the man who ran the show. The sun was sinking low at the end of the day and he held up a flat board, moving it into the field of projection so we could see the sun storms around the edge of the sun.

Even I was interested now. He had turned off the narration tape to do the sunset show in person. Kris stood right in front of him, hanging on every word. He smiled down at her. "About twice a month we see the green flash."

Her eyes were big. "What's that?"

"It's caused by the spectrum of light being split by the atmosphere. The various colors of light are separated, and when green comes along it flashes just as the last rays of light leave."

"Oh, wow!" Kris breathed. "Do you think we'll see it?"

"I can't promise," the man said. "It only lasts for a tenth of a second, but it's something special when it does happen."

We waited. I knew it wouldn't happen, but maybe Kris wouldn't be too disappointed. I was almost angry at the man for building her up to be let down. My daughter had been on the receiving end of too many disappointments lately. Then it happened. A flash of liquid jade.

There and then gone.

I held my breath, overwhelmed by the loveliness of it.

"I saw it!" Kris shrieked. "It was right there." She pointed at the horizon.

I swallowed around the lump in my throat. It had been like a glimpse of heaven. Suddenly I wanted Neil so badly my heart throbbed with the longing. I walked out of the camera-shaped building and stared at the shoreline.

I felt Kris and Kelli press close against me. "Don't cry, Mom," Kris said. "We're here."

"We'll help you, Mom," Kelli said. "We'll like living in San Francisco."

I looked down at the love shining in their eyes and knew some way I could go on because I had these two precious daughters. Neil lived on in their lives and in my heart.

I nodded. "Yeah, it will be all right."

Beni from the new church called that night. "Kate, I don't know if you noticed, but the singles group is having a holiday mixer tomorrow evening."

I'd noticed, all right, and had no intention of going. It was much too early for me to be thinking of singles meetings.

"I don't know, Beni," I began, but she interrupted me.

"Don't make up your mind right away. If you do decide to come, bring a covered dish and a gift that would do for either a man or woman."

A gift exchange? "But Christmas is over."

"I know, but this is our Christmas and New Year's meeting combined. Most everyone brings gag gifts, but a few buy more serious items. It will be fun, Kate. No pressure, I promise."

I felt pressured, and I didn't like the idea, but I agreed to come to the silly social because I didn't know how to say no. "All right, I'll come if I can bring a friend."

"Sure, Kate. That will be fine."

I hung up the phone and called Mazi. She might not be single, but she certainly could use the fellowship. She was strangely reluctant, for someone who thrived on fun.

"Oh, I don't know, Kate. I know you go to church and all that, but I really don't get that God stuff."

"It isn't a worship service, Mazi. Purely social, I promise." I sounded like Beni.

I caught the shrug in her voice. "All right, I'll go to keep you company."

I hung up the phone and called Alissa, who happened to be free tomorrow night. "Come planning to be here a while. I have no idea how long this thing will last."

"Doesn't matter," she assured me. "I only live a few minutes away. It's not like I'd have a long drive home. And I can use the extra money."

Poor Alissa was always broke.

The night of the mixer I dressed in a black skirt and shell, topped by a jacket of turquoise, green and gold paisley pattern on black velvet. Neil had liked me in this. Wearing the jacket made me feel as if I was taking a part of him along with me.

Mazi was resplendent in a black sleeveless dress topped by a sheer chiffon peplum jacket with bell sleeves in a warm golden brown. The knee-high slit showed a fetching glimpse of sheer black hose. For once, she looked perfect for the occasion.

The girls admired us, and assured me they were looking forward to an evening with Alissa, who had promised to play Chutes and Ladders with them. Mazi and I set off for our night on the town.

We left our casseroles in the kitchen area and laid our gifts under the tree. A nice-looking man with silver hair and mustache claimed Mazi's attention and, figuring she could hold her own, I drifted over to chat with Beni.

"I'm so glad you could come." She introduced me to a few people and then excused herself to check on the food. I stood there with a cup of punch in my hand, wearing a silly grin.

I hated these things. Right now I could be home soaking my tired feet in a tub of hot water.

A tall, extremely buff blond guy walked up. He paused, punch in hand. "So, Kate. You're new to the area, right?"

I nodded. "We've only been here since the end of November."

His brow furrowed. "We?"

"My daughters and I. Kris and Kelli."

"Oh. You have kids."

"Ages seven and five."

His eyes glazed over. "Ah, yes. Well, if you'll excuse me. I see someone I need to talk to. Nice to have you tonight."

I watched him walk/run away and figured he wouldn't be asking for my phone number, which was fine with me. I took a fortifying sip from my cup. And smiled.

Mazi, meanwhile, had exchanged the older man for another just as old. The top of his head barely reached to her chin, and Mazi wasn't tall. Everywhere she went, he trailed her. If she stopped for a glass of punch, he was thirsty. If she joined a group, he was there. I saw her distinctly flash her wedding ring at him, but he didn't appear to heed the silent warning.

She wore a hunted expression, and I figured I'd better do something. I cornered Beni. "Who's the guy hanging around Mazi?"

Beni squinted in the man's direction. "Oh, that's Earl Ray. He's a pest, but he's harmless."

"What does he do?"

She grinned. "Mostly he chases women."

I snorted. "Well, right now he's chasing Mazi. How can we head him off?"

She shot another glance in Mazi's direction. "Don't look now, but I think he has competition."

The white-haired man was back, elbowing Earl out of the way. The two men were joined by a tall, lanky redhead with a friendly smile and a terrible haircut. Suddenly my friend's hunted expression disappeared and Mazi was her usual bubbly self.

During the evening I had a chance to get acquainted with several people from church I'd not met before, and I was surprised to see Mazi enjoying herself so much. Maybe this was a start. For both of us. Maybe I'd come out of my self-constructed shell, and Mazi would see that organized religion wasn't the same thing as Christ-based faith. If she got acquainted with the people at the singles group, God could start to move in her life and she would agree to attend morning worship service. For a moment I was filled with relief; I was slowly starting to feel and think like the old Kate. Neil would be proud of me. Better yet, I felt proud of myself. I was far from healed, but I realized that I was closer to forgiving God.

How magnanimous of you, Kate.

I shook the thought aside and filled my plate with smoked sausage and crackers. Mazi was chatting to one of the women while still surrounded by half of the available men present. She seemed to be doing just fine, so I carried my plate to a vacant table. It was as if I had turned on one of those bug-zapper lights. Evidently the men were hungry for a new face. Soon I had my own little entourage offering to refill my punch and fetch more crackers.

The man on my left introduced himself as Sam Whitley, and he proceeded to monopolize the conversation, telling me about his gas station and how hard it was to get dependable employees. I wasn't sure if he was giving me his résumé or interviewing me for a job.

Hollis Temple, across the table from me, speared a bite of ham and munched on it, while pointing the fork at me. "Have you been to Chinatown?"

I assured him that I had, and Fisherman's Wharf, and for the time being I was through with the tourist stuff. He looked disappointed and retired behind a piece of cherry pie. If he was planning to ask me to visit either sight, I had successfully nipped the plan in the bud. I considered bringing out pictures of the girls as added insurance to head off any other invitations.

The gift exchange was a hoot. Mazi got a Christmas pin in the shape of a wreath and as big as a teacup. The "jewels" flashed on and off like a traffic light. She immediately put it on, which seemed to earn her brownie points with the others.

My gift was a set of pig bookends. The pink porkers lolled, happy mouths curved in sappy expressions that seemed to match the way I felt. I silently christened them Kate and Mazi.

The gas station man, Sam, got a tie with an alligator on it, but not the little tasteful alligators that in an understated way suggest that you are wearing a classy piece of clothing. This alligator was big and green and glittered. His wide-open mouth displayed big pearly-white teeth. Sam grinned good-naturedly and tied it around his neck. I liked him better after that.

The party started to break up after the gift exchange, and I went to the kitchen to collect our dishes. Mazi joined me, laughing at something one of the women said. I was proud of the way she had fit in, because I knew she had been hesitant to come.

When we got home she consulted her watch. "Only eleven. Early yet. Come over to the house for a few minutes. I'm too wound up to sleep."

I followed her across the hedge, hoping that she'd wind down quickly. I could fall asleep on a rock. "You looked like you had fun tonight."

"Oh, yes, I did. Thanks for inviting me. Funny, I had an entirely different opinion of church people. If they are all like this bunch, they're not bad."

"People who go to church are just like people who don't go to church. The only difference is they have God in their life."

"Yeah." She paused, key in lock. "That's the part I don't understand."

I swallowed. Were we about to embark on a theological discussion? I wasn't sure I was up to it. "I'd be glad to answer any question you might have—if I can."

"I know you would. Trouble is, Kate, I don't know the questions. But not tonight, okay?"

"Sure. I'm right next door anytime you want to talk." I would pray for her, pray that God would allow me to plant a seed and he would make it grow.

She unlocked her door and we went inside to slump into soft overstuffed chairs in the living room. Mazi brought cups of hot tea, which seemed to fit the bill tonight on a chilly San Francisco evening. I'd eaten too much, and the light taste of chamomile was exactly what I needed.

Mazi kicked off her shoes. "Did the men come on to you tonight?"

"Some. You?"

"They tried." She giggled. "You notice that little guy, that Earl Ray?"

I nodded.

"He wanted to take me for a romantic stroll on the beach."

I grinned. "What did you say?"

"I told him I was allergic to sand."

I leaned back, cradling the cup of warm liquid in my hands. "I think I almost got an invitation to Chinatown, but I headed it off."

She shook her head, smiling. "Did you see that big guy, George something, crushing soda cans with his bare hands? That always slays me when they do that. It's like, 'Hey, woman, look at me.' Real macho stuff. As if crushing soda cans is a trait a woman would want in a husband."

I laughed, knowing exactly what she meant. "I got an invitation to join Ted Johnson in a one-on-one study of Revelation. At his house. I declined."

Mazi laughed. "You know what, Kate? The men were all nice guys. When they discovered I was there with you as a guest, and that I was married, they were perfect gentlemen. Kind. Witty. Thoughtful."

"I know. They're just lonely." Like me. Lonely, desperate for someone to love.

My best friend's eyes twinkled. "You know the really amazing thing? The men were coming on to us." She leaned over and smacked my knee playfully. "We've still got it, girl!"

"Now, if we could just remember where we put it."

"Or what to do with it."

We sat there giggling like a couple of schoolgirls.

Out-of-our-silly-gourd sophomores.

Chapter 13

New Year's Eve had never been a big event for us, so I guess that's why this year the girls and I had stayed home and worked puzzles. We were in bed asleep, blissfully unaware, when the New Year started. Mazi had suggested Chinatown again, but I'd decined the offer.

Neil and I had usually stayed home with the girls anyway on the holiday. Popcorn and a rented family-friendly video was about as wild as we got. Neil always brought home a bottle of sparkling white grape juice. At the stroke of midnight we'd lift stem glasses and drink a toast to the Madisons' happiness and well-being. Later the girls would polish off the bottle of grape juice.

Last year we'd observed the same rite, unaware of the changes looming on our horizon.

Now it was mid-January, and impulsive Mazi had decided that we needed a New Year's Eve celebration.

"The year won't go right without one."

I'd said, "Whatever." My life would be the same no matter what.

I closed the salon at three-thirty this afternoon, and everyone made a beeline for their cars, focused on colds and flu. A nasty viral bug had swept the shop. As I watched my staff leave, blowing red noses and coughing, I felt a now-familiar ache in my heart. I would put on a brave front tonight, but I had never felt less like celebrating in my life. Hopefully Mazi wouldn't insist that we stay at her place until midnight.

I stopped at the supercenter and picked up a bottle of sparkling grape juice. We had microwave popcorn at the house, and for the girls' sake I would go through the motions, but I would be relieved when the evening was over. I realized how much I had come to depend on Mazi. Maybe too much, but she was willing to help, and I was so willing to let her.

The video I chose, *The Best Little Christmas Pageant Ever,* was a holiday behind, since Christmas had come and gone, but I always enjoyed watching a bunch of scruffy kids teaching a group of church members the real meaning of Christmas.

The house was empty when I got home. The girls were already over at Mazi's. Alissa had asked for the evening off. The young woman had smiled and said she had a date. Something about the way she said it sent up a red flag and I started to worry that I might soon be looking for a new baby-sitter. I remembered the applicant pool I'd interviewed before hiring Alissa, and I cringed.

The phone rang. Mom calling from Kansas.

"How's the weather out there?"

"Nice, balmy with a warm breeze."

She sighed. "We're in the middle of a blizzard."

Well, I didn't miss that. Cold, blowing snow and storm-blocked roads were one part of the Midwest I could do without.

"Are you and Dad all right?"

"We're fine. I'm just worried about you and the girls."

I pretended a confidence I didn't feel. "We're doing all right. The girls have adapted to their new school, and things are going well at work." If you didn't count the flu going around, fussy, difficult-to-please customers and high-strung stylists. I'd become so good at negotiating peace I was thinking about sending my résumé to the United Nations.

"Well, we know you're a grown woman, but your dad and I still worry about you, Kate."

I had a hunch about the purpose of tonight's call: Mom wanted to ride to the rescue. Trade wintry Kansas for sunny California. Who could blame her? I didn't really need her. I wasn't proud of my thoughts, but I didn't even want her here right now.

"Really, Mom. The girls and I are adjusting." I couldn't bring myself to say "doing fine," because we weren't exactly blooming in our new environment, but we were gradually coming to grips with our new life. "Why don't you and Dad plan to come see us sometime in spring?" By then I'd be more in control of my emotions, although control had never been a major character trait of mine.

"I suppose that would be better. It's difficult to travel this time of the year. Airport delays, terrible road conditions. What are you planning to do tonight?"

"Oh, we're going to the neighbor's for a delayed New Year's Eve party."

"New Year's Eve? That was two weeks ago. You be careful, Kate. I worry about all of those strange people I hear about walking the streets in San Francisco. You're too innocent to cope with them, honey."

Right. Really innocent. I needed my mommy. I wondered what her reaction would have been to Tina with the striped stockings or Mrs. Ferguson and Homer. I knew how she would have reacted to the battleship demeanor of Mrs. Harrod. Mom might look more like a frivolous sailboat, but that's one battleship she would have torpedoed on sight.

"I have a routine, Mom. Home, work, the grocery store. There's not a lot of opportunity to encounter foul play."

"What about church?" Her voice had a "gotcha" ring to it.

Rats. I'd forgotten church. "That, too. We've visited a nice church and we're fitting in just fine."

"That's a relief, dear. Then I guess you don't need me."

"I always need you, Mom, but not at the moment. My job takes up all my spare time and the girls are in school all day. I'd rather you wait and visit when we can spend time together." I paused. "I'll take you and Dad to Chinatown and Fisherman's Wharf."

"That sounds interesting. Are there a lot of strange people hanging around there?"

"Oh—hey, Mom. I hear the kids. Can I call you later?"

"Your father and I are going to a prayer study tonight. He's waiting in the car right now. I'll call you tomorrow."

"Great. Have a good time, Mom. Drive safely and don't drink too much."

Mom poohed. "Kate, you're an incurable tease."

I grinned. "Give Dad my love."

"The same to you, darling. And kiss Kelli and Kris for us."

I hung up as the front door opened and Kris and Kelli burst inside the foyer. I walked through the kitchen to greet them.

"Mom! Mazi's husband is *sick,* but she said we can still have our not-really-New-Year's-Eve party!"

I cast a quick look toward Mazi's picture window, half expecting to see the elusive Warren "Is she sure? We might disturb him." Plus, I wasn't crazy about the thought of coming down with a roaring case of the flu.

"He's upstairs in bed," Kelli said "He's sort of cranky."

"Well, probably he doesn't feel good." The chattering girls followed me into the kitchen explaining that Mazi really wanted us to come. Really, really.

I was reluctant to go over, with her husband ill and probably wanting quiet instead of a houseful of company, but one look at the girls with their flushed, excited expressions, and I caved. After all, it was Mazi's place to worry about her husband, not mine.

"Okay. Let me change clothes and we'll go." I considered my usual jeans and sweatshirt, but instead pulled on navy blue dress pants and a rose-and-navy-print blouse, a final birthday gift from Neil.

The girls had gone back across the drive by now. I grabbed a packet of microwave popcorn and the bottle of juice. At the last moment I decided to take the video, wishing I had more to contribute, but Mazi liked to cook. She probably had six trays of snacks already prepared.

She met us at the door, beaming. "I'm so glad you could still make it. Warren's upstairs so he won't expose you to the virus." She beamed. "It looked for a minute like I was going to spend the evening alone. Just me and the TV."

"Miss a belated New Year's Eve party?" I deadpanned. "You know me—a real party animal."

The girls had spread a quilt in front of the television. The cats were scattered around them. Kelli lay stretched out on her stomach, chin propped in her hands, while Mimi walked up and down her spine. Mystic and Minto curled up next to Kris with their topaz eyes cracked open slightly to stare at me.

I carried my offerings to the kitchen and Mazi eyed them as if she'd never seen sparkling grape juice before. "Juice?"

"It's a Madison family tradition."

"Oh. Well, sure. We'll drink a toast at midnight."

I dropped into my usual chair and relaxed, weary from the day's stress. Instead of getting easier, it seemed as if the personnel problems at work were coming more frequently. Maybe I wasn't cut out to be a manager.

Mazi had set the table with her best china and crystal goblets. We were getting the full treatment tonight. Everything looked delicious, and suddenly I was hungry. She had a cheese ball to die for. One dab on a cracker and I could have eaten the whole thing.

Mazi paused in filling her plate. "I fixed beds on the sunporch for the girls to have a sleepover, if that's all right."

I started to protest, but they begged to stay, so I gave in. But that meant I'd have to go home alone. An empty house, all by myself?

Mazi couldn't get enough food tonight. She went back to the table several times to fill her plate. I could never understand her eating habits. One day she ate as if there was no tomorrow, and the next she starved herself, consequently throwing her into a really foul mood. I wondered if I should point out temperance in all things, but then decided Mazi's eating habits were none of my business.

Around midnight we poured the white grape juice into the footed crystal glasses. I watched, worried, as Kelli and Kris took theirs.

"Those goblets are probably expensive. I'd hate for them to get broken."

"My dear Kate. The only way Kelli and Kris are going to learn to care for and enjoy nice things is by use. If the glasses get broken, well, they're just glasses. I want the girls to remember they drank out of the best tonight."

I realized she was right. We had to use things to appreciate them, and Kris's and Kelli's ability to develop memories hadn't died with Neil. I needed to adopt more of Mazi's attitude. Things were, after all, just things, and that included crystal goblets.

Mazi was doing everything to make us comfortable. She'd even made popcorn balls for the girls. I filled my plate with shrimp and water chestnut pastry cups, filled mushrooms and more of the cheese ball. I had no right to criticize Mazi's overindulgence. After all, tonight was special.

Mazi got up from the table. "I need to check on Warren. I'll be right back."

She left the room, and again I worried that we might disturb him. But then, the girls were quietly watching television and Mazi and I weren't exactly tooting horns and yelling. It was a very low-key celebration.

She came back into the room and answered my questioning lift of the eyebrows. "He's fine. Sleeping."

The girls watched the video and even Mazi got interested, although she left the room a few times to check on Warren, which made me nervous. If he was that sick, we really shouldn't be here.

The girls couldn't make it much past midnight. Once we'd shared our ceremonial toast, they sacked out on their pallets. Everything in me wanted them home tonight. With me. They were tired, but we could have gone home. However, Mazi begged us to stay and I could see she was lonely. She switched the television off and we nursed our grape juice.

"Warren really should see a doctor in the morning." Actually I didn't really care about his state. I was royally miffed at him for leaving Mazi alone so much.

She laughed, staring into her glass. "He's not as sick as he thinks he is. Warren takes good care of Warren."

I detected a hint of bitterness beneath her good-natured manner. Well, who could blame her? Sure he must make good money, judging from their home, but nothing could take the place of having a companion to share that home. Nobody knew that better than me.

Mazi left the room again and I helped myself to more cheese ball. If I didn't stop eating, my first act of the New Year would be a stringent diet.

My host returned and I asked, "So, what do you think the next year will bring?" I popped a jalapeño popper into my mouth.

Mazi was once again her usually bubbly self. I noticed she discreetly put her plate in the trash. "For starters, maybe we'll both find the gold at the end of the rainbow."

"And we'll be stars on TV."

She pursed her lips "The White House will call for advice on how to plan a state dinner."

"We'll open a restaurant in Chinatown."

"And top the list of the world's best-dressed women."

I toasted her with grape juice. "It was a lucky day when I moved into your neighborhood."

She nodded. "A lucky day for the both of us. Do you still miss Oklahoma?"

I thought about it. "I miss Liv. She was my best friend. Moving here was hard and, yes, there are days when I'm still mad at God for taking Neil and turning my world upside down."

Mazi smiled. "That's just the pain talking. You'll feel differently someday."

I nibbled on a cracker. Maybe I'd get over my anger at God, but I didn't think I'd ever adjust to California—too much traffic, a job that was proving to be more stressful than flying. "I don't think I will, but I'm learning I can't run away from my past or my fears. Some days I feel like I've made matters worse by leaving Oklahoma City." I paused for a moment. "Do you think God is trying to teach me something and if so, what?"

"Wow. You know more about God's ways than I do. If He's trying to teach you anything, maybe it's patience. Or stronger faith?"

I sighed.

"And who knows. Someday you'll meet someone and remarry—"

I shook my head. "I've heard too many horror stories about stepfathers. I won't subject Kelli or Kris to a stranger and make them call him father. No one will ever take Neil's place. For them or for me."

She grinned. "Have you met our postman? He's kind of cute and he's single."

At that she reached over and said softly, "You never said how your anniversary went. That night, when the kids told me it was your anniversary, I said a prayer for you, and you know I don't pray."

My mind skipped back to January 5. Bummer of a day. Neil and I would have been married nine years. I didn't think the kids had remembered and I wasn't sure Mazi even knew.

I'd watched my top stylist, Connie, leave that afternoon and suddenly I'd known I couldn't go home in my state. I'd have been bawling all night and upset the girls. I'd needed to do something. Get away by myself. It had struck me that I hadn't been by myself since Neil died. Unless you counted the nights I slept alone, wishing he was there beside me.

I had called Mazi. "Look, I've got something to do. Can you feed the girls supper?"

"Sure, Kate. Everything all right?"

I realized my agitation was probably saturating the telephone line. "I just need a little time alone."

"Take all the time you need," she offered. "We'll be right here."

I hung up the phone and stared out the window. So now I had time alone. What was I going to do with it? I decided that I needed to celebrate our anniversary. Not the way it would have been if Neil were alive, but something to set the day apart so it wouldn't be just another day.

I pulled out the telephone book and looked for restaurants, deciding on a little French bistro not too far from the salon. My burst of independence didn't include a drive across town.

I combed my hair, retouched my makeup and dabbed cologne on my wrist from the tester that sat on the counter. Good stuff. I smelled like a celebration.

The restaurant was cozy without sacrificing elegance. White tablecloths, green linen napkins, waiters in black suits and white shirts and a manner that fell somewhere between haughty and friendly. I ordered coq au vin and an endive salad. The food was delicious. I tried not to enjoy it, but found that I did. I also enjoyed being alone, although it didn't feel as if I were really alone. Neil was there, sitting opposite me. Smiling. Eyes openly adoring me.

I lifted my water glass to him. "Here's to nine perfect years, darling." I drank deeply. Set my glass down. Smiled.

Clearing my throat, I made him a promise. "I'm going to make it, Neil. I'm stronger than I thought. At first I was so mad at you for leaving us, but now I forgive you. I know you didn't want to leave us, and I know that somewhere up there you're watching over us.

"What?" I cocked my head. "You *bought* me something? You shouldn't!" I pretended to carefully slip the ribbon off a gold-foiled box. Opened the lid and gasped.

"This is too much!" Diamond earrings—the exact pair from Gaylord's Jewelry window.

I brought my hand to my heart. "How did you know?"

I grinned and leaned to kiss him. Then I caught sight of the young couple seated at the next table, who were staring at me as if I'd just sprouted wings.

Straightening, I lifted the menu to cover my face and dispensed with my game.

Pretending to peruse the dessert menu, I secretly kept an eye on the young couple, who had returned to their conversation. I had a feeling they weren't married. I also had a feeling they weren't going to be. They had two kids with them, a boy and a girl, maybe a little older than my two. They weren't behaving very well. The young mother tried, but the kids were on a roll.

The children didn't like the food, didn't like the restaurant and, what was really obvious, they didn't like the man. I remembered the way Kris and Kelli had reacted to Gray Mitchell.

The woman glanced my way and I smiled. She reluctantly smiled back, and I knew she sensed my sympathy. Kids. They had a way of making their feelings known.

Later I had left the restaurant and drove toward home, but a mile away I pulled into a small park at the top of a hill and turned off the motor. I could not believe this was me. Sitting alone in a parked car late at night. The Kate who left Oklahoma would never have dreamed of doing something so ill-advised.

I watched the moon bathing the Golden Gate Bridge in mellow light. The past months had brought changes not only to my life, but to me.

I had done things I'd never have dreamed of doing. Made choices I wish I'd never had to make. I let my thoughts turn to Neil and I felt a peace gently settle around my heart, as though he'd put his arm around me and said, "You've done well, Kate. You're going to be fine."

I stared at the moon for a long time before I started the motor and drove home. I had a feeling Neil would have been pleased with the way I'd celebrated our anniversary. Maybe I'd make this a tradition, getting away by myself for a couple of hours each year to take stock of life and to remember him, the love of my life.

I fingered my imaginary "gift" and thought, Well, hey. Life stinks sometimes, but it's the best thing going.

When I had pecked on Mazi's door and she'd opened it she'd been sporting an anxious frown. "You all right, Kate?"

"I'm fine, Mazi. Sorry to be so late. I'll tell you all about it later. Are the girls asleep?"

"Yeah. I'll help you carry them across."

Mazi had taken Kelli, and I'd carried Kris. We'd stepped across the hedge and headed toward the back door. Kris had lifted her head sleepily. "Is everything all right, Mommy?"

"Everything's fine, sweetheart. Mommy just needed some time alone tonight."

"We were worried," Kelli had murmured, picking up the thread of conversation.

"Nothing to worry about. How about hot chocolate before we go to bed?"

The girls had come alive. "Can we stay up and watch television?" they'd asked in unison.

"Not a chance. Tomorrow is a school day. One cup of chocolate, then off to bed you go." Mazi had deposited Kelli, and I had put Kris on the porch step as I hunted for my keys.

The two girls had raced ahead inside ahead of me.

I'd glanced up at the moon one last time. I had worried and dreaded this day for weeks; all my fears had been for nothing. I'd had a lovely anniversary.

And I loved my pretend earrings.

And until this moment I had never told another soul about my make-believe anniversary.

Not even my daughters.

Week three of January I decided to treat myself. I had worked so much overtime that I figured the salon could do without me for a few hours. I was looking for new bills as the postman arrived with a handful. I liked the way he looked— sandy hair, not really tall, but muscular and with eyes as blue as the bay on a sunny day. I liked his manner, too. There was something about him that said he would be dependable. Not flashy, just an all-around good Joe.

Golly, Neil. I'm moving along too fast now, darling.

"Morning, Kate."

"Good morning, Lee." I'd bumped into him several times and we had gradually progressed to first names. I felt comfortable with the familiarity.

"You doing all right?" he asked.

I sighed, and suddenly I found myself telling him how much I missed Oklahoma.

He leaned against the side of the porch railing. "I'm a transplanted Texan myself. I still miss it. My boys live there, you know."

I didn't know. "I think the worse part of moving is leaving your friends behind. I really miss my neighbors and my church family. I'd never realized how long it takes to make new ones."

He gave me a friendly grin. "Someone like you shouldn't have trouble making friends."

"No. I guess I don't, but you only make one at a time. It takes a while to gain back as many as you've lost."

He laughed. "Are you keeping score?"

I blushed, thinking I must have sounded like an idiot. "That wasn't what I meant."

His expression turned serious. "I know exactly what you mean. I've got a few friends here, but nothing like I had in Dallas."

I'd told him about Neil and our life in Oklahoma, but he'd not said much about his past. I drew a deep breath and asked a question I would never have believed I'd have nerve enough or even want to ask.

"Have you remarried?" Maybe I needed to know that a person could start over when the time was right.

He studied the toe of his shoe. "No, never remarried."

Why had I asked? When would I learn to keep my thoughts to myself? This was a subject that he probably didn't want to talk about.

He shook his head. "The ex said I stifled her 'artistic nature.'"

"Really." I didn't know her, but already I'd formed a preconceived notion—I wouldn't like her.

He flashed another boyish grin. "You heard right. I stifled her artistic nature. She took a few art classes and suddenly she was Rembrandt reincarnated."

"Did she have real talent?"

He shrugged. "Well, I couldn't see it, but she found someone who could. She eventually ran off with an artist. Last I knew they were both eking out a living in SoHo, painting desert sunrises."

"Well, to each his own," I said. There was no accounting for taste. "Tell you what—we have a singles group at church. Why don't you join us sometime? I think you'd enjoy the class."

He shook his head. "I don't have much free time. I'm moonlighting at the post office while I do my real work on my time off."

His real work? What would that be? I must have looked confused, because he explained.

"I'm writing a novel."

"Oh. Well...that must be fun. What's it about?"

"Gophers."

I blinked, sure I'd missed a turn somewhere. "Gophers?"

He nodded, his eyes alive with excitement. "See, it's an imaginary kingdom. There's a king gopher and a queen gopher, and they have all kinds of problems."

The first of which would be that they were gophers. "I see. It sounds...interesting."

"It's real cutting edge. Nothing else like it out there."

Yep, you could put money on that. "When will it be finished?"

"I'm working on the final chapters now. Then I'll get an agent and sell it. I don't anticipate any trouble finding a publisher. Mark my words, it'll be the next Great American Novel."

And I'd dance *Swan Lake* at the first Barnes & Noble autographing.

"You want to read it?"

"Oh, I don't know. It sounds great, but I have so little time."

"That's okay. I understand, but if you ever get a few free minutes, just give me a call and I'll run it over."

"I'll do that, Lee. But now I have to get busy. I'll see you around."

I took the mail and hightailed it out of there before he offered to drive home and fetch the manuscript. I was lonely, not desperate.

Chapter 14

"Guess who!" Mazi was framed in my doorway, arms loaded with packages.

"Mazi, you have got to stop this." Shaking my head, I opened the door wider to allow access to her and the bulging shopping bags. "You are shamelessly spoiling my children."

"So?" She shrugged. "Isn't that what children are for?"

A typical grandparent assumption—or one from a lovely, giving woman who longed for her own brood but had never been able to conceive. I trailed her into the living room and watched while she set the various shopping bags and colorful sacks on the coffee table, then peeled out of her light jacket. Outside a faint drizzle cast a gray pall over the city where little cable cars reach halfway to the stars. February had arrived with no letup in gray skies.

"Other than mall pillaging, what else have you accomplished today?"

I plumped a sofa pillow and stacked a mound of Kelli's picture books before I sat down cross-legged on the couch. Three perms, a highlight and six cuts had cleaned my plough. The salon was always busy holidays, but with Valentine's Day looming every client on my book needed attention.

Kicking off her three-inch patent leather heels, Mazi dropped into my overstuffed floral print and sighed. "Other than spending money? Zip. What about you?"

I told her about my hectic workday. She said I worked too hard, and the sincerity in her voice made me weepy—not an uncommon state, you understand. Instead of easing, my grief had only been getting worse. Nights longer. I'd stopped counting the times I'd reach for Neil and he wasn't there beside me. Warm. Loving.

"Work distracts me." I picked at a loose thread. I deliberately made my days long and arduous so that when I got home I'd drop into bed so tired I'd pass out and I wouldn't think about anything.

The plan hadn't worked.

We sat in the gathering twilight in silence. There wasn't anything I couldn't tell Mazi or her me; we were wounded soul mates—she by a husband who apparently cared little, I by widowhood. So now our silences were comfortable—not the solitary kind of stillness that occupied my waking days and sleepless nights, but compatible without words.

Mazi studiously examined a red acrylic nail. "I could eat the north end of a southbound horse. Got any of those wheat crackers?"

"Sure—and there's cheese, I think. Unless Kelli found it. Get me a hunk while you're up."

Mazi shoved her way out of the cushion and moseyed into the kitchen while I leaned back and studied my stocking feet. Apparently today she was eating. I never knew. Some days she ate more than I did and others she ate lettuce like a rabbit. I supposed that was how she maintained a neither slim nor full figure. I needed to cut back on my own snacking. I'd finally started gaining weight after being a beanpole all my life. I'd put on all I'd lost after Neil's death, and then some.

Within minutes she was back carrying a tray of provolone and crackers. Two cans of diet soda accompanied the late-afternoon snack. I hate diet soda; I read somewhere once that the chemicals made you fatter than sugar.

"This stuff's going to kill you," I warned when Mazi popped a tab and handed me a can.

"I know, but I'll go happy." She scooped up a cracker and cheese and dramatically devoured the snack, shaking her stylish bob with ecstasy. "Ummm, ummmm, *ummm.*"

Grinning, I reached for a cracker, too tired to chew cheese.

"You should have been with me today. We'd have had a ball together."

"Oh...you know me. I'm not all that interested in shopping, and besides, I can't afford it."

Her eyes softened. "I know. I wish I could help."

I shrugged. No one could help.

She dropped back onto the chair, now holding a fistful of crackers and cheese, and blessedly changed the subject. "I found this new makeup foundation. 'Sweet,' as Kris would say. One of the salesclerks offered to give me a free makeover and—voilà—chic, no?"

"Beautiful." Mazi was blessed with a flawless complexion. I admired the clerk's artistry. Her skin positively gleamed with a tan light. She was a true winter palette. Gorgeous brown eyes, brown hair, so dark it was nearly black. I couldn't help but wonder why her husband chose to spend so much time away from home. With no children, only the two of them, you would think they would be closer than ever. She had once confided that Warren could come home more often, but frequently chose not to. I knew my friend had to be puzzled and hurt by her husband's lack of interest, though she vowed she was very content.

"I have my shopping," she contended when I asked. "And now I have you." Her eyes would glow with real affection when she spoke about our friendship. I had the faint impression that true friends had eluded Mazi, that she'd shut herself away in a world of shopping and phone-sitting, waiting for her husband's infrequent calls and even more infrequent visits. If you ask me—which nobody had or likely would—Mazi was a neglected wife. Her husband was a cold fish, but one she openly adored.

Spousal neglect had not hindered her; she was a bubbly, overachieving fireball most days. It wasn't uncommon for me to get up in the middle of the night to check on Kris or Kelli and notice lights burning in Mazi's house. She had a passion for housecleaning into the wee hours of the morning, although I couldn't see how eighteen hundred square feet could possibly require so much maintenance. I sometimes didn't touch the house for a week, but then I would have to get a shovel and dig my way out. Mazi cleaned or baked or shopped incessantly. She made me tired to watch her. How she carried those extra pounds that she was always trying to lose was a real puzzle.

She bit into her third piece of cheese. "So I had the makeover. Of course, I loved the product so much the clerk sold me on the whole line of skin care. Then I made the mistake of looking at eye shadow, and then these new slanted brushes. From there I moved to lipstick, then blushers."

"Then perfume," I said, now familiar with Mazi's peccadilloes.

She nodded. "Fragrances."

"And the sum total of this afternoon's damages?"

"Four hundred and twenty-seven dollars." She shook her head. "Warren will shoot me. My makeup drawer looks like Imelda Marcos's shoe closet."

I laughed. "And this from a girl with a military background?"

"Daddy might be a retired admiral, and Mom a navy nurse, but I'm afraid the discipline they tried to instill in me didn't work. The word isn't in my vocabulary."

I knew she spoke the truth; I'd seen her makeup drawer. And the boxes of shampoos, conditioners, gels, spritzes and sprays she'd purchased, used once and discarded.

Then there were the lotions: creams, spray-ons, oils, moisturizers and hand-pump concoctions promising overnight skin renewal. Oh—and the bath washes. Tubes and tubes and bottles and bottles of shower gels and nonsoap soap. A shrink would say Mazi was searching for something, but in my amateur opinion, it wasn't makeup, shampoo, conditioner, lotion or shower gels. I believed Mazi's endless quest for something went much deeper.

She polished off the remainder of the cheese and crackers, and stretched her legs out before her, legs fashionably attired in black hose. "I wish I hadn't eaten that."

"Skip supper," I suggested. If it hadn't been for Kris and Kelli I could have lived on peanut butter sandwiches—and frequently did.

With a sack of peanut M&M's thrown in for additional protein.

Mazi's gaze traveled the homey sitting area. "Where are the kids?"

"One of Kelli's classmates is having a birthday skating party. Kris was invited to crash the activities." Yawning, I stretched, feeling the inevitable 6:00 p.m. slump. "Want to share a salad?"

"Nah—I'm full." Mazi sighed. "I have some cold meat loaf I'll eat later. Talk to the postman today?"

"You mean our postman who's writing the Great American Novel?" I looked up. "He'd already been here by the time I dropped Kris and Kelli by the rink and got home."

"Too bad." She grinned. "You notice the abs on that man?"

I was a little surprised by the observation. Mazi was straight as an arrow and never looked at other men. Oh, she'd been flattered at the singles mixer, but she'd made certain the men knew she was married.

Maybe she wasn't as crazy about Warren—oh, that was nuts!

So a woman window-shopped; that didn't mean she was buying, even from a woman who was a shopaholic. Still, the remark seemed odd coming from her. To hear Mazi tell it, the sun rose and set on Warren. Me, I wanted a man to come home to every night or at the very least, a man who came home occasionally.

Mazi didn't have either.

Days passed uneventfully. Gray Mitchell hadn't called again. I laughed—nonhumorously—and stacked a cereal bowl in the dishwasher. Did I dare wonder why? A harridan alone, raising two hooligans who acted as though they had come straight from the bowels of the Land of No Discipline...

I caught my bitter thoughts and realized that lately I'd become a shrew, thinking horrible thoughts about my most treasured blessings. An honest-to-goodness, full-fledged, card-carrying shrew. I wouldn't trade my children for five Gray Mitchells, as nice as he was, so why was I blaming my kids for my lack of appeal? Wait. Not a lack of appeal. I wasn't a troll. I was a young widow, semiattractive, good bone structure but fallen arches, doing the best I knew how to raise two young daughters.

And I resented my condition like anything.

I dumped soap in the dispenser cup and slammed the door. The gentle swish of water filling the appliance penetrated the silence. The girls were asleep; Mazi was home in bed nursing a head cold. That left a long, empty night stretching ahead of me.

Channel surfing is an art. Honestly. There should be some sort of contest where contestants vie for prizes on how long it takes to surf from, say, local stations to Fox news without a single glitch. A challenger should master navigating swiftly and uninterruptedly through fast-talking evangelists, steak knives, the weather channel, *Mayberry* reruns, *M*A*S*H* reruns, *Cheers* reruns, *Matlock* reruns—oops, another fast-talking fellow, talking heads, talking heads, talking heads.

I tossed the remote aside and stared at the illuminated screen. *God, it isn't fair. I'm thirty-two years old! Other thirty-two-year-old women are putting their children to bed, then settling down in their husband's arms for adult companionship. How long can one woman discuss the pros and cons of Barbie hairstyles?*

I tried to remember the times I'd actually had time or Neil had invited me to "settle down in his arms" after a long workday. Lately I'd had trouble recalling the past. Yesterday I'd had to think for a moment about the tiny mole on Neil's cheek. Was it on the right or left side?

I lay down, cradling the sofa pillow, holding on to something. Despite my good intentions, prayer didn't help; I felt my pleas went no higher than the ceiling fan.

Work didn't help. I'd worked so many hours lately Kelli had naively asked if I now lived at the salon. They missed their dad something fierce, but in their youthful way they had accepted that Neil was with God.

Why couldn't I be so generous?

I rolled off the sofa and picked up the two-day stack of mail. Bills. Utilities. House payment. My eyes wandered the cozy living room. I couldn't afford this house. I had lived here almost three months and already I knew that I didn't have the energy to maintain the lawn, and I sure didn't have money to hire a gardener. Kris could help when she was older, but the grass was going to be over the roofline in five years.

Buying the house had put a severe pinch in my income. I didn't dare use Neil's insurance; I'd safely tucked that away in an annuity for leaner days, though I couldn't imagine times any thinner than right now. Everything—utilities, food, property taxes, gasoline, everything—was higher in California. Even a simple movie and popcorn turned into a penny-pinching contest. One bag of corn, one drink and three straws; I wasn't used to this.

Even tithing had gone awry. Neil and I had always given God a tenth of our income; yesterday I'd found in my wallet three folded checks written to the church—on hold until I caught up on bills. IOUs to God. Of course, since I wasn't going to church all that much, I thought maybe it didn't matter, but then in my heart I knew this was just another check mark for indifference.

Well, fine, I thought, pitching the unopened mail back onto the desk. So my faith wasn't strong enough to believe in His provisions. Why should it be?

I was talking to God now, not me.

"You promised to meet my needs and You haven't." I was stunned when I realized I'd spoken the words out loud.

Hateful thoughts poured out of my mind. Unreasonable finger-pointing. Even as I made the silent accusations I knew—I *knew*—that if anyone had reneged on promises it was me. *Oh, God, if You'll only get me through Neil's death I'll never ask for another thing.*

Oh, God, if You won't make me fly again I'll never ask for another thing.

Oh, God, please keep me safe and I'll never ask You for another thing.

If I couldn't blame God, then I had to have somebody to blame, because none of this was my fault. I'd been a devoted wife, a doting mother, a reliable employee, an avid churchgoer and where had it gotten me?

Into a house I couldn't afford, alone, frightened half out of my wits, with a wallet full of IOUs to God.

That's where.

Early-morning sunlight streamed through the panes of La Chic. I opened this morning flashing a cheery smile at the first two clients of the day.

"Susan is running a few minutes late, Mrs. Watts. Would you like some coffee?"

"I'd love some, dear."

"You, too, Mrs. Stone?"

"Me, too, dear."

I brewed a pot, then poured coffee into two china cups—one black, one with sugar and cream—and carried them to the two ladies now happily chatting. Two women—with husbands and nothing more to do than keep a hair appointment.

It's not fair, God. Somehow I had to pull out of this pity party I'd fallen into. I'd thought I was doing better, but now I seemed to be slipping back into my old pattern of worrying and feeling sorry for myself.

"Here you go." I dispensed the cups, then went to my own station and flipped on the curling irons.

The phone rang. I took the handset out of my smock and said good-morning.

"I *quit.*"

I recognized Melody Turner's nasal twang moments before she slammed the receiver down in my ear.

She quit. Great. Simply great. That was the second stylist that I'd lost this week.

Punching the off button, I took the short but succinct notice to be final. Well, fine. Melody had been skating on thin ice for weeks. She was habitually late, and inexcusably rude to clients. Good riddance.

Smiling, I moved to the desk, and walked right out of my three-inch pointy-toed black mule, which turned my ankle. Pain shot up my right hip. The one day I'd decided to "fit in" with the other stylists and wear a shoe that was about as comfortable as an ice pick in my ear, I'd turned my ankle. Muttering under my breath, I quickly stepped back into the fashion nuisance, nodding politely to the two waiting women. I would switch Mel's clients to the new girl, due in any moment. I marked a distinct black *X* through Melody, and then carefully copied her day's appointments to Michelle's relatively empty column. Some clients would be upset when they heard that Melody had "unexpectedly" terminated her employment, but most of them would be thrilled that the minor inconvenience had not interfered with a scheduled cut or color.

Susan and two fellow stylists breezed into the salon through the back door. In moments the salon had taken on the normal sounds of everyday life. Dryers were humming, the smell of shampoo coming from the bowls, the scent of fresh coffee in the air.

The tightness in my neck and shoulders started to ease. My first client wasn't due until nine. I checked my watch and decided that I had time for a first cup of coffee. I was out of coffee at the house this morning, and anyway too hurried to make a pot if there had been some. Kris had misplaced her math book, and Kelli was cranky, complaining of a sore throat—her third in the past month. Both girls were struggling with their new routine. Where school had once been happily anticipated, they now dragged out the door as though facing a guillotine. Kris had managed to make some friends, but Kelli complained that nobody sat with her during lunch. Other than the birthday skating party, the girls had not penetrated a social circle. My heart broke, but I was too busy to grieve.

I was too busy to *live*, working overtime to pay for a house I now didn't want.

I poured coffee, glancing up to check the wall clock over the shampoo bowls—8:50. The new girl was due in at nine o'clock. I was aware Melody's first customer was sitting on the long white sofa, leafing through a *Vogue*, blissfully unaware of the crisis.

I carried my coffee back to my station.

Eight fifty-five. I was starting to get antsy. If this were my first day at the salon I would be here by now—early, even. I don't like to be rushed, so I would have arrived thirty minutes before my scheduled time. Set up my station. Caught my breath.

The clock hand ticked off another minute.

Relax, Kate. You were impressed by Michelle Tate. She seemed bright, energetic and dependable.

What if she didn't show? Melody had nine clients with appointments but no stylist! It wasn't possible to fit nine people into the other stylists' appointment books if Michelle didn't show. I reached for the coffee and took a fortifying swig.

The woman flipping through *Vogue* eyed her watch, then the wall clock.

I took another sip of coffee, pretending interest in the long row of gels, mousses and conditioners lining the back of my station.

The woman glanced at me, then back to the magazine.

Please, dear God. Don't do this to me.

Another five minutes crawled by. Then ten.

My client had arrived right on time, and I headed her straight for the shampoo bowl, smiling patiently at the orphaned customer—though she still was clueless.

"She'll be here any minute," I chirped.

Fuming on the inside, I wondered what kind of person took a job, then never showed up! I couldn't do that. Good ole dependable me would have been there regardless. Hell or high water. I'd have been *here*.

That's your problem, Kate. You're too dependable. Too responsible. You should go wild—do something totally absurd. Abandon your customer with a head full of lather and go shopping. Buy something thoroughly extravagant. Go have a picnic. Go back to Oklahoma. I was giddy with worry.

Overreacting, Kate. Calm down.

I glanced at the clock, frantically scrubbing my patron's head. Bubbles lathered. The woman shifted in the chair.

"Ouch."

"Sorry."

The hose slipped out of my hand and I lunged for it. It sent a geyser across the shampoo bowls. I wrestled the gyrating hose as if it were a python. My customer shot out of the chair like a wounded hen. She stood there watching me chasing the stupid hose around the chair bottom in my equally stupid mules, looking as if she was going to hit me. I finally regained enough sense to reach up and turn off the water.

Miraculously—I would *never* again accuse God of ignoring my pleas—the front door opened, and inside marched Michelle looking as confident as four aces. My knees buckled.

Hurriedly draping my furious client in towels, I excused myself, clopped to the front and took the young blonde aside. Then in my typical shrewish pitch—mind you, there wasn't a dry thread on me—I asked why in the *cat hair* she was almost fifteen minutes late!

The young girl's brow lifted with resentment. "It's only twelve minutes after nine."

I lowered my voice, trying to maintain a pleasant demeanor for the customers between clenched teeth. "You were due at nine o'clock."

Michelle straightened. "You said ten o'clock—'Be here at ten o'clock.' That's what you said. I like to come early when I start a new job...."

Her voice faded and I suddenly felt light-headed. I groped for a chair and sat down trying to reroute my thoughts. I remembered. I *had* told Michelle to come in at ten. I'd figured that Melody and Susan would be in early, and Michelle, since she would be building a customer base, could come in later.

I got up and went into the break room, leaving a confused newbie to cope with the stares.

You're losing it, Kate. I sank to the nearest chair wondering what Kris and Kelli would do when I was institutionalized.

I hated this change in my life, and more to the point, I was not coping. I was only fooling myself if I said that I was. I knew that I had to accept my new role in life, which right now seemed about as plausible as a pig on roller skates.

Chapter 15

The phone rang around six Saturday evening. Mazi's perky voice came over the line. "Let's howl tonight."

"After the day I've spent, howling is the last thing I planned to do. I'm going to soak in a hot tub."

"Ah, come on. There's this great chick flick on at the Palace. Only three-fifty a ticket because it's not a first-run kind of theater. Let's go."

"A movie? But the kids—"

"I've already arranged for Alissa to baby-sit. She's thrilled. She needs the—"

"Extra money," I finished.

We laughed.

"Okay, you're buying the popcorn."

"And you'll get the Milk Duds."

Alissa arrived shortly after dinner. The girls were almost ready for bed, so she had nothing to do but her homework and kid patrol.

"Make them go to bed early," I warned. Tomorrow I should get up and take them to church, but increasingly it was easier to sleep in.

At first the girls had protested; they liked church. But last Sunday, when I'd failed to set the alarm, they weren't upset. They had seemed content to play video games and read. That ought to tell me something. Back in Oklahoma I wouldn't have missed two Sundays in a row without someone holding me accountable, but here nobody knew me.

I gave the kitchen countertops a final wipe down and rinsed the dishcloth.

A movie.

I'd rather stay home.

Mazi showed up decked to the gills in a spiffy-looking new red pantsuit. I looked positively dull in my gray pants, black silk turtleneck and rose-patterned tapestry vest.

"Have you lost weight?" I asked.

She pivoted in front of me. "Five pounds. Does it show?"

"It shows. You look fabulous."

"That's me. Fabulous Mazi."

Kris and Kelli ran to hug her. Kelli gave her the once-over and I braced myself because I never knew what would come out of the child's mouth.

"You're wearing red. Are you someone's Valentine?"

I thought Mazi's smile dimmed a bit, but if so, she recovered. "How about letting me be your Valentine?" She parodied Elvis's "Let Me Be Your Teddy Bear," rolling her eyes and singing.

Kelli laughed and clapped. "Okay, you're my Valentine. Where's my candy?"

"Are there going to be men at the movie?" Kris interrupted, her expression anything but sunny.

"I would imagine," I said. "There usually are." I hadn't been to a movie since Neil died, but unless they'd passed some law, the theater wasn't divided by gender.

"Is tonight like a date?" My eldest daughter wasn't easily satisfied.

"No!" I said. I didn't know where she came up with those things.

"You gonna talk to men?" Kelli demanded.

"Not unless I have to." I was starting to feel like a teenager getting the parental third degree.

"We don't want you talking to men," Kelli said sternly.

"Yeah, Mom. We're a family and we don't need anyone else." Kris met my eyes suspiciously. "Kids at school say you'll be getting married again."

I glanced at Mazi and Alissa, not sure how to handle this. Mazi stepped in. "Tell you what—I'll keep an eye on your mom and if a man looks like he's getting too friendly, I'll scare him off, okay?"

"How?" Details were important to Kelli.

Mazi pretended to concoct a plan out of thin air.

"Well, I could spill a cup of soda on him."

"Or cut his tie in half," Kelli suggested.

"Tell him she yells when she's mad," Kris suggested.

"I don't *yell,* I speak loudly to get your attention," I rebuked, trying not to laugh.

"Tell him she has seven kids." Alissa joined the fun.

"And six dogs," Kelli contributed.

"Five cats!"

"Four fish." Mazi was laughing now.

"And a partridge in a pear tree," the five of us sang in unison.

"She snores." Kelli grinned, dancing just out of my reach.

Now, that stung. "I do *not* snore." This certainly had no relevance anyway. "I can stay home if you want."

"No, we're going to the movie and we're going to have fun if it kills us." Mazi caught my arm. "Be good, girls. We'll see you later."

She pushed me out the door and we walked to the car and got in. I turned the key, then snapped my seat belt shut. "What do you think? Were they serious about men?"

"They're still grieving, Kate. Give them time. They'll adjust. People do."

I supposed she was right, but how could I expect the girls to adjust when I wasn't doing all that well myself.

We eased our way through the crowded aisle, trying to avoid feet. Two seats were empty in the middle of the row. Coke ran down my right wrist. Someone had jostled me as I left the lobby. Settling down, I shoved the bag of corn at Mazi.

The movie had started. The plot involved a group of older women in England who had posed nude for a calendar in order to raise funds for cancer research. I was almost certain I wasn't going to like the story. Older women and nudity were not funny.

Mazi shoveled corn into her mouth, enthralled as the plot unfolded. Soon I was equally caught up and found myself truly enjoying the picture.

"Would you do that?" I asked when the women began to plot the calendar.

Mazi turned to give me a wide-eyed stare. "Me? With this body? I take a shower in my housecoat."

"You don't."

She laughed. "I should, purely for humanitarian reasons."

Once or twice I glanced over to see my friend wiping tears out of her eyes. The story was touching in places, funny in others; the kind of chick flick that makes close friendships even dearer.

"Warren would like this," Mazi mentioned a couple of times. "I need to bring him to see this."

I'd just like to *see* Warren. I was beginning to think the husband was a figment of Mazi's imagination. Oh, I'd caught glimpses of a man coming in and out of her house, but the guy was as elusive as an echo.

"Isn't this sad?" Mazi asked once, holding a tissue to her nose.

"Yeah, Maz. Just what I need. A good cry."

Mazi laughed and whispered, "I'm going to the rest room. Be right back."

"Don't talk to any men."

I laughed at my own wit as she walked up the aisle and promptly sucked a piece of popcorn down my windpipe. Where was Mazi when I really needed her? I was choking.

I flailed my hands and struggled for breath, feeling my face turning blue from lack of oxygen. I gasped for air like a beached fish.

The woman on my left must have realized I was about to pitch face-forward into the row in front of me, because she leaned over and whacked me across the back, and the lodged popcorn kernel shot across the row of seats with the aplomb of a runaway bullet, slicing between a white-haired couple seated in front of me.

The man turned halfway in his seat and stared in my direction.

Mazi returned, fumbling for her seat as she stared at the action on the screen. When she saw tears streaming down my cheeks she absently pressed a tissue into my hand. I wiped my eyes, no doubt smearing mascara until I resembled a raccoon on a crying jag, and blew my nose.

I don't think she ever knew what had happened.

"Great movie," she murmured, her eyes glued to the screen.

When we left the theater we were both bone-dry from weeping—me from choking—and laughing. On the ride home we discussed at length what we perceived the moral of the story to be, which was: what would you do to help eradicate cancer?

The answer was anything it took.

And to my immense relief, I had encountered only one man—a scruffy-looking teenager at the snack bar when I bought my Coke.

When we got home I helped Mazi across the hedge, catching her elbow when she tripped. "These high heels. I don't know why I wear them," she complained. "They're going to cause me to break my neck one day."

My sentiments exactly. I'd pitched the mules when I'd got home from work last week, vowing to go barefoot before I bought shoes like that again.

Mazi fumbled with the locked door, her hands unsteady. "Night, Kate. It's been fun."

"Hey—are you okay?" She'd been a little unsteady all evening.

"Fine, just a little tired. Talk to you in the morning."

I stared after her, puzzled. There'd been a frenetic touch to her laughter tonight. I'd noticed her placing her hand on her chest during parts of the movie as though she was having difficulty breathing, and while she always wore high heels, she hadn't ever complained about them before. I made a mental note to check on her in the morning. She was probably coming down with a virus, and being Mazi, she wouldn't complain.

I stepped back across the hedge and paid Alissa. After she left I checked on the girls. They were both sleeping soundly.

Later I lay in bed and stared at the thin shaft of streetlight coming through the blinds. I felt as if I should pray before going to sleep, but the longer I went without talking to Him, the easier it was to skip evening prayers.

I rolled to my side and closed my eyes, but instead of counting sheep, I thought about the movie and the extent one friend would go for another.

San Francisco had given me one priceless thing: Mazi.

If I could only hold on a little longer, I would adjust.

Patience.

I needed a boatload.

Tuesday afternoon I was sitting in the porch swing, wondering which of the many tasks waiting for me I should do first, when I saw Lee, the postman, coming up the walk. An alarm immediately sounded. I'd studiously avoided him since our previous conversation.

He climbed the porch steps and handed me a stack of bills. I didn't need to look; I knew they were bills.

"Hey, there. Getting some fresh air?"

"Got home early, which doesn't happen often, and I was sitting here enjoying the day."

He hoisted himself onto the porch railing. "I, on the other hand, am running late. What a coincidence. If you hadn't been early and I hadn't been late, we'd never have had a chance to visit."

I grinned. "Don't you have other customers waiting anxiously for your arrival?"

"Nope. You're the last house on my route. I'm done for the day." He paused, and then plunged deeper. "Would you like to go get something cold to drink?"

"Thanks, but the girls will be home in half an hour."

"Then could I bother you for a glass of water?"

I thought of the fresh pitcher of iced tea sitting on my kitchen counter. It never hurt to be nice; being nice didn't mean accepting a date with the man.

"I can do better than that. Stay where you are."

I returned in a moment with two frosty glasses of iced tea. Lee had moved to the porch swing. When I handed him a glass, he smiled. "Thanks."

He moved over to accommodate me. I sat down, easing to the right as far as possible, my daughter's admonition about speaking to men running through my mind. Apparently he sensed my uneasiness, because he kept to his side.

I set my glass aside and absently leafed through my mail. I was starting to feel overwhelmed by the avalanche of statements with a balance due.

I sighed and he glanced at me. "Problem?"

"Yeah. Lots of problems. All of them are costing money. Moving expenses, both girls need shoes and school clothes. The hot water heater quit. Thermocouple. That one word plus labor cost me a hundred dollars. This move has been a disaster."

Lee swallowed tea and crunched an ice cube. "Maybe it just seems that way. You've not been here long."

"Long enough to know I'm in over my head." I shook my head, knowing I shouldn't dump my problems in his lap, but frustration took over. Words spilled out. "Honestly, I think I made a mistake. I should never have uprooted the girls and left everything familiar because I trusted God to lead me in the right direction."

"Well, maybe it will eventually work out better than you think. You've been here how long—just a few months?"

I nodded.

"Give it time, Kate. I've been writing my novel for three years. You can't rush the good stuff."

"Right. Your novel about gophers." I had to tell Mazi about this.

He leaned toward me, his eyes holding mine. "I wish you'd let me read it to you some night."

Read it to me? Was this his idea of a date? Evidently it was. Talk about cheap. I didn't know many writers, but the few I had met seemed almost fanatical about "their novels." One of the women in my church back in Oklahoma talked about her characters as if they were real people. She was insulted if you didn't ask how they were doing.

Maybe you had to be a little quirky to be a writer. If so, Lee definitely fit the pattern. He swigged iced tea. "A lot of important writers have readers who read their books and make comments. You could be mine. I'd acknowledge your help and you'd see your name in print."

In a book about gophers? I could probably live without that. "I don't know, Lee. Between work and my children and taking care of a house, I don't have much free time."

"No room for a man in your life?"

"Not at this time." Not anytime as far as he was concerned.

He sighed. "I miss my wife at times like this. She could work and bring in the money and I could spend all my time on my novel. It's difficult to go to work at the post office when genius is burning."

"I'm sure it must be."

"Writing is lonely work, Kate. I sit in front of my computer with no one to talk to. No one to enjoy the beauty of the words I write. All I want is someone to share my life, ease the loneliness. Is that too much to ask?"

"Probably not. You need to pray about it." All he wanted was a roof over his head, clothes on his back, food in his belly and someone to provide it. I wasn't available. No wonder his wife preferred painting sunrises.

He started to say something, but I cut him off. "Here come the girls. It's been nice talking to you, Lee."

I set my glass on the porch railing and walked down the steps to meet my daughters. When I looked back, Lee had left.

"Was that the postman, Mommy?" Kelli asked.

"Yeah. We were visiting while he rested and drank a glass of tea."

"Do you like him?" Kris frowned.

I watched Lee's retreating back and felt utterly foolish. And I suppose I was. What a discussion.

"I like everyone, honey. Don't you have homework?"

Kelli nodded. "Can we get a cat?"

"Not right now. We have Sailor. He probably wouldn't be happy if you brought in a rival."

She thought about this. "I guess you're right. I can play with Mazi's cats."

We entered the house and I set out a snack of celery and peanut butter. "Chicken strips for supper tonight."

"And corn dogs?" Kris asked.

"Sure—why not?" I watched the girls as they ate. Were they happy here? I had never asked, because I was afraid to. Now I felt I had to know.

"Do you girls like living in California?"

Kris looked noncommittal. "It's all right. We're getting used to it."

"I like Mazi and the seals and the beach," Kelli said.

"And that's all?"

She thought for a minute. "Well, I like Chinatown."

"Do you have friends here?"

"We have Mazi and Alissa," Kris said.

"What about at school?"

"No one special." Kris finished the last of her milk. "If I get my homework done can I watch TV?"

"I guess so."

They left for their rooms and I started dinner. Almost automatically I reached for the telephone. "Hey, Mazi. You doing anything tonight?"

"Not a thing. Why?"

"How do you feel about chicken strips and corn dogs for dinner?"

She laughed. "I'll bring the salad. Okay?"

"Sure. We need something other than junk."

"One taco salad coming up."

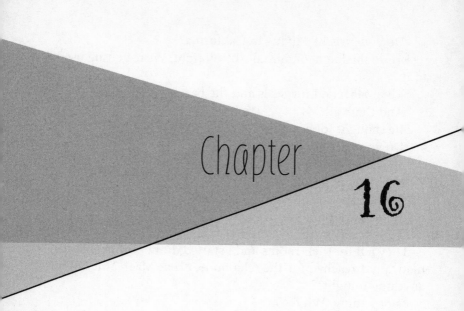

Chapter 16

"What a nightmare." Mazi slid closer to the wheel, trying to see through the sheet of heavy rain. The windshield wipers could barely keep up with the steady deluge.

I stared out the window at the passing motorists. Maybe it was true; laughing released endorphins and made you feel better. I was glad Mazi had insisted on going out for coffee this evening.

Mazi mumbled under her breath, intent on manipulating the crowded freeway. I lay back, rested my head against the car's leather interior and thought about the past week. There were still billboards advertising Valentine's Day, which had come and gone with an outbreak of sentimental gush. Roses or something equally thoughtful had decorated every stylist's station, expressions of love from husbands or significant others. With Mazi's help, Kris had purchased a single red rose at the supermarket, along with a sprig of baby's breath, and stuck the arrangement in a bud vase. She and Kelli had proudly handed it to me on my way out of the house on Valentine's Day.

"It's from me and Kelli. And Daddy," Kris had added.

At that moment I was too overcome to do anything other than pull her close and hug her.

I'd set the vase on my station and I thought it looked just as impressive as the other floral tributes. Certainly as much love had gone into the giving of the gift.

"I shouldn't have bought the house." The words slipped out of my mouth before I realized I had spoken out loud. Mazi glanced over, frowning. Not a word had been spoken about bills or mortgages tonight.

"You're really not happy here?"

Biting my lower lip, I shook my head, allowing my true feelings to surface, allowing myself to express without fear of censure all I kept deeply compressed in my heart.

"Oh, Kate." The car slowed. Mazi fumbled in her oversize bag for a clean tissue and pressed one into my hand.

I took it and blew my nose. "Watch the road," I cautioned. It was a terrible night for travel. Slick wet highways glistened like polished glass.

Mazi's tone gentled. "Why don't you like it here? It's San Francisco. Cable cars, delightful weather most of the time, so much to do and see."

I lifted my shoulders with apathy. "If you have someone to do and see it with."

Mazi fell silent and I knew I'd insensitively touched a raw nerve. Until I'd moved next door, Mazi had spent much of her time alone. She'd never admit that she hurt, but God had given me eyes to see and ears to hear. Sometimes, in order to make even the vaguest sense of what had happened, I pretended that God had a purpose in taking Neil, that He had sent me here to be with Mazi.

Maybe she needed me more than Neil needed me.

She had no real belief in a supreme being, but Neil had had

no trouble at all trusting his life to the Lord. In those flights of fantasy it was easier for me to accept Neil's absence; it gave his death meaning. But the reasoning never stayed with me for long. I still thought there was no viable reason for God to take Neil and leave me to raise two small daughters alone. Tears smarted when I felt Mazi's hand creep tentatively into mine.

"Well, no one has to tell me about lonely."

I gently squeezed her hand back. *Forgive me, God, for reminding her that this isn't a perfect world.*

Sometimes I would think that if I were only holy enough, prayed hard enough, all I'd have to do is put on my righteousness and God would protect me from all evil.

Faith didn't work that way.

"I should have stayed in Oklahoma," I admitted. "Kept the house, raised the children and begun a new phase of life."

"You did begin a new phase."

"No, I ran, Mazi. And I've been running ever since—at full speed, for the last few weeks. I'm only spinning my wheels. Leaving Oklahoma didn't lessen my hurt. It didn't bring Neil back. The only thing I've accomplished is to sink myself up to the eyeballs in debt."

Mazi wiped her nose with a tissue. The hypnotic *slap slap* of the wipers was sprinkled in the conversation.

"Are you considering moving back?"

Was that what I was doing? I never dared let myself think that far ahead. I was too scared. So far my rash decisions had proved disastrous. I missed teaching, missed demonstrating new products, doing an occasional platform demonstration. I missed the fresh young faces and the talented hands that I'd helped mold to be exceptional stylists. Flying had been the downside, but I had loved my work.

I was gradually getting the hang of managing the shop, but I'd never like it. I had a good crew now, well trained and working to my specifications. I was developing a good rapport with my customers. I'd learned to drive in San Francisco traffic. I knew I was making progress, but it seemed as if I'd get on top of one problem and another would crop up. Like the broken pipe in the bathroom. And it was amazing what plumbers cost in this town. I sighed. What was I, an Okie to the bone, doing here?

"Oh, Kate. It hurts me to see you so unhappy." Tears openly ran down Mazi's cheeks. "You'll go back, won't you? You'll go back, and I won't be able to stand it without you. I am so selfish. I want to keep you and the girls here, with me."

"I can't go back. There's no way out. I owe far more on the mortgage than I can ever hope to regain without making major repairs." Just this week I'd discovered that the house needed new heating and air-conditioning.

"Warren and I have savings...."

That was Mazi. Begging me not to go back but unselfishly offering me a way to go home. I reached over and touched her arm. "Don't even think about it. I could never repay you...and I wouldn't borrow anyway." Neither a borrower nor a lender be—that was Neil's mantra. But I was head over heels in debt to Mom and Dad for the down payment on the house.

"But if you make the repairs you can recoup your losses when you sell."

"Maybe, but who knows if I could sell for the price I would have to ask? The former owner practically gave me the house, and truthfully, the children are so confused right now I don't know how they'd take to another major upheaval in their lives?"

I knew both girls longed to go back to Oklahoma, back to friends and classmates and familiar surroundings, but going home was harder than it sounded.

"Oh, Kate. Mrs. Lewiston, the former owner, is a sly old fox. She didn't *give* you the house. She'd tried to pawn the thing off on some unsuspecting buyer for over a year." Mazi shook her head. "Nobody would pay her asking price. Then she tried the old 'I want the house to have the right family,' and she found two interested parties."

"Two?"

Why wasn't I surprised that I was the only gullible patsy?

Mazi shook her head. "The other person dropped out a couple of days before you hit town. He'd had a house inspector and—"

"They found the problems." Great, Kate. Another case of your impulsive nature resulting in calamity.

"Did Gray Mitchell know about this?"

"Any house that age will have problems."

Huh. And he'd seemed so nice. Another Kate boo-boo.

Mazi sniffed. "I feel guilty that I haven't been going to your salon. It's just that I've gone to my regular stylist for years, but I'll come to you if it would help. You know I can't bear the thought of losing you."

I smiled, turning to face her. "I understand. And I don't expect you to change. I have to stay, Mazi. I don't have a choice. But even if something amazing happened and I could go home, I would always keep in close touch. We could fly back and forth, visit each other. You wouldn't lose me. Maybe you could even talk Warren into moving there. He travels so much, and you have no close family here—what difference would it make if you lived in California or Oklahoma?"

"You hate flying!"

"For you I'd do it."

"Something amazing? Isn't that God's territory? I thought you were mad at Him."

"I am mad at Him, but I still believe He exists. He could work something—if He wanted to."

He just didn't want to in my case.

"Then why do you sound so hopeless? I don't necessarily buy this religion stuff, but it seems to me that the folks who do buy it enjoy a certain advantage. Have you completely lost faith?"

"Not completely. I rant and rave a lot—blame God for what's happened—but I know there's a higher power, and right now

I'm just peeved, I guess. Mad at God, mad at the world. Mad at Neil for leaving me."

"I don't think Neil had a choice."

Of course he didn't. And now neither did I. As Grandma used to say, *You made your bed—now you lie in it.*

Straight ahead I spotted a long stretch limousine sitting on the shoulder. A uniformed driver struggled to change a flat tire in the driving rain. I assumed we'd whip by, but Mazi immediately let up on the gas.

"Look at that poor guy. He needs help."

I reached for my cell phone to alert the highway patrol, but by now Mazi had pulled in back of the stalled vehicle. I turned to stare at her.

She shrugged. "Hey, my dad taught me to change a tire in five minutes flat. I can help."

"Are you *nuts!* Two women alone stopping to help a stranger? How do we know this isn't some elaborate setup to mug us?"

I didn't know much about California, but I'd heard enough to know you'd have to be out of your mind in any large city to stop in a situation like this one.

"We don't know. We just take our chances. If you're worried you can wait in the car."

If I was worried? I was in a perpetual state of anxiety. Didn't she know that!

Before I could argue, she sprang out of the car, popped an umbrella and waded through puddles to the driver now standing with hands on hips, staring at the flat tire.

"Deranged," I muttered under my breath. Mazi acted so weird sometimes. Wired. Irrational.

My hand closed over the heavy-duty flashlight she kept under the passenger seat for emergencies; I could turn the light into a lethal weapon if I needed to.

My daddy had taught me the good-ole-boy way of handling disputes.

Jerking the door open, I climbed out of the car, sucking in a breath when cold rain hit me in the face. I jumped several puddles on the way to the limousine, feeling my way down the side of the long sleek automobile. I couldn't cut, perm, or color enough hair in my lifetime to own this thing. Whatever star or celebrity lurked behind the dark tinted glass failed to show himself.

Drinking champagne, eating caviar while the peons wallow in mud, I thought.

Mazi was chattering a mile a minute to the bewildered driver. Poor guy—he looked as if he was in the middle of a nervous breakdown.

"I got a real problem," he said. "I gotta get these people to the airport, and considering the road conditions and the traffic, by the time I can call someone to change the tire and get them there, they'll miss their plane."

Mazi chewed on her lower lip. "I have the perfect solution. Kate, you take my car and drive them to the airport. In the meantime we'll get the tire changed and follow you."

I jerked her aside. "Are you out of your mind? You don't know these people. This could be a plot to kidnap us."

She shook her head. "Use your head, Kate. Why would anyone hire a stretch limousine and let the air out of the tire on the off chance a couple of women might stop in a driving rain?"

"There's something wrong with your logic," I groused. "I just haven't spotted it."

"You can think about it on the way to the airport." She strode back to the driver. "Tell your fare my friend will drive them to the airport. I'll help you fix the tire and then we'll follow them. Will that work?"

He looked relieved. "Oh, lady, you have no idea." He opened the door and peered inside. "Sir, I think we have the problem solved. Miss..." He looked at me.

"Mrs. Madison," I muttered, thinking this had to be the stupidest thing I'd ever done.

"Mrs. Madison will drive you to the airport." Mazi handed him her umbrella and he held it aloft.

A man—no one I recognized, which didn't mean much since I wasn't a celebrity hound—got out and bent to help a younger woman gloriously arrayed in furs and diamonds out of the car. I took a deep breath, allowing that Mazi had a point. No one was going to put on a show like this just to kidnap a couple of hapless females. I figured they were legitimate.

I hurried back to Mazi's car after arranging a meeting point and got in behind the steering wheel. The young woman got in the back and the man settled in the front passenger seat. The driver placed their luggage in the trunk. I started the car and drove off, leaving Mazi, who by now had stripped out of her coat. In her chic black pantsuit she looked drenched. I saw her grab a lug wrench and set to work.

At first I concentrated on driving. I wasn't used to Mazi's car, and the road conditions and traffic claimed all my attention. Finally I relaxed and glanced at my front-seat passenger.

He grinned. "You're doing fine. We're going to make it."

"I know how long it takes to get through security nowadays."

"It does, but I'm sure it will be all right. We do appreciate you doing this for us."

The woman leaned forward. "I hope we're not delaying you too much."

"No. My baby-sitter will stay as long as I need her. I'll call from the airport and let her know where I am."

"You have children?" the man asked.

"Two daughters, seven and five. We haven't lived in California all that long and I haven't done much driving at night, particularly in the rain."

"You moved here from where?" the man asked.

"Oklahoma. My husband was a firefighter and..." I stopped, unable to go on.

"Was?" the young woman asked softly.

"He died while fighting a fire."

"And you're raising them alone."

I sensed the man's appraising glance, but I didn't look in his direction.

"Yes. It's all mine. Family, home, two mortgages." I tried to laugh and failed. "The all-American dream."

We reached the airport and I stopped in front of the terminal. "I'll let you out here and then go park to wait for your car and my friend."

The man didn't move to open the door. "What can I do to repay you for your kindness?"

I smiled, recalling Neil's classic reply when he'd helped someone in trouble. "Nothing. Just return the favor to someone else."

"No. Really." The stranger insisted. "Allow me to express my gratitude."

"Okay," I conceded. "You can send my friend a bouquet of flowers." I rummaged in my purse, took out a business card and handed it to him. "I'll see that she gets them."

The good Lord knew Mazi didn't get enough attention. Fresh flowers would make her day, and after all, it had been her idea to help them.

I waited until he had helped the woman out and then drove off to find a parking place. Of course I had to park a full city block away and got even wetter walking back.

Once I got inside I looked for my passengers, but they were nowhere in sight. I didn't know what gate they were boarding from and I didn't want to squish my way through the airport in my rain-soaked shoes. Besides, I needed to hang around the entry waiting for Mazi.

It was a good twenty minutes before they showed up, and I was so relieved to see her safe and unharmed that I grabbed her for a hug. She grinned. "Did you make it in time?"

"I guess so. I haven't seen them since I let them out in front."

The driver sighed, his expression relieved. "I don't know what I'd have done if you hadn't come along."

Mazi suddenly stopped in her tracks. "Say, your boss looks like that dot-com guy. Anyone ever mentioned the uncanny resemblance?"

The driver covered a smile with his hand. "I believe that he is aware of the similarity."

"Yeah, amazing similarity, but Gates lives—ah, whatever. I don't know where he lives." Mazi led the way to the double doors. When she shoved them open she let out a howl of anguish.

"What's wrong!" the driver and I said in unison.

"My nail! I broke it!"

"Broke it?" We both stepped forward to confirm the crisis. One jagged acrylic hunk dangled from her third finger.

"Ohhhh, no! My nail tech is on vacation! What will I do?"

I tried to calm her, the driver tried to calm her, but this was apparently a crisis of monumental proportions. Mazi had broken a fake nail.

"No problem. You need to get in out of the rain. You're going to catch cold." I glanced at Mazi, who was dramatically wringing the injured finger and muttering under her breath. "What will I do? What will I do? Pilar is on vacation!"

"Crybaby," I teased. "Stop by the salon in the morning and I'll have one of our nail techs repair the nail for you."

I draped my arm around her shoulders and we sidestepped puddles on our way to the car. "You know, the proverbial Good Samaritan. Yada yada yada."

"Yeah, yada yada yada—you're sure? No charge?"

I laughed. "Of course."

If only my problems could be solved so quickly and effortlessly.

Later I checked on the girls to make sure they were properly tucked into bed, and then headed straight for the shower. I stood under the hot spray and let the water chase away the chill. I still couldn't believe that two lone women had stopped and changed a flat tire on the freeway for a set of strangers, but then with Mazi, anything was possible.

I dried off and soothed lotion over my body, then slipped into a warm robe. Outside cold rain pelted the street.

A few minutes later I paused in my daughter's doorway, a cup of steaming chocolate in my hand, and for the first time in months realized that I was blessed. Before me lay one of my two angels—perfect gifts that God had entrusted to my care.

I recalled the morning Kris was born: it had stormed all night. I remember watching jagged lightning fork outside my window, hearing thunderous claps that shook the hospital foundation. Toward dawn I'd delivered Kris—six pounds, five ounces, with a thatch of golden hair. Neil had been enthralled. He'd stood at the nursery window pecking on the glass, beaming from head to foot. He'd handed out candy cigars to every man, woman and child on the floor.

Kelli had come into the world around midnight on a cold, snowy March evening. We'd slipped and slid all the way to the hospital. I almost fell getting out of the truck, but an orderly in nothing but short sleeves had been there to catch me, which was no small feat considering that I'd gained forty pounds during pregnancy. I'd barely reached the delivery room when Kelli made her appearance.

Neil had shown up a few minutes later, prepared to spend hours helping me breathe. Inhale. Exhale. Rubbing my back. Offering words of encouragement. We'd practiced the procedure over and over again; we were prepared for natural birth. But by the time my devoted spouse parked the truck and took the elevator up five floors, I was holding our seven-pound-three-ounce daughter in my arms. If I lived to be a hundred years old I would never forget the look on my husband's face. He was floored. Speechless for the first time in his life.

Later he confessed he'd had no idea babies came so fast, and I told him that if men shared the responsibility of birthing children there'd be only two in every family. Kelli's labor was quick, but certainly not a picnic.

I caught back a laugh, remembering the good times, remembering Neil's utter devotion to his family. Knowing how disappointed he would be in me right now.

Life is what you make it, Kate.

How many times had he reminded me?

If you're counting on circumstances to make you happy you'll never reach your goal.

I tiptoed into the room and set my mug of chocolate down on the bedside table, then tucked one of Kelli's blankets closer. She stirred, opened one eye and smiled up at me. "Hi, Mommy."

"Hi, darling."

"Did you and Mazi have a good time at the coffee shop?"

"We had a wonderful time. Thank you."

"Did you bring me anything?"

"A blueberry muffin. You can't eat it until morning."

"Okay." She dropped back to sleep instantly. Yes. I was richly blessed. Two very important parts of Neil had been spared and left for me to love and nurture. As long as I had my daughters, I would have Neil. If that wasn't blessed, then I didn't know the meaning of the word.

Right now, gazing down on my sleeping daughter, I saw with complete clarity what I had been so blind to for months. I could go on without Neil. I didn't want to; never in my wildest imaginings had I considered raising Kelli and Kris alone, but I could.

And I would.

With God's help.

"Kelli has never 'manhandled' another person in her life."

I sat across the desk from Principal Meadows, stunned. When the school had called this morning to tell me that Kelli had been involved in a classroom altercation I hadn't believed the person on the other end of the line. I thought it was a prank call until the person insisted that I come to school. Immediately.

Kelli now sat beside me, sullen.

"Mrs. Madison." The attractive redhead struggled to remain civil. "When Janine refused to give up the red magic marker, Kelli wrestled her to the ground and took the pen away from her."

"She'd had it long enough," Kelli stated. "I asked her first, *and then* I took it."

I turned in my chair to gape at my daughter. I half expected to see her head pivot and hear vile words pouring out of her mouth. My daughter did not "wrestle" other children to the ground!

Mrs. Meadows leaned forward, features softening. "I understand there have been numerous unsettling changes recently in Kelli's life, but we simply cannot permit ruffians to rule the classroom."

"My daughter is not a ruffian."

Our eyes rotated to the victim, Janine, a five-year-old preschooler. The child had vivid slashes of red marker running down both cheeks. The poor kid looked a mess. It was hard to argue an adequate defense with that kind of prosecutorial proof.

I mentally groaned. "I am so sorry, Mrs. Meadows. Kelli and I will have a long talk, but I can assure you she will not repeat her actions."

Kelli drew her knees up under her dress and stuck her tongue out at Janine.

When I left the school with Kelli in tow, I was mad as hops. This little incident had not only caused me to cancel a client, but now I had to go back to the salon and make up for lost hours. If I'd been in Oklahoma—

I caught my thoughts. I wasn't in Oklahoma. I was here. In San Francisco.

And when I got home tonight I was going to bypass "time out" and deliver a good old-fashioned tongue-lashing in a not-so-thoughtful tone.

Chapter 17

I hung up the phone and sat staring at the wall. Neil's parents were coming.

On Tuesday.

Coming here.

I pictured Madge—tall, blond, with an overbite and an attitude—and Harry, short, solid, stoic. He reminded me of Neil in an odd way. Not in looks or personality, but occasional flashes of Neil's common sense and compassion.

I think Neil was what Harry would have been like without Madge.

Actually, I loved them both. It was just that for as long as I could remember, my mother-in-law had strong convictions about everything; she was never wrong.

Put Madge and my mother in the same room and you would have a clash of icy wills that would make World War III look like a kindergarten tiff. Neil had called their verbal tussles "the Battle of the Broads."

That pretty well covered it.

Anyway, Madge and Harry were coming for a week...and I didn't want them. Not now. Not when I was still having trouble accepting my new role.

Kelli came in, trailed by Sailor. "Who called?"

"Maws Madison."

"Maws! Did she want to talk to me?"

"She'll talk your head off in a few days. They're coming to visit."

"Awesome!" Kelli turned and scampered out of the room. "Hey, Kris! Maws and Paws are coming!"

Kris yelled back, "Really? When?"

"Tuesday!" I joined the shouting match.

"Tuesday, Tuesday," Kelli chanted. "Maws and Paws are coming on Tuesday!"

So okay, for the girls' sake I could act excited.

I decided to move Kelli into Kris's room, mainly because Kris had turned territorial and refused to give up her space. For once, Kelli accepted the situation without trying to negotiate. I bought enough groceries to feed half an army and stared in dismay at the total on the register receipt. I couldn't afford company, but then I couldn't very well feed Maws and Paws chicken strips and corn dogs either.

On Tuesday I took off work early and drove to the airport. The plane was thirty minutes late. The elder Madisons came through the gate looking like wrung-out chickens. I hugged them generously and decided it really was good to see them. Like having a little part of Neil back.

"Did you have a good flight?"

Harry opened his mouth and Madge spoke for him. They'd been together for so long they'd perfected the ventriloquist act.

"*Terrible.*" Madge twitched the strap of her handbag firmly over her shoulder. "Airport security is so tight it took hours to board the plane."

"Thirty minutes," Harry said.

"The woman in front of us talked so much Harry could barely hear what I was saying."

Harry smiled like a Cheshire cat.

"The pretzels were stale."

"About what we're used to."

Madge shifted her attention to him and I intervened. "Let me take your carry-on bag, and then we'll collect your luggage."

The interruption had thrown Madge off course. She stopped and stared at me. "Kate! You look terrible. Dark circles under your eyes... I thought you said you were coping well!"

Well, talk about a conversation stopper. I had thought I'd looked fairly decent today, if not exactly fetching, in my loose beige slacks and top and tapestry vest. Evidently I needed a brighter light over my mirror.

I smiled. "We'll play catch-up later. Luggage first." Which only postponed the inevitable, but I knew that before my in-laws left I'd have to discuss my feelings and what I planned to do in the future.

As if I knew.

We spent another fifteen minutes collecting bags, then we were ready to go.

As we exited the busy terminal, Madge blinked against the bright California sunshine. "It's so *warm*."

Compared to Vermont in February, I supposed it was.

They began to peel out of their coats and heavy sweaters before getting into the car. Apparently the traffic intimidated them, because Madge didn't speak again until we cleared the terminal traffic.

"Is California always this frantic?"

"Oh, no. Some days it's worse."

"Oh, my." She didn't say much more until we stopped in my driveway, and then she looked at the house, the surrounding houses and the quiet street. "Well, this is a *nice* neighborhood."

"We like it. Here, let me help you with that carry-on." I followed as Harry packed the luggage into the house.

Madge picked a dead leaf off the ivy before she stepped up on the porch. "You shouldn't let that climb on the walls, Kate. Ivy puts out roots that grow into your house and destroy the wood."

She made it sound as if the entire structure was held together by a fragile framework of ivy roots and leaves.

"I'll keep that in mind." I liked the ivy, and it wasn't growing on the house anyway. It had been trained to grow on a lattice.

We stepped inside the foyer. First order of business—a good cry. I hadn't seen Madge and Harry since the funeral, and they were still as much in the grieving process as the girls and I. One glance at Neil's picture and we all dissolved in tears.

I dried my eyes, ushered them to Kelli's room, where they were to sleep, and headed for the kitchen. I opened the refrigerator and started lunch—grilled chicken, salad and fresh fruit.

During lunch, Harry openly appreciated my culinary skills. "Good chicken, Kate. Always knew you could cook."

Madge speared a hunk of lettuce and carefully inspected it. "Did you wash this?"

"Yes, and hung it up to dry."

She glanced at me, then burst out laughing. "You're quicker with a comeback than you used to be."

I grinned. "Your son taught me all I know."

A little before four, the girls came home from school. I watched their spindly sprint to hug their grandparents, heard their gleeful shouts of "Maws, Paws," and I knew the Madisons' visit was needed. God had let me coast on my laurels long enough. With Neil's parents around, I'd have to go to church or come up with a very good reason not to. Madge wouldn't let me shirk Sunday-morning worship. She attended church faithfully, and if you were part of the Madison family, you did, too. And if she sometimes tried to order God around the way she did Harry, well, it was only habit and I was sure He could cope. Harry did.

Maws and Paws had come bearing gifts for the girls. New blouses and books. Kelli and Kris were as excited as on Christmas morning. After dinner we sat in the living room and talked until bedtime. Madge had insisted on washing dishes, and compared my brand of dishwashing liquid with hers. Mine didn't measure up.

Harry decided to take a walk, but she vetoed that. "You don't know what kind of criminal lurks out there."

"He'd be safe here," I said. "It's a protected neighborhood."

Madge shot me a disapproving glance. "I read the papers. I prefer not to have my husband gunned down in a drive-by shooting or kidnapped for ransom."

Since no one in our family had been listed in the Forbes 500 in my lifetime, I figured we were safe on the ransom part.

Kelli's face paled. "There are kidnappers out there?"

"No, of course not," I said, but Madge interrupted me.

"I hope you're not letting the girls run loose."

"I don't keep them penned up like horses. They live here. They have to leave the house once in a while."

Harry took off his hat and turned on the television. "Just thought I'd get some exercise. Try to keep in shape."

Since he was built sort of low down and high around, as the saying goes, he'd have to *get* in shape first.

Sailor ran through the living room and bounded into Kelli's lap.

Madge frowned. "That dog should be kept outside. I never allowed Neil to keep a dog in the house."

Kelli's lower lip jutted. Badmouth Sailor, badmouth his master. Madge should know that by now. "Sailor lives here."

Madge lifted disapproving eyes. "Kate, that child is more like your mother every day."

"But I *like* Sailor," Kelli said.

I stepped in, figuring I'd better head this off before fur flew. The conversation turned to Poor Kate. Apparently great thought and planning had been given to my circumstances and it had been decided, unbeknownst to me, that the girls and I would move to Vermont and draw sap off trees.

That was where I got off the train. That had been the plan when Neil was alive, but not now. I had no idea what my future held, but I didn't think it held maple syrup.

"Are we *really* moving to Vermont with Maws and Paws?" Kelli gave me a questioning look.

I dodged the question. "Tomorrow is a school day, remember? Don't you have homework?"

"No."

"Then go take a bath."

She glowered at me, and I realized Madge had a point; she did have a few of my mother's facial expressions.

"All right, but I don't want to."

Ah. The last word, and it had been hers.

"Madge. Harry. The girls and I really don't know what our future holds. We're waiting to see."

Kris curled up on the floor, with Sailor lying beside her. Madge looked forbidding, but apparently she knew when to let the matter drop. She changed the subject and we spent the rest of the evening talking about Neil and the past, which just made me more homesick for Oklahoma.

The following week I let the kids skip school one day, and we took Madge and Harry to Cliff House and to see the seals at Pier 39. Harry was as impressed with the Camera Obscura as Kris had been. We didn't see the green flash, but he had a wonderful time anyway. Madge loved the restaurants and shops and I enjoyed the day with family.

On Thursday, feeling I had neglected Mazi, I invited her to dinner. She came in looking tentative, but after a few minutes she warmed to Harry. She had a tendency to walk carefully around Madge with an expression on her face that reminded me of Sailor, who had the same reaction to my mother-in-law.

After dinner we sat in the living room having coffee, and Madge grilled her. There wasn't any other word for it. I tried to head her off, but she was like a bulldog with a bone. Mazi left early.

The door had barely closed behind her when Madge announced, "That woman has a drinking problem."

I erupted. "What a terrible thing to say! What would make you say something like that?"

Madge held her ground. "Several reasons. First, no one can be that hyper naturally. She'd bolstered herself with liquid courage."

"Nonsense. She was nervous. Usually she's quieter." Who wouldn't be jittery with Madge's third degree?

"She's twitchy. Her hands were never still."

"Nerves," I repeated. "Just nerves."

"Well, she acted tipsy. A couple of times she had to grab hold of something to keep from falling."

I faced her, hands on hips. "Anything else?"

"Yes, there's something else. Her husband's never home. She's lonely. She doesn't have many friends. She's too dependent on you. She's worried about something. It all adds up to an insecure woman who finds strength in the bottle." Madge tapped one well-manicured, long, bright red fingernail on the chair arm. "It's obvious."

Harry folded the paper he'd been reading. "Give up, Kate. If Madge says she's a drunk, she's a drunk."

"Then why haven't I seen it?"

Madge shrugged. "Because you don't want to see and you don't listen."

I almost choked. Don't listen? To Mazi? My dearest friend in the world right now? I knew everything about her. "I do listen. I just don't pry or jump to conclusions."

Madge ignored the statement. "That woman is not a good influence on my granddaughters."

That was rich. I wondered if I was a good influence. Sometimes I thought Mazi was the one constant in Kris's and Kelli's chaotic lives.

The girls, who had been silent, leaped to their friend's defense. "We love Mazi," Kris declared.

"She is so a good 'fluence." Kelli glared at her grandmother. "You take that back."

Maws and granddaughter stared at each other in a standoff reminding me of a couple of gunfighters at the O.K. Corral. To my surprise, Madge blinked first. She glanced at Harry, who was ignoring all of us and was now engrossed in a football game.

Kris's expression was as dark as Kelli's. Madge pursed her lips. "Well, obviously my opinion means nothing."

"Of course it does." I took a breath and tried to calm down. "We just know Mazi better than you do." Maybe Mazi didn't present the best first impression, but nothing short of personal observation would ever make me believe that she was a closet drinker.

"Perhaps you know her too well to see what's right under your nose. You mark my words, that woman has a problem and I don't like her having so much influence over my granddaughters."

Harry snapped off the TV. "Bedtime."

Having Madge and Harry in the house ratcheted up the tension several notches. I almost hated to go home. I'd arranged to take a few hours off each day, but spending too much time in my mother-in-law's vicinity was about to be harmful to her health. So I'd decided to go back to my normal schedule.

The girls missed Mazi, who discreetly stayed clear of the house and my company. I didn't know if she was being polite or if she was just plain scared of Madge. I was starting to realize how much I depended on her to lift me out of my emotional slumps. I missed our talks.

Friday night I took the long way home from work and found myself parked in the church lot. The building was dimly lit with the wall sconces. I wondered if they left them on all night. The soft golden light spilled out as if welcoming the weary wanderer. The church itself resembled a Thomas Kinkade painting.

The haven beckoned me in a way I didn't understand.

I sat there looking at the white floodlit steeple reaching up to the star-spangled velvet of the sky. Finally I got out of my car and approached the front door, expecting it to be locked. To my surprise, the door swung open on silent hinges. I stopped inside the warm foyer, listening. A murmur of voices rose and fell from the lower level, so I knew I wasn't alone.

I sat down in a back pew and let the calming silence embrace me. The wooden cross over the baptistery, the electric candles in the wall sconces, even the five-foot palm tree by the side window all contributed to the feeling of a place set aside. I sat with my head bowed and my hands clasped. Hot tears rained down my cheeks.

I didn't speak the words out loud, afraid of being overheard, but I needed answers. My life had spun out of control and I needed to know why.

What did I ever do, God, to make You so angry? Why did You tear up my life this way?

I waited, but no answer came. Silently I raged, *Listen to me. Don't turn away—not now. I want to understand. I need to know.*

Maybe I was approaching this in the wrong manner. I remembered Job demanding answers and God replying, "Where were you when I laid the foundation of the earth?"

Good question.

Okay, I'm sorry. Let's start over. I'm not demanding answers, but I would like to know.

Nothing.

I knew my Bible. There had been a time when I read it every night. So I knew that God hadn't abandoned me. He'd promised to be there always, and deep down, past the hurt, I knew He kept His promises. I had walked away. Still, a deep gulch separated us from the intimate relationship I'd once known, and I didn't know where to find the bridge. I was wandering in the darkness, too lost to see the light.

I knew my excess baggage. I was angry at God, angry over Neil's death. But closer to home, I was angry at Madge. How dare she criticize Mazi, calling her a drunk? Mazi had been the one person to see me through endless dark days. How could I take Madge's false accusations seriously?

When I finally left the pew, I felt no better than when I'd arrived, but I figured it wouldn't be long until the group in the basement broke up and left. Having distanced myself from the church lately, I didn't want to be discovered sitting in the back of the building crying.

My life was a mess and I couldn't see any way to fix it. My problems had turned into a bottomless pit with no way out. I had just been fooling myself when I thought I was learning to cope. Madge had seen through my feeble facade and zeroed in on the real problem. I was not capable of making the right decisions for my daughters' welfare. What I saw as progress she made me see was just treading water. Maybe I should move the girls to Vermont, but what had been something to look forward to with Neil now sounded like a prison sentence. I started the car and drove home, dreading having to face Madge in this mood.

Saturday we took Madge and Harry to Chinatown. They were fascinated, of course. Who wouldn't be? They bought gifts for the girls and Kris talked them into buying kites, wildly colored, fanciful shapes that would look great soaring against a blue sky.

Harry bought them each a doll—round-faced cherubs with straight black hair and elaborate silk costumes. Harry loved the streetlights, but Madge thought they would be hard to clean.

As if she might be called on to bring the Windex and paper towels the next time she visited.

Why is it that some people always look for the fly in the custard, and if it's not there, they'll catch one and install it. Madge always managed to find something to fuss over even if she had to create it. The trait made me mad. There was enough turmoil in the world to go around; nobody had to look for it.

Kelli told her about the Chinese New Year parade. She made it sound like something extremely exotic, which it probably was, but Madge wasn't buying it.

"Firecrackers? Wasn't that dangerous?"

Since her remark was addressed to me, I immediately turned defensive. Never mind I had felt the same way—she was questioning my care of the girls.

"We didn't go. Maybe next year."

"Just the same, what if someone throws one into the crowd?"

"We'll worry about that when it happens." I was ashamed of the shortness of my answer, but she was even more prone to worry than I was. The girls had begun outgrowing the fears I had instilled in them and I was trying hard not to inflict them with my new worries, but Madge was turning them into a quivering mass of nerves.

Kelli looked anxious. "Is Chinatown dangerous?"

I resisted the impulse to tell her any place was dangerous given the proper circumstances. She needed reassuring. I shook my head. "Chinatown's all right. We don't have to worry."

She relaxed. "Okay." I noticed she held tightly to Harry's hand the rest of the way.

Kris was quiet, clutching the bag that held the kites. I smiled at her and she gave me a half smile. I sighed. Think Tuesday, Kate. The day the in-laws were slated to go home.

Madge bought souvenirs for her friends, and Harry found a wooden back-scratcher he had to have. I tried it and liked it so much I bought one for myself and a second for Mazi.

Harry nodded. "I like Chinatown. Something different. I get tired of maple syrup all the time."

Madge rolled her eyes, but she didn't say anything. I was on his side.

"I know what you mean, Harry. We all need a new experience once in a while."

"Keeps a body from becoming bilious," he agreed.

Well, I might not have put it exactly that way, but I knew what he meant. We stopped for pizza on the way home, and for once Madge didn't find anything to complain about. Taking the good with the bad; it had been a passable day.

Monday noon a thick, gray, soupy fog rolled in, turning San Francisco into a twilight zone. Familiar landmarks and street signs vanished. I got lost twice trying to get home. Streetlights barely penetrated the gloom.

The airport was socked in.

No flights out, no idea when the fog would clear. I kept the girls home from school Tuesday. Since I had already decided to take Tuesday off so I could deliver Madge and Harry to the airport, and since all of our clients canceled because of the weather, I stayed home.

Actually it would have been better if I'd gone to work, even if there was a fairly good chance I might have driven off a pier into the ocean. Madge, for some unfathomable reason, decided to clean out the freezer.

If she had asked, I would have admitted things probably needed rearranging, but not today. We were all on edge from the fog and the canceled departure date.

Mounds of frozen peas and corn littered the kitchen floor. The sink overflowed with cartons of melting ice cream and popsicles. One good thing—she had unearthed a forgotten container of lasagna, which I slid into the oven for lunch.

"Madge, I appreciate all the work you're doing," I said. "But really, it's so unnecessary."

"Don't say another word, Kate. I'd never forgive myself if I hadn't done what I could to help you get this disaster straightened out."

Disaster?

She placed her hand on my arm, staring deep into my eyes. "Trust me, Kate. I only want to help."

"How come you never clean our freezer?" Harry asked.

Madge sent him a steely look. "I do clean our freezer."

He turned surly. I figured the fog was getting to him, too. "We've had that freezer since Neil was little, and it has so much ice inside you could hold the Iditarod dogsled race in there if you had room."

The doorbell rang and I gratefully left to answer it. This day was rapidly going downhill, dragging me with it. I opened the door to find an enormous bouquet of flowers. All I could see of the deliveryman was a pair of legs extending below the mass of blossoms.

"Kate Madison?" a disembodied voice asked.

"Yes, that's me."

"Flowers for you."

I helped him place the arrangement on a table and he left, looking relieved to be rid of the enormous weight. I stepped back to examine the bouquet, the heavenly scent penetrating the room. Who on earth would send me flowers? A card peeked from between delicate yellow roses and bird-of-paradise blooms. I carefully opened the envelope and read the message.

"The flowers are for your friend. I hope you enjoy your home here in our lovely city. Thank you again for your act of kindness."

Attached to the note was a simple letter from my mortgage company. It said "The outstanding loan on your home has been reduced by $110,000.00. Official notice of this arrange-ment has been sent to you via the U.S. Postal Service. Con-gratulations."

It was signed by the president of the company.

My heart stopped. I actually felt it. It stopped. Although fog still blanketed my windows, sunshine burst out in my heart. I read the message again, hardly daring to believe.

That amounted to half the mortgage.

No name on the note, but I knew who the flowers were from. The stranger in the long black limousine.

My life had been turned upside down for the second time in five months.

Chapter 18

Odd how priorities change.

Once I would have immediately run to Mom to share my still-unbelievable good fortune. Now all I could think about was Mazi; I wanted to tell Mazi about the incredible news.

Slipping into a light jacket, I paused at the back door and listened. The television was blaring. That meant Harry had persuaded the girls to switch to *Judge Judy*. Ordinarily I would storm the compound and demand more suitable children's programming, but not this afternoon. This afternoon I was so full of sheer joy that nothing could spoil my mood. Not even *Judge Judy*.

Hefting the tall bouquet, I left the house, pulling the back door closed behind me with my right foot. Hundreds of thoughts sifted through my mind as I carried the monstrous floral offering down the walk and stepped over the low box elder hedge. For so long I had been blind to everything God *had* been doing in my life. When I couldn't fly, He had provided a different venue. True, California had yet to feel like home, but He'd given me a house that I adored though I couldn't afford. It was my lack of faith that kept me in a perpetual financial mess. So far I'd met my mortgage payments and utility bills and still fed my children.

And now this had happened. I'd performed a simple act of kindness and in return God had sent a Good Samaritan to pay down my mortgage. This happened only in books and movies. Not real life.

I stopped long enough to pinch myself.

Ouch!

I wasn't dreaming. Elation bubbled over. I was wide-awake!

"Mazi!" I balanced the vase on my knee, turned the back doorknob and let myself into the house. Weeks ago we'd dispensed with formality. Now we both came and went in each other's homes when we liked. It wasn't unusual for me to come home from work and find a complete meal in my refrigerator, compliments of "Chef Mazi."

"Mazi!" I called. "You'll never guess what just happened!" I rid myself of the bouquet, setting the heavy vase on the kitchen table before I walked through the silent house, flipping on lights. Gray light filtered through the slanted blinds.

"Hey, Maz!"

Don't tell me she's off on a shopping trip, I thought. Not now—not today when I needed so desperately to sort through my revelations and share my incredible news.

I cleared the formal dining area, where a long walnut table and six sage-green upholstered chairs sat. The window treatments were of the same sage hue, elegantly framed by white crown molding. A large cabinet holding Mazi's china collection sat against the north wall.

I switched on a living-room lamp and paused, allowing time for my eyes to adjust. Where— My breath caught when I saw my friend lying on the sofa, wrapped in a brown throw. I immediately lowered my voice. "Hey, Maz, are you sick?"

Mazi wasn't one to nap, especially this hour of the day. In the time that I'd known her, I'd never seen her take an afternoon nap. She slept late, mostly because she didn't shut down until the wee hours of the morning.

When the figure on the sofa didn't stir, I thought about quietly backing out of the room and phoning later. It was the only courteous thing to do.

But my news was too good to keep.

I crept closer. "Hey, sleepyhead. Wake up. Have I got news for you. Smell that heavenly aroma? There's a bouquet of flowers on the kitchen table from an admirer—"

The form on the sofa never moved.

Puzzled, I knelt beside the sofa and gently shook her. Maybe she'd been out shopping and worn herself out. When I couldn't get a response, my heart began to bump.

"Mazi?" I stood up, my eyes scanning the prostrate form. She was unconscious. I could detect shallow breathing, but I knew this was no ordinary sleep.

I shook her, hard this time, so hard her straight brown bob fell across her pale features. Still no response. By now my heart was beating like a hummingbird's.

Dear God, no—please. I felt sick to my stomach.

I bolted out of the room, raced to the kitchen phone and dialed 911. My fingers shook so badly I could barely hit the keypad. A thin sheen of perspiration dotted my forehead.

I managed to give the address before I dropped the receiver and raced back to Mazi. I could hear the faint thump as the phone swung back and forth, hitting the wall.

She was lying deathly still, the throw still cast aside from my efforts to revive her.

In the short time it took for an ambulance and paramedics to arrive, I called Madge and Harry and told them I was riding to the hospital with Mazi.

"It's alcohol, isn't it, dear?"

I wanted to smack Madge Madison.

"It isn't alcohol. I don't know what it is."

"Well, don't worry. Harry and I will look after the children. You help your friend."

I hung up and returned to Mazi's side. There were no signs of alcohol—no telltale bottle present, no half-filled glass. Since I didn't drink I didn't know if all alcohols were detectable—but Mazi wasn't a silent drinker. I'd bet my life on that. Yet I couldn't help but recall her odder moments. Generally she was sunny and happy-go-lucky, but other times she had a detectable irritability. Sometimes she had complained of depression, but I'd figured who wouldn't be depressed with a husband like Warren?

One day she'd nearly fainted. I'd helped her out of the stuffy dressing room and we'd laughed, saying it had finally happened: she'd overdosed on shopping.

I thought about how she'd clean the house while the neighborhood slept. At times her energy seemed limitless, but did that mean she was a drunk?

My heart resisted the thought. I would have known; we were best friends, together more than not. I would have noticed signs. Mazi would have shared that part of her life with me.

In the distance a low wail signaled the ambulance's approach. I hurriedly wrapped the throw around Mazi and straightened her appearance. I didn't want anyone to see her in this condition—inert, mouth slightly open.

When the knock sounded at the door I was there to admit the paramedics. "She's in here."

The three men bore a variety of medical paraphernalia, which they carried to the living room and put on the floor. Then they immediately set to work.

"When did you find her?"

"Maybe fifteen minutes ago." I stood back, eyes glued to their actions. If anything happened to Mazi... I couldn't finish the unthinkable.

Dear God, please don't let me lose her, too. Surround her with Your grace.

The men talked back and forth as they attempted to stabilize my friend. When I caught the phrase "stabilize and transport" I knew she was still alive.

Or so I desperately prayed.

"May I ride with her?" I asked when the attendants lifted Mazi off the sofa and onto a stretcher.

"Are you family?"

"No. Close friend. Her husband's out of state."

The men nodded and proceeded to wheel the gurney through the dining room.

I hurriedly pulled the front door closed behind us and trotted after the men to the waiting ambulance. Seconds later they'd loaded Mazi. I scrambled in behind.

When the emergency vehicle pulled away from the curb, lights flashing and siren blaring, I caught a brief glimpse of Madge, Harry and the girls peering out the front-room window. Throughout the neighborhood, drapes were pulled back and people watched the spectacle.

The attendant continued to work on Mazi. I reached over and took her free hand and held it tightly. I was so scared my breath came in irregular puffs. If anything happened to her I couldn't bear it. She was closer than a sister now.

The attendant hooked an IV into his patient's arm and set the drip. So far nobody had speculated about what might be wrong. I caught words like blood pressure 170 over 93. Heart arrhythmia. Shallow breathing.

"Is it her heart?" I ventured.

The young paramedic remained detached. "We won't know anything until the doctor sees her, ma'am." He gave me a warm smile. "She's stable for the moment."

Stable for the moment; I didn't like the sound of that. I tightened my grip on her hand and leaned closer to whisper to a lifeless Mazi, "You're causing quite a stir, you know."

I knew she would love it.

For the time being, I'd forgotten my happy news. Right now I prayed for Mazi. Funny how one moment you can be on top of the mountain and the next moment all of your priorities are rearranged. Friendships matter; love matters. Money is only a tool in this world.

Was that odd or was that God?

I think I believed the latter.

I sat in the empty waiting room, staring at the CNN news reporter on the overhead television. The president was making a speech; there had been another drive-by shooting in Ohio.

Mazi had been in the emergency room for over an hour, and no one had been out to speak to me. I wondered about Warren. Should I call him now or wait until I knew more details?

What if Mazi was this minute dying? Wouldn't Warren want to be here? I racked my brain, trying to remember where the missing husband was working this week. Ohio? Mississippi? Arkansas. Little Rock. I'd been with her so little this week I didn't recall her mentioning Warren's location. No matter. He couldn't just appear in the emergency room. He'd have to book a flight....

A blue-coated doctor emerged from behind the double doors and I sprang to my feet. When he sailed by without comment, I sank back to the hard chair. Should I wait and call Warren when I knew more? What if I alarmed him for nothing? Then again...

Over the next half hour I repeated the action twice before a physician headed in my direction. His name tag read "Dr. Phil Harding."

"Are you with Mrs. Hollingsworth?"

"Yes." Inside my chest my heart thumped like a three-sided tire.

The graying doctor consulted his chart. "She's had a mild cardiac episode. She's awake but confused."

Heart problems? Mazi? "But she's so young for heart problems."

I was so relieved that he hadn't said alcohol, but I was totally unprepared for his next words.

He shook his head. "When will women learn? Diet pills can be a dangerous drug—even the over-the-counter ones."

I stared back at him blankly. "Diet pills?"

He glanced up, meeting my rattled gaze. "You didn't know she used diet pills on a regular basis?"

Numbly I shook my head.

He frowned. "She told me she has for years. The abuse has finally caught up with her."

Vaguely his words penetrated my shocked senses. Suddenly threads of Mazi's somewhat bizarre behavior started to make sense. Diet pills were responsible.

"I'm so sorry. I'm her closest friend, and I had no idea."

"She probably didn't want you to know." He scribbled a notation on the chart before he looked up. "Diet pills are as addictive as alcohol. Once a woman gets hooked on them, either by prescription or with over-the-counter products, she's powerless to stop usage. She's driven by motivation and the hope of a quick fix—the constant fear that she might regain any weight that she's managed to starve off. The behavior becomes an endless cycle once a woman buys into the idea of being ultrathin."

I bit back the urge to cry. For the past few months Mazi had been my anchor, my emotional foundation. In that time I had not once stopped to ask about her problems. I was so absorbed in my own worries that I had lost sight of others.

The sun rose and set on Kate Madison.

Had this blind self-absorption bled over into my children? My family? Certainly my friends. I was so ashamed.

"Will there be any lasting damage?"

"There could be. There's always the risk of liver injury. She's lucky. Strokes and renal failure can be side effects of diet pills.

Of course we'll run tests. I'll want to keep her here for a couple of days, but my guess is that this is her wake-up call." He gave me a stern look. "I hope, as her friend, that you encourage her to heed the warning. This is not an easy habit to kick."

Snapping the chart shut, he strode briskly back through the double doors.

Mazi took diet pills.

I sank back into my chair trying to let the moment sink in. Why had she never told me? There had been numerous times she could have mentioned her dilemma, shared her struggle. How many times had we split entrées, ordered one dessert and two spoons? Had drunk skinny lattes with sugar-free vanilla syrup, avoided cookies while mall shopping and split a whole-wheat pretzel instead?

Why hadn't I noticed her battle?

I knew she liked to nibble, but who didn't nibble occasionally? And show me the person who didn't adore peanut or almond M&M's. Mazi could eat a whole bag, but the next day she'd drink diet soda and eat lettuce and fat-free cheese all day for penance.

My heart ached for my loyal friend. I felt incredibly selfish and self-centered. I had not once noticed what lay behind Mazi's frequent bouts of stomach complaints and insomnia.

Warren. I had to call Warren and tell him what had happened. After a vain search for quarters, I walked to the hospital gift shop for change. I spotted a phone on the far wall and headed for it. Mazi had once insisted that I take her husband's cell number in case of emergency.

Had she known then that she was playing with fire, that it was only a matter of time before her self-destructive habit would overcome her?

I rummaged through my purse and located the small address book I carried. Phone numbers were noted after each entry.

The phone rang three times before a man answered. I'd spoken to Warren so infrequently I wasn't sure I had the right party.

"Warren?"

"Yes? Who's this?"

"It's Kate. Kate Madison."

When the name failed to register I tried again. "Your next-door neighbor. In San Francisco." Lest he forgot where home was.

"Oh—Kate. Yes. Is something wrong?" I could hear a television playing low in the background.

"Warren, I'm sorry to have to call, but Mazi's in the hospital."

"Oh?"

The response indicated little more emotion than if I'd just informed him that his shoe was untied. What sort of cold fish had Mazi pledged her life to?

I repeated my statement. "Mazi's in the hospital. They say it was a cardiac incident. She seems to be fine now, but the doctor wants to keep her here a couple of days for tests."

The background noise ceased; I assumed that Warren had hit the mute button on the remote. He cleared his throat.

"Is she all right?"

"The doctor says she's stable for the time being, but he won't know anything for certain until test results come back." I briefly explained about the diet pills.

"Yes, I know she takes them."

"And you don't mind!" My words came out sharper than I intended.

"Mind? Why should I mind? She has a weight problem."

I wanted to somehow beam myself through the phone line and slap him silly. What an awful thing to say when his wife is lying in a hospital bed, threatened by something you'd condoned.

"Unsupervised diet pills are harmful, Warren. Doesn't Mazi know that?"

"She never felt well when she took them, but they controlled her appetite. She rarely takes prescription pills. She usually stays with the over-the-counter brands. Health food stores, that sort of thing." Resentment now colored his tone. I could tell he didn't like my attitude, but then I didn't care for his, either.

I clutched the receiver. "When may I tell Mazi to expect you home?"

"Home? I'm in Arkansas."

"Yes." What I longed to say was a very sarcastic *So?* He made the distance sound like earth to Mars. We had a crisis here, not a class reunion.

"By the time I fly from here to there the emergency will be resolved. My wife is okay. Isn't that what you said?"

"She's stable. I don't know what the tests will show."

"But she's being properly treated?"

"As far as I know. I'm not a doctor."

"When the tests come back you call me. If my presence is warranted, then I'll see about booking a flight. Right now Little Rock is experiencing blizzard conditions. I'm not sure I can even get a flight out. I have two important accounts to call on in the morning—"

I interrupted his excuses. "More important than your wife?"

The challenge lay between us like a coiled rattler. This was none of my business; this was Warren and Mazi's affair, but at the moment I felt as if I was the only person in the world who cared about Mazi Hollingsworth's welfare.

Warren said sharply, "I beg your pardon?" Tension hummed over the wire as thick as lowland fog.

"Listen, Warren. Here's the hospital number."

I rattled off the digits, barely allowing him time to jot down the numbers.

"I don't know what room Mazi will be in, but if you care enough about your wife to call and inquire about her condition, ask to speak to Dr. Harding in Emergency. He can fill you in."

I hung up.

Bonehead.

He hadn't bothered to ask what hospital.

Chapter 19

Thin sunlight cast a light orange glow in the sterile hospital room. Mazi lay on the narrow bed, drifting in and out of consciousness. She knew I was with her, but she was confused and perplexed. She wasn't certain where she was or what had happened.

Oddly enough, she hadn't asked for Warren.

The long night, filled with uncertainty, had provided me time to think about the people God had placed in my life. Devoted friends. My children. Neil.

Mom.

Madge.

Mazi.

All three would give their lives for friends and family. Tonight's life-threatening experience with Mazi had made me realize how much I loved the three special women in my life, and how little I'd appreciated two of them.

I rested my head on the side of the mattress and listened to the activity of a busy hospital. Shift change. New nurses coming and going—compassionate men and women who got small recognition and still smaller pay for the jobs they performed.

I should have known about the diet pills. Within minutes of meeting her, Madge had caught on that something wasn't right with Mazi. She misinterpreted my friend's distracted behavior, but she'd been on the mark otherwise.

Face it, Kate. You missed the warning signs because you are blind to any trouble other than that on your doorstep.

I wasn't the only woman in the world who had lost a husband, but I had acted as if I was. I'd cried, whined, ranted and raved, even tried to run away from my problems, and God had let me pitch my fit. I'd been acting like a spoiled child, throwing a first-class temper tantrum.

Sure, I had a right to be angry. I didn't have a right, however, to reject God and teach my children that trouble meant they could abandon trust and belief in times of crisis. Regret and remorse filled me until I thought I couldn't breathe.

How hardheaded could I be?

Mazi's eyes fluttered open and I eased closer to the bed. Her eyes focused on me, and I could see the uncertainty in her expression.

"Kate? Where am I?"

"You're in the hospital."

She swallowed against a dry throat. "Why? Am I hurt?"

"No. Do you remember anything about last night?"

Her eyes closed. "I was upset. Warren called. He wasn't coming home this weekend."

I spoke softly. "Remember the flat tire we fixed?"

She nodded.

"Well, the limousine owner sent you flowers—a simply unbelievably gorgeous bouquet. The size alone rivals the Rose Parade."

I was exaggerating, of course, but I needed her to know and to feel the excitement.

She managed a faint smile. "He did?" Her eyes remained closed. "Does Warren know I'm here?"

"He knows. I called him last night. He'd be here right now, but Little Rock is having a blizzard and flights are canceled."

Forgive me, God, but how can I tell her that her husband cares so little that he didn't plan to fly home unless she worsens?

"The bouquet is large?"

"Honest, Mazi. I've never seen anything like it."

"Imagine that. I thought he would forget."

My news could wait—forever, if need be. Mazi was my only concern and joy at the moment. I took a deep breath, not certain of how much to tell her regarding last night's events.

"The moment I got the bouquet, I brought it over. I yelled, but you didn't answer."

Her face remained expressionless and I figured she knew where I was going.

"Your door was unlocked, so I stepped inside and called you. When you didn't answer I went looking for you."

"And you found me," she whispered.

"I called for an ambulance and they brought you here. You were very ill, Mazi. How long have you taken diet pills?"

She opened her eyes and tears slid silently down her cheeks. "A while now. I knew they weren't good for me, but it seemed like I couldn't get through a week without them."

I squeezed her hand. "I'm so sorry. I was so wrapped up in my own troubles I never thought about you and any problems you might have."

Mazi used her free hand to wipe her eyes. "Oh, Kate, my life is such a mess. Warren is seldom home and when he is here, he's so cold and distant. I'm afraid he doesn't love me anymore."

I didn't think his blood ran warm enough to love anyone. Warren was a first-class moron, but of course I didn't tell Mazi. But she had to know.

"You are deeply loved," I told her. "I've been almost jealous sometimes at the way the girls carry on over you, and I love you so much."

I hadn't realized the extent of my feelings until tonight when I'd thought I'd lost her.

She seemed to brighten at that. "Really, Kate?"

"Really, Mazi."

She blinked at the teardrops clustered on her lashes. Then her facade crumbled. "I think he's involved with another woman."

Poor Mazi. Foolish Warren. How could any man not see what he had in this warm, wonderful woman?

"Why didn't you tell me? I would have understood."

She shook her head. "How could you possibly understand? Neil was everything that Warren isn't. Warm, caring. Devoted husband. I'm a military brat, Kate. We moved around so often I never got to make close friends, the kind of friends that you confide in about your problems. I was brought up to believe that my problems were *my* problems. You don't bother others with them."

"For the most part, problems are best shared with friends."

Mazi choked on sobs. "You think I don't know how cold and indifferent my husband can be? I do, but I love him, Kate. And you're so perfect."

I handed her the small box of hospital tissues and she blew her nose. Perfect? Me? The one who couldn't cope, the wimp afraid of her shadow? The dedicated Christian who had tried to run away from God? I could think of quite a few adjectives that might describe me, but *perfect* wasn't one of them.

"If only you knew how imperfect I am. When Neil died, I shattered into a thousand tiny pieces. I didn't have anything holding me together—not faith, not trust in a God I knew held my future. Nothing. I have wandered around in a faithless stupor, unable to function or care for my girls the way I should have. If it hadn't been for you, I don't know where I'd be right now."

Mazi wiped at tears. "Certainly not sitting in a hospital room with a foolish friend."

"You don't understand, Mazi. I've been so afraid."

"Afraid of what?"

"You wouldn't understand. You've lived all over the world. You aren't afraid to stay home when Warren's gone. You accept and cope. I haven't coped. I haven't even come close."

She gave a rueful laugh. "You call what happened to me last night coping?"

"Well, no, I guess not, but you function. Most of your decisions are good ones. The only decisions I'm capable of making are wrong ones."

"You've done the best you could. You sold your house, you moved out here where you didn't know anyone. Look at all you've accomplished."

"I never felt secure. I always worried."

"Who does feel secure? No matter what we have, it can be taken from us in a minute."

Aha. That was it. "No, that's where you're wrong. God's love cannot be taken from us. We *can* be assured, if we are children of God. And He is able to handle the uncertainties of our lives."

Now I was thinking and sounding like the Kate Neil had fallen in love with.

"I'm afraid of snakes and frogs and tornadoes and earthquakes. I'm afraid of the ocean and of bugs and germs. You name it, I'm afraid of it, but those aren't eternal fears. I have no eternal fears because I'm confident in the One who holds my future. I simply forgot when Neil was taken away so unexpectedly."

I thought I caught a hint of a smile. "Well, I'm afraid of some of those things, too. Maybe the eternal fears more than the snakes and frogs. Being brave doesn't mean you're never afraid. It means you do what you have to do even if you're scared."

I squeezed her hand and leaned over to whisper, "I think God has His eye on you, Mazi Hollingsworth. You can run, but you can't hide. Trust me."

Her expression sobered. "I've had plenty of time to think about God and His acceptance, haven't I?"

I nodded. "I think you're past the age of accountability."

Mazi reached for another tissue. She wiped the tears from her eyes and blew her nose. "You've got so much faith. I wish I could have just a small dose." She stared at me, her lips quivering. "I'm addicted to diet pills, Kate. I've never admitted it before, but it's true. I found a new doctor last week—he put me on even stronger ones. That's why I've been so trembly and unsteady lately. I can't come to God in this condition."

I drew a deep breath and explained the plan of salvation: repent and accept. So easy even a child could understand.

She looked at me with the beginnings of new hope dawning in her eyes. "Give me a little time to think it over. But I promise I will."

The nurse came into the room, and I stepped out into the hallway. While people flowed around me, intent on their own purpose, I prayed for Mazi.

A warm peaceful calm filled me. I knew God wasn't mad at me; He never had been.

Doctors and technicians came and went. I called work and told them I wouldn't be in, and then called home and told Harry what happened. Around eight o'clock I wandered down to the cafeteria for breakfast. I'd had a rough night. I needed sustenance. The long, lonely hours sitting by Mazi's bedside, praying that I wouldn't lose her as I had lost Neil, had left me rattled.

An older woman carried her tray to my table. "May I sit here?"

"Of course."

She looked exhausted. Thin, gray haired, shoulders slumped. She touched my heart.

"Are you all right?" I asked.

She managed a smile. "Just tired. I've been here all night. My husband had a stroke." She stopped and took a sip of coffee. I could see she was struggling for control. "I'm afraid I'll have to put him in a nursing home—if he ever leaves here."

I reached across the table and took her hand. "Do you have anyone with you?"

She nodded. "My daughter is coming today." She smiled, even though her lips trembled. "Even so, I am not alone."

Silent camaraderie flowed between us. I knew, without her saying, where she found her source of strength.

A younger woman approached our table. Her daughter. I murmured goodbye and left, returning to Mazi's room. She peered up sleepily when I entered.

"I did it," she said. "I asked Him and it happened, just the way you said. Oh, Kate. I never knew I could feel so—loved."

When I hugged her, our tears mingled. I grabbed a tissue and blew my nose. We were rapidly going through the tiny box between the two of us.

"Now we are blood sisters. Sisters in Christ."

She grinned, the former Mazi mischief flaring briefly in her eyes. "I think our meeting was one of those God jobs. Don't you?"

"I have for a long time, because California sure hasn't cut it for me." I winked at her.

She sobered. "I'll pray that He'll give you wisdom to know what to do, Kate. The right thing for you and the girls—"

I slapped my forehead. "I can't believe that I forgot to tell you! That man, the one who sent the flowers—oh, Mazi." I took another deep breath. "He paid off half of my home mortgage."

She stared at me, mouth agape. "He did what?"

"There was a card with the flowers. It said he'd paid down my mortgage, and I'm sure he did. I'm going to call the bank to verify it."

Her eyes shone with wonder. "Oh, Kate, how wonderful. Who do you suppose he was?"

"I have no idea. I wish I knew, so I could thank him." Thank him? The word didn't begin to describe my gratitude.

"Maybe he was an angel."

I laughed. "No. I think he was a rich Good Samaritan who could return a favor in a way that most of us only dream about. If it hadn't been for the flowers he sent you, I'd never have gone to your house yesterday."

"You'd never have found me in time," Mazi mused. And I knew her thoughts; no one would have found her, certainly not Warren.

"We'd never have had this talk."

"And I wouldn't have accepted God's gift," she finished. "So He did have a hand in it."

"God works in mysterious ways."

I was learning that His ways were not my ways. I made plans, all right, lots of plans, and they fell apart, like the sand castles the girls built at the seashore.

Kate Madison was through building on the sand.

Three days later, having taken the afternoon off, I drove Mazi home. I helped her inside her house, since she was still feeling a bit weak, and there on the table sat the bottle of diet pills.

She picked up the bottle and put it in a plastic grocery sack. "Don't leave yet. I may not have the strength to do this by myself."

She went through the house gathering up bottles of pills and dumping them in the bag. She must have bought every brand on the market, the way she bought perfume and lotion. Prescription drugs were less evident.

When she finished, she handed me the sack. "Okay, you can go home now. There are no pills in the house, and if I feel I can't get through the night without them, I'll call you."

"I can sleep over if you want."

"No, I have to do this on my own. The girls have been without you enough. Tell them I'm all right, and thank them for their prayers." She reached to hold me tightly. "Thank you for everything."

I hugged her back. "You've helped me, too, Mazi. That's the way it works with friends."

She smiled. "God has given me a new life. I promise you, Kate, I'm not going to waste this one. I know it won't be easy, but with God's help, and even if I get bigger than a blue-ribbon guernsey, I'm through with pills for the rest of my life."

I was so proud of her I could have cried. Instead, I hugged her again and then went to face my in-laws and Kris and Kelli. The girls met me at the door.

"Is Mazi home?" Kris asked.

"She's home. You can go over later. Give her a chance to settle in first, okay?"

"We drew pictures for her!"

"She'll love them. You can take them over after lunch."

"I've got lunch cooking." Madge came into the living room. "Chicken strips and corn dogs."

I laughed. "I'll bet I can guess who chose the menu."

She grinned. "Nothing like a well-balanced meal."

The girls ran to tell Harry that Mazi was home and she was all right. I followed Madge out to the kitchen and watched her put napkins and condiments on the table.

"I need to apologize. I was too self-centered to notice anything strange about Mazi's behavior, but you did. I'm sorry I didn't trust your instincts."

Madge put plates on the table. "Don't be so hard on yourself. You've never been around anyone who is addicted. You wouldn't have known the symptoms if you tripped over them."

I shook my head. "That's no excuse. You noticed right away."

She looked out the kitchen window, not answering. I wondered what I had said wrong.

"Madge? Are you all right?"

She turned to face me. "I wasn't always a pillar of faith, Kate. I recognized an addiction because I had the same problem once. Hers wasn't the addiction I suffered, but it was an addiction, and I certainly knew the symptoms."

My mouth dropped. Madge? The leader of the Women's Missionary Union, a dozen committees under her belt, president of the kitchen committee?

"That's right. But alcohol, Scotch, was my addiction. I should have caught the difference between alcohol addiction and pills in Mazi's behavior. I knew something was wrong, but I jumped to the wrong conclusion."

"Oh, Madge. I never dreamed. Neil never mentioned—"

"Neil never knew. It was long ago and at a time in my life where I didn't know up from down. I was young, on my own and fell into the wrong crowd. I met Harry and he introduced me to God. I've never gone back to my former lifestyle, but that's only through grace."

I smiled. "You'll be glad to know Mazi has now met God, too."

Madge broke into a smile. "Wonderful news. I'm so glad."

"Yeah, me, too." I picked up a carrot stick and nibbled on it. "I've really enjoyed having you here."

She grinned. "I know I've gotten on your nerves. I tend to do that, but I've always appreciated you as a daughter-in-law. I never want to lose you, Kate. I hope you know that."

I swallowed. Never in this life had I ever expected to hear her admit that. "You won't lose me, Madge. I'm family. You have me for better or for worse."

"Even when you remarry?"

"I'm not going to remarry."

"You will—and you should. Neil would want you to be happy. Just don't forget me and Harry. We love you, too."

I was so touched by her admission I was speechless.

She reached down and moved the saltshaker a few inches, looking at me sideways. "I cleaned the garage."

I opened my mouth, then shut it before I said, "That's nice. I'm sure it needed it."

She laughed. "Almost bit your tongue on that one, didn't you?"

I dredged up a weak smile. "Well, you didn't have to do that. I wanted you to relax and have fun, not spend all your time cleaning up my messes."

She placed a platter of chicken strips on the table. "Tell you what, Kate. If you ever give it up here and move back to Oklahoma, just give us a call. Your mother and I can have you packed and moved in a day. I'll say this for Kay—she's one pain in the neck, but she's a hard worker."

After lunch the girls carried the pictures they had colored across the hedge to Mazi's. I tagged along, carrying a plate of leftover chicken and corn dogs. Only traces of fog remained.

Madge and Harry were off sightseeing with someone they had met at church. I knew they would soon be going home. Life would be back to normal, and I'd be glad, but I realized I would miss them.

Mazi opened the door and made a big fuss over the girls and their paintings. She posted the colorful drawings on the refrigerator door using ladybug magnets. Even Kelli was satisfied with the showing.

The girls hovered over Mazi, as if they, too, realized how close we had come to losing her. I wanted to ask if Warren had called, but I was afraid to. It would hurt her to admit he hadn't cared enough to check in.

I wanted to wring his neck.

The doorbell rang in the middle of all the confusion and Mazi insisted on answering.

"I'm not an invalid." She bit into a corn dog and set off for the foyer. A moment later I heard a man's voice. When I went to look, I could barely see the newcomer for the enormous bouquet he held in his hand.

"Oh! Oh, my!" Both hands covered Mazi's mouth, her eyes as round as baseballs. "For me. Warren?"

Warren edged his way inside, and I cleared a place on the walnut table in the foyer so he could set the vase down. The house was starting to look like a funeral parlor. Straightening, he grinned. "There you go. I bought the biggest bouquet the florist had." He set his suitcase down and took off his hat. "Nothing but the best for you, Mazi."

"Oh, my. I *see* you did. Warren! They're lovely."

Well. I learned right then and there love comes in varying sizes. Some flashy and showy, others in quiet desperation. When all is said and done there is no pat explanation of love.

Mazi's husband turned several shades of pink. He reached out and took her hand. "You're looking good, Mazi. Healthy as a May hedge in bloom."

She tittered. Honestly. Tittered.

"Why, thank you, Warren. You don't look so bad yourself."

I gathered the girls and they said goodbye and gave Mazi a final hug. I reached out and touched her arm. I knew the Hollingsworths needed time alone. Warren had come through by the skin of his teeth. *Thank you, God.*

"You'll call if you need me, okay?"

"Sure." She squeezed my shoulders. "Don't worry about me. I'm not alone anymore."

"You mean Warren's here."

"Him, too."

I thought that was a good healthy admission that Mazi was on the right track. She'd be a powerful warrior. A powerful witness for the love of God.

She watched from her doorway as we crossed the hedge, and I turned for one last wave before going inside the house. The girls, having eaten grease for lunch, settled for vegetable soup and grilled cheese sandwiches for dinner. Madge and Harry phoned to say they were going to be late. I'd given them a key so they could let themselves in.

The house settled down for the night. I sat by my bedroom window looking out on the quiet streets. I wasn't afraid anymore. The fear, doubt and confusion that had been my steady companion the past few months was gone. And I knew to whom I owed the thanks.

I thought back over the events leading to this moment. I'd changed in ways I'd never thought possible. All my life I'd been a worrywart, afraid of everything. Afraid of life itself. Even worse, I'd been turning my daughters into miniature, frightened replicas of myself. I shook my head, thinking of the damage I could have done to them if I'd continued that sort of irrational behavior.

The move to California had been good for me in many ways. I'd been pushed out of my comfort zone. Forced to make decisions, to do things the old Kate couldn't have done. I'd failed occasionally. My thoughts turned to the night I'd sat in the empty church wallowing in defeat. I'd let Madge cause me to doubt myself, to doubt what I'd accomplished.

Sitting beside Mazi's hospital bed had forced me to realize that life is a series of wins and losses. But through it all God is there, lifting us up, carrying us over the rough spots. I knew now whether we lived in California or in Oklahoma we would be all right because God would be with us.

I could do all things through Christ.

I thought of California, land of opportunity. I'd come, I'd seen, I'd survived. And now I wanted to go home.

Slipping to my knees, I allowed tears to fall for what I hoped would be a finale to my folly.

"Dear God. I am so sorry. I know I was wrong, and I'm asking You to forgive me. I've tried to do it on my own and I couldn't. Now I'm through being in charge.

"If I die in a plane crash, or if You do call me to serve in Africa or Bosnia, or any other of the one hundred and one different things I've worried about, I accept Your will because, Father, I do not want to live out of Your will. I only ask that if it happens, You won't leave me alone."

And in the still small voice I've silently heard so many times, the answer echoed back to me.

My dear child. When have I ever left you alone?

Epilogue

One of my favorite things has been and remains to be watching an airplane take off—that I'm still on the ground goes without saying. When Neil and I first married, we'd pack a picnic lunch and drive to a dirt road close to the airport. On a sunny day we'd spread an old army blanket over the hood of his pickup, and we'd lie like sunning lizards, staring up into the wild blue. The roar of the powerful engines would seep through our bones. Jets lifted off half a mile from our vantage point, and we watched the big aircraft climb and climb until there would be nothing left but a thin vapor trail, way way up.

The girls and I had said our goodbyes to Madge and Harry earlier.

"Kate, honey, don't let Kelli stay out after dark." Madge shook her head. "There's a lot of crazies running around."

Kelli's eyes rounded. "Is a crazy person going to get me?"

I drew my daughter under my protective wing. "No, honey. Maws is being goofy."

Kelli eyed her grandmother, and Madge caved. "Well, of course your mother isn't going to let anything happen to you." She leaned closer and gave me another hug.

"Come on, Madge. The security line's past the door."

"Hold your britches, Harry. I'm coming. I'm coming already." Madge gave me a devious wink. "The old coot."

"I heard that."

She'd nudged Harry to move up in line. "Get moving. I'm right behind you."

So now the girls and I were parked on an access road, lying on the hood of my car. The aircraft carrying my in-laws back home was nothing more than a tiny speck of vapor trail.

The girls and I had watched in silence.

Kelli heaved a deep sigh. "I'll miss Maws and Paws, but I'm glad it's just us again." She snuggled closer and took my hand. "Just us family."

"Mmm, me too, honey. Me, too." I'd miss Madge and Harry, too. With them around, and Kelli and Kris, I'd always had a little piece of Neil remaining. And the house was never quiet when they were here, and never cleaner. Madge had organized every drawer, closet and cabinet, and I'd pit the sparkling-clean interior of my deep freeze up against any woman's in the Bay Area.

Planes systematically took off and soared. We could feel the powerful engines even at this distance, and I relished the familiarity. I lay on top of the hood, eyes closed. It all seemed to fall into place now.

The house was half paid off.

I was slowly but surely coming to grips with the fact that Neil was gone—the best part of my life, but not the only part.

And someday, God willing, my life with the girls would take on new dimensions. With the sun warming my face, I thought about the poignantly sweet verse in Ecclesiastes. "To everything there is a season, a time for every purpose under heaven."

A time to plant
And a time to pluck what is planted;
A time to kill
And a time to heal;
A time to break down
And a time to build up;
A time to weep
And a time to laugh.

"A time to mourn, and a time to dance..."
Lying here, with the warm sun on my face, I was filled with an overpowering sense of God's miraculous love.

What I did from this day forward would depend on my choices. I could remain here and adjust or I could go back to Oklahoma, back to deal with old memories in familiar surroundings. Basically, the world was mine once more. I prayed God would give me wisdom and understanding, to do His will and nothing less.

Good or bad, I think I finally had my head screwed on straight.

"Just put it down over here," Mazi called to a man loading the moving van.

I paused, taking a second hitch at a heavily loaded cardboard box I was carrying. The van had arrived a little before six this morning; all but the last remaining household items were loaded. I'd listed the house last week, and already we had two interested buyers.

Kelli came out of the house carrying Sailor in his cage. Kris had her arms full of CDs as she herded her younger sister and the cage into the car.

Mazi paused, pillaging a clean tissue out of her jeans pocket and dabbing her eyes. She'd been blubbering nonstop since early this morning.

I set the heavy box on the van tailgate and turned to comfort her. Moving day was never easy.

"Ah, come on, Maz. You promised you wouldn't cry."

"I know." She blew her nose. "I lied. God forgive me."

Last night we'd hardly slept. We'd sat up drinking diet sodas and talking long into the night. Mazi was driving to Oklahoma with me and the girls, and helping us to get settled in an apartment until I could buy a house. The cramped situation was only temporary. Two houses in our old neighborhood were for sale; one I had admired and loved for years. It was larger than the one Neil and I had previously owned, with lots of closets and storage space. The girls would be back in their old school. Life seemed to be going pretty smoothly right now.

"Have you talked to Warren about moving?"

Nodding, Mazi summoned a weak smile. "He finally admitted that he left me alone too much, and this morning, before he kissed me goodbye, he told me if that second house in your old neighborhood hasn't sold, he'd take a look at it."

Well, maybe I'd be wrong about Warren, the coldhearted mackerel; the possibility was entirely valid. I'd been known to be wrong a lot lately. If he'd move Mazi to Oklahoma, I'd forgive him for the years of neglect.

And maybe he knew Mazi would do the same.

Having her in Oklahoma would be the best of both worlds. My eardrum was healing nicely, and the doctor said in another month I could return to teaching and travel. Flying no longer scared me. I'd discovered there are worse things in life than death. Mazi would be living three doors away, looking after the girls when I was away. No box elder hedge to step over, no swaying ground beneath our feet. No smell of rotting garbage.

There'd be nothing to separate me and my best friend but Okie sidewalks.

"Then why are you crying?" I demanded. This was a happy day!

"Because." Her face corkscrewed and she started bawling. "I'm so *happy!*"

"Goofus." I hugged her and headed back to the house for my purse and keys. The girls had loaded Sailor's cage into the car and were anxiously tooting the horn. Postcards of Cliff House, Chinatown and Fisherman's Wharf were tightly packed away, lovely memories of our time in San Francisco.

I took a minute to wander back through the empty rooms. The house was a good home, even though it needed repairs. Oddly enough, this parting didn't feel the same as when I'd left the house that Neil and I had shared. Of course, nothing felt the same, but then, it wasn't supposed to.

New life.

New beginnings.

I reached for my purse and then slipped on my sunglasses. Just before I closed and locked the door, I stuck my head into the foyer and whispered, "I'll pray that the right person buys you, that you will be a home to some lucky family, not merely a house."

Minutes later Mazi piled into the passenger seat and fastened her belt. "What have I forgotten? I know I'm forgetting something."

"You took the cats to the kennel?"

"Yes—yes. Shut the windows and turned off the coffeepot. Set the security alarm."

"Then we're set."

She heaved a happy sigh. "You're right. We're set."

I slid behind the wheel and waited to follow behind the large moving van. The cross-country trip would take the better part of three days, but nobody, even Kris and Kelli, minded. The Madisons were going home.

As I pulled away from the curb, I glanced back in the rear-view mirror, watching the ivy-covered cottage with its charming porch boxes gradually recede. No, nobody minded leaving.

Personally I think all of us were anxious to see what God had up His sleeve next.

* * * * *

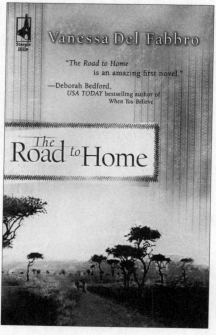

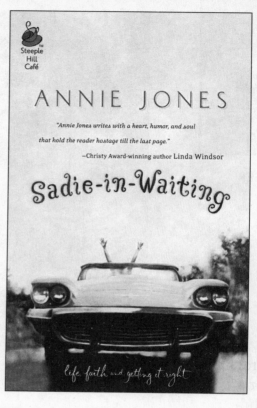

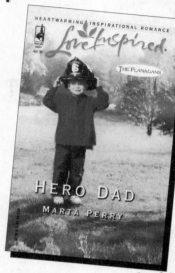

Love Inspired

THE FLANAGANS

SERIES CONTINUES WITH...

HERO DAD

BY

MARTA PERRY

Firefighter and single dad Seth Flanagan was looking for a mother for his son. Then he met photojournalist Julie Alexander. The introverted beauty made him wonder if God was giving him a second chance. As he watched his toddler son break through the barriers around Julie's guarded heart, Seth realized he was ready to love again. But would their budding relationship be destroyed when he learned her real identity?

The Flanagans: This fire-fighting family must learn to stop fighting love.

Don't miss HERO DAD
On sale April 2005

Available at your favorite retail outlet.

Love Inspired

THE McKASLIN CLAN

SERIES CONTINUES WITH...

SWEET BLESSINGS

BY

JILLIAN HART

Single mom Amy McKaslin welcomed newcomer Heath Murdock into her family diner after he'd shielded her from harm. And as the bighearted McKaslin clan and the close-knit Christian community rallied around him, the grief-ravaged drifter felt an awakening in his soul. Could the sweetest blessing of all be standing right before him?

The McKaslin Clan: Ensconced in a quaint mountain town overlooking the vast Montana plains, the McKaslins rejoice in the powerful bonds of faith, family...and forever love.

Don't miss SWEET BLESSINGS
On sale April 2005

Available at your favorite retail outlet.

www.SteepleHill.com

LISBJHTR

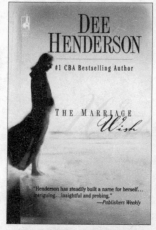
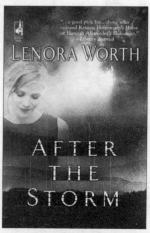

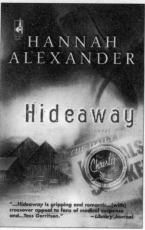